WAYNE'S CALLING

A PALADIN

Richard M Beloin MD

authorHOUSE®

AuthorHouse™
1663 Liberty Drive
Bloomington, IN 47403
www.authorhouse.com
Phone: 1 (800) 839-8640

Published by AuthorHouse 09/27/2018

ISBN: 978-1-5462-6050-9 (sc)
ISBN: 978-1-5462-6049-3 (e)

Library of Congress Control Number: 2018911274

Print information available on the last page.

ACKNOWLEDGMENT

The front and back covers were designed by Jason Walker of MONSOON DESIGN c/o monsoondesign.com

DEDICATION

This book is dedicated to all my Vermont family and friends.

CONTENTS

CONTENTS

PROLOGUE

Sarah Dutton, age forty two, was a seven year widow in Denver CO. This was year 1871 and she had an eleven year old son, Wayne, which she had raised as a single parent since age four. Her husband, a bank teller, had been shot dead during a bank robbery. At the age of thirty five, she went to work as a seamstress in a local garment factory. This was not enough income to support herself and her son, so she went to work in the evenings at a local diner, as a waitress.

Now at forty two, she was under the care of a local doctor. The diagnosis of breast cancer in 1871 was a terminal diagnosis since the disease had already spread. Her doctor informed her of the care she would need in the months to come. He was adamant, that a close family member would be needed to provide this care, and an eleven year old son would not be that person.

As the disease progressed, she had to quit her job at the garment factory and later her waitress job. With her savings used up, she felt her choices were dwindling. She had good friends at work and a good boss at the diner, yet they could only help so much, and they certainly could not provide continuous care for a dying person. Other than dying, who was going to care for her son?

Sarah made the most crucial decision of her life. She would send a long telegram to her only living relative, her brother, Sam Swanson and his wife Cora. They had remained close over the years and managed to visit once a year at Christmas. Sam had offered to support Sarah over the years, but Sarah had refused. Sam and Cora were childless. They would take the train every Xmas, and arrive with gifts for Sarah and Wayne. They would stay a week and entertain Sarah and Wayne. Occasionally, Sam would visit at other times when in Denver on business.

Today, Sarah sent this telegram:

> *UNFORTUNATE NEWS, I AM DYING OF CANCER AND NEED YOUR HELP -STOP- WOULD YOU AND NORA CARE FOR ME TILL END --STOP–AND RAISE MY SON -STOP- PLEASE SARAH*

The answer came the same day:

*PACK YOUR BAGS -STOP- WILL
BE ON NEXT TRAIN AND WILL
ARRIVE IN TWO DAYS. –STOP-
YOU AND WAYNE ARE COMING
HOME. SAM*

Sam and Nora arrived in Denver and were met at the RR platform by Sarah. After hugs, smiles, and many tears, Sarah explained that Wayne knew of her diagnosis, but he did not realize that she had only a few months to live. She also explained that her doctor in Denver had notified Hawthorne's home town doctor, and had arranged for a supply of laudanum. Cora made it clear that she would serve as her nurse day and night, till the end. Sam would try to support Wayne anyway he could by getting him involved with ranch activities.

The next weeks saw a general decline in Sarah's health. She was having constant back/bone pain and required regular doses of laudanum. She could not eat and quickly became emaciated. Her doctor was called when she developed a fever. He said, "Sarah has pneumonia and it's a blessing.

Keep her comfortable and well sedated–and pray for a quick end".

Sam had been at Wayne's side for the past weeks. All his duties were passed on to his foreman, Brad. Sam's philosophy on life had struck Wayne, "it's hard to come into this life, then we live our lives and again, it's hard to leave this life–and we all will."

Sarah was buried in the Swanson cemetery next to the ranch house. Sam stayed with Wayne for the next couple of weeks to assist him in grieving. After a week of withdrawal, Wayne started showing interest in his surroundings. That is when Wayne asked after dinner, "what happens to me now?" Cora answered, "we would like you to stay with us forever. You are part of our family and would be happy to see you to adulthood. Tears came to Wayne's eyes and Sam said, "we'll take that as a yes, and welcome to the Swanson household and the Double S ranch in Colorado.

***

CHAPTER 1

Formative Years

Wayne remembered his uncle's words the next morning. "Well Wayne, you're no longer a city boy, you're a rancher in training. So today we go over your daily chores." As they were walking to the barn, "we start with the chickens, feed them a scoop of chicken mash and spread a half scoop of seeds over their penned yard. Add fresh water to their troughs and clean the poop under their roost. Finally pick the eggs twice a day and bring a fixed number to your aunt, and the remainder to the cookie at the bunkhouse. In the evening herd them back in the coop with fresh water and a half scoop of mash—the most important thing, lock the door to the coop against predators."

Thinking this was his job for the day, would give him many hours for play, but Uncle Sam added a few other jobs:

- "Care for the horses left in the barn after the ranch hands are back on the range.

Feed them a half scoop of oats and add hay in their hay trays. Pump water till their troughs are full. Bring a daily supply of hay from the hayloft, and muck their stalls."

- "Help your aunt with the daily garden harvest, weeding and watering."
- "In the afternoons, you become cookie's helper. He has multiple jobs to do to include: tack repair, blacksmith projects, post hole digging, building repairs and even laundry for the Cowboys. Finally, by dinner time you might help him with dinner prep work, or you may have private time. You will learn many living skills from this man."

At the end of the first week, Wayne was getting into the routine. Uncle Sam needed to go to town regularly for business activities and he said, "tomorrow we are all going into town. Wayne, you need clothes, and we need groceries and other items."

On their way to town, Wayne asked, "how far are we from town and how long does it take to get there?" "The ranch is six miles from town and it takes us some 45 minutes with this buggy." "Is this a new town?" Aunt Cora answered, "Hawthorne is a town in its infancy, having sprung up from the discovery of a silver deposit that lead to a full underground mining operation. A second business appeared out of the need for building lumber. The third source of employment were the many ranches within 10 miles east and 10 miles west of town."

"Is this a large town?" "The town presently has 200 people and the essential businesses are all geared toward services to include: a bank, mercantile/hardware, diner, livery, sheriff, telegraph and two saloons. The town is fortunate to have its own doctor, and new businesses are sprouting up regularly. The promise of a railroad spur is high on the list for the mining company and the ranchers."

"Why is the arrival of a RR so important?" "Now, the silver is hauled by wagons to the nearest RR spur some 50 miles away, our goods arrive once a week by wagons, and our cattle have to be herded some fifty miles to the RR yard. We cannot ship lumber out of town because of costs, and the only way into town is by horse or stagecoach. A RR would solve all these problems, but would also turn our nice town into a city overnight–with all its social problems."

When they got to town, Uncle Sam took off to do his business at the bank. Aunt Cora chose clothes for Wayne, everyday pants, shirts, socks, underwear and one set of dress clothes for Sunday. At the end of her selections she added a Stetson and Cowboy boots. The clothes did not impress Wayne, but the hat and boots certainly did.

Sam came back from his business rounds and selected some items at the hardware department, while Cora picked the food items needed to keep the larder full. Wayne asked, "what about food for Cookie? Sam said, "Cookie does his own shopping and is independent of the household supplies." "Good, that means that I get to go to town with him, heh!"

On their way home, Sam suddenly stopped at the livery and invited everyone to come inside. As they entered, they saw a small black horse with a bridle and saddle. Wayne stepped closer to read a note stuck on the saddle and it said, "A Cowboy in training needs a horse, welcome home Wayne."

"How did you know that I was dreaming of owning my own horse." "Wayne, we are aware of your changing needs as you grow up, and we will always try to stay ahead of your wants and needs." The livery owner, Bruce Hawkins, spoke up, "this is a medium size Morgan standing 14 hands. He is gentle, intelligent and will serve you well till you are ready for a full size horse. He will make a smooth traveler and a quick cattle cutting horse. Unlike most Morgans, he has a few white spots on his front legs and forehead" "Well he looks fine to me, and he is all mine. I am going to call him Domino because of the combination of the white spots mixed with his black coat." "I will show you how to ride, saddle, and care for your horse. I expect you to exercise him everyday, and brush him down afterwards."

His first summer was spent getting use to a ranch routine and learning to ride a horse. He rode Domino at least two hours each day throughout the ranch's grasslands. One day Brad, the foreman, came to Wayne and asked, "I am leaving tomorrow for a two day trip running the fence line, and wanted to know if you would like to join me" "Yes sir, I would love to do this. What do I need?" "A bed roll, a slicker and your horse. I provide everything else."

Running the fence line was a routine undertaken every month. Brad explained after starting the trip, "your uncle's ranch is 10 sections. Each section is 640 acres or one mile square. So to cover the perimeter we have 3 miles north, 3 miles east and 3 miles south to get back home. At mid- point, we have a line shack for overnight lodging."

They had been on the trail for one hour when they saw several broken wires. Brad said, "look at all the grey and brown hairs stuck to the barbs. This means a pack of wolves were chasing deer or antelope. To repair this, you make a loop out of each barb wire end and add a piece of single strand mending wire to connect the loops. The mending pliers will tighten the connection and cut off the excess wire."

After several repairs, they got to the line shack at dusk. "Bring the horses to the lean-to in the cabin's rear, unsaddle and rub them down. I will start the fire in the stove to cook dinner." The beans and bacon made a fine dinner. They got a good night's sleep and resumed their trip the next morning. Wayne got to repair several broken strands, and expected to be doing this job by himself in the near future. In mid afternoon, Brad softly says, "off your horse and hold mine as well." He grabs his rifle and without warning shoots at a dog running after a yearling. They were at least 100 yards away and Brad hit that wolf on his first shot. Wayne knew then, that shooting well was going to be his next project.

By September, it was time to start school. Wayne was allowed to ride Domino to school and leave him at the livery for day care–the livery being a 5 minute walk to the school. The next several years were the same from year to year. School was a good time with other kids and learning was also interesting. During the summers, Wayne was allowed more training days with the ranch hands on the range. He even was allowed to skip school for two weeks during the spring roundup. This brought him to the summer of 1874 when he was turning 14 years old.

***

On his birthday, Uncle Sam handed him a brand new Winchester 1873 in the new caliber 44-40. "This is a fine hunting rifle and is effective to 100 yards. I expect you to learn to shoot this gun well and accurately. I will teach you the proper handling and shooting, then it will be up to you to improve your accuracy by practicing.

"I am ready, when can I have my first lesson?" "Right now. To load it, you add 15 bullets in this side loading gate, then you rack the lever which will bring a live round to the top chamber and cock the hammer. If you don't fire, then let the hammer down slowly. Now let me see you run the lever and dry fire." He did this for several times, and his uncle showed him how to keep the butt against his shoulder, and hold the front of the gun with his left hand. When Uncle Sam was satisfied with his technique, Wayne loaded the gun and proceeded to shoot it for the first time.

Something magical happened when he fired that rifle for the first time. He could not explain it but his uncle saw it in his face. "Now aim for that old bucket I set at 50 yards." He hit it 12 out of 15 times, reloaded the magazine twice more and buzzed through these last 30 rounds. At the end Sam was looking at the box of shells with 5 shells left over. He said, "well young man, I can see that buying a box of shells at 50 cents a box is going to run into mega bucks. So if you want to shoot a lot, you have to make your own bullets and reload them yourself." "I will make a deal with you. If you can make bullets, reload them and become proficient with a rifle, I will buy you a brand new Colt in 44-40." All Wayne said was, "man, you have a deal."

Two days later they went to Hawthorne on business. They went into Harrigan's gun shop. The attendant, showed them how to melt lead, pour it into a bullet mold, use the hand loading tong tool to reload the 44-40 with new primers, prepare the cases, add black powder and our recently cooled bullet. Wayne was totally mesmerized by the process and even Uncle Sam was impressed. They left the store with 5 pounds of powder, 2000 primers, 1000 casings and 60 pounds of lead. He also bought three bullet molds for the 200 gr. 44 cal, bullet, and three handloading tong tools for the 44-40.

On their way home, Wayne asked, "I understand buying all the reloading components, but why three molds and three handloading tools?" "The hired hands on a ranch should stay proficient with their firearms. It is to my benefit for this to be ongoing, but at the cost of loaded ammo, I could not afford this training. Now if the boys get together in the evenings, they can make bullets and or reload some, heh. Now we can afford to have them maintain their gun handling skills."

It was a learning curve for everyone–Wayne, Uncle Sam, cookie as well as all the ranch hands, and the foreman included. Yet they all learned how to make bullets, and reload them. Everyone got to enjoy the practicing sessions. Wayne had a mission–learn the rifle proficiency and accuracy ASAP, so he could get his hands on a Colt pistol.

Brad was an old gun handling expert that was not well advertised. He helped Wayne and gave him many useful tips. One day Brad said, "you are ready to do a demonstration for your uncle. Go get him and I will set up the targets." When he arrived, Wayne said, "Uncle Sam, you said that when I became proficient with my rifle, that you would consider giving me a pistol. So let me demonstrate." He grabbed his rifle and at full speed, he shot the bucket at 25, 50, 75 yards once each, then hit the bucket twice at 100 yards and repeated the process once more, and for the last 5 rounds, he shot the 100 yard bucket 5 times in a row. He turned around and saw Brad with the biggest smile on his face. Uncle Sam said nothing but stepped to his saddlebags and took out a brand new Colt in 44-40 with a nice black holster/belt rig, and said, "I knew you could do it. Now Brad will teach you the basics of pistol handling and probably too many other tricks of the gunfighter trade. Meanwhile, I will continue to buy reloading components, heh!"

***

Wayne's next two years in school were uneventful but he learned how to study and work independently. His favorite subjects were, accounting and social studies, He especially enjoyed reading about the state's judicial system, and how lawmen functioned—he could not figure out why he found this so interesting. Approaching the age of 16, he graduated having reached 10th grade. He was then working full time as a ranch hand and spending as much time reloading and practicing the draw and pistol shooting. Brad's help was beyond belief. He had skills that only a gunfighter would know, yet he would not talk about his days before the Double S Ranch.

Sam and Cora had a habit of surprising him on his birthdays. This day was certainly no exception. After dinner and a 16th birthday cake, Uncle Sam said, "we are getting older and we are in the process of writing a will. Our lawyer is insistent that we need to name an heir. To fill that need, he insists that we legally adopt you and name you as our sole heir. What do you think of that?"

Wayne had not anticipated this issue, he had always assumed that he was their son, even if a paper did not exist to that effect. Wayne softly said, "So, you took me in, fed me, clothed me, trained me as a Cowboy, gave me living skills, loved me and now you want to give me the ranch?" Silence in the room.............!Cora says, "that's about the size of it, heh!"

"And what did you get out of all this giving?" "The love of life, to have you with us all these years!" "Oh well, in that case, it's OK with me under one condition—that I get to call you pa and ma instead of Uncle Sam and Aunt Cora." Instantly, hugs and tears were enjoyed by all.

After the hot emotions cooled down, Sam said, "tomorrow we are all going to the courthouse in town. We need to fill out adoption papers, visit with Judge Atchison, and sign all legal documents. We will also meet with our lawyer, name you as our legal heir, sign all documents and register them with the court. Then we go to the bank to add your name to our account and you will have the right to make withdrawals and sign bank drafts." "But I am not 21." "We know, but we have a dispensation from Judge Atchison, that gives you the right to come to town to do our business. That includes the bank, and other businesses in town. After the bank, we will visit all the merchants we use, and show them the dispensation, which will give you business rights as our representatives."

***

The next 5 years saw a teenager grow into manhood. He became an experienced cowhand and earned the respect of his coworkers, especially of the foreman, Brad. To Sam's surprise, Wayne had a talent with business management. He was very secure in handling the books, he was ardent in maintaining the buildings and he proved to Sam that he was a progressive. He subscribed to cattlemen's publications and was quick to see the advantage of crossbreeds.

He convinced Sam to start diversifying the herd, by adding Herefords, Angus and even Shorthorns to the native cattle. These crossbreeds proved to be more durable and were livelier. They had a lower birthing mortality, and were more resistant to disease. The result was an increase in productivity with more meat on the hoof in the same time period—even on poor terrain during bad winters and droughts.

The ranch prospered. The bunkhouse was enlarged to support 8 full time cowhands plus a foreman and a cookie. The herd was now up to 2500 head and the last roundup took almost three weeks even with Sam and Wayne helping out. The one thing that would make ranch life much easier would be the RR spur with cattle holding and loading pens. This would also mean the growth of the town to city status.

Despite the busy ranch schedule, Wayne managed to find time every day to practice his draw and accuracy with a handgun. Brad not only provided the expertise, but he provide the ethics and philosophy of being a shootist. Above all, to respect life and realize that a gun can be a tool to maintain goodness and justice—not just killing.

The only gun he added those 5 years was a Winchester 76—the Centennial model. The caliber was 45-60 and would shoot a 210–350 grain bullet at 1300–1500 fps. loaded with 60 grains of black powder. This was a centerfire cartridge that was reloadable. The carbine model fit in the horse scabbard and was recognizable with a brass butt plate. It had a ladder sight that was good to 500 yards. Wayne did a lot of shooting with this rifle and was accurate to 400–500 yards. He enjoyed using this gun for pleasure but never realized the importance in mastering the firearm's potential–which he had achieved.

One fine day, saw Wayne going to town for supplies and for cash to cover payday. Little did he realize that this day's events would be crucial in directing his future.

***

Wayne took the buckboard to town. The cookie needed groceries but did not have time to do his own shopping. He was needed on the range to help move 1000 cattle to a different pasture. Wayne drove up to Ed's Mercantile. Ed Sorenson was one of the early businessmen to set up a mercantile in Hawthorne's early years. Wayne had known Ed since he came to his uncle's ranch ten years ago.

Wayne stepped up to the counter and said, "hello Ed, today I have three lists for you: groceries for the family house, groceries for the cookie, and a list of hardware and feed items for the ranch. I have to make a quick trip to Miller's Bank, and will be back to help you load." "Ok, I will have things gathered and totaled by then."

It was a quiet time of day, and Wayne took a short walk over the boardwalk to the bank. As he arrived, he noted a lone rider across the street holding the reins of three horses. As he put his left hand on the door knob, he instinctively removed the hammer loop off his pistol. Once he stepped in the bank, he saw a sight that no one ever wants to see. The sheriff was in the lobby, his gun pointing at three men who were pointing their pistols at the sheriff.

Wayne said, "whoa, what is going on here?" The middle robber said, "young fella, get down on the floor, face down, or you are going to die." Sheriff Jim Smithfield, who had known Wayne for years, said, "better do as they say Wayne. This is not your fight." "So you are going to fight these three men by yourself?" "I may not survive, but I will take at least the leader of the gang when I go down. So get on the floor, please." "Well I can't do that." As the robbers heard Wayne, they all started to turn their guns towards Wayne. That is when Wayne drew his gun and fanned three quick shots that sounded like a single explosion. All three robbers dropped to the floor–all three shot in the head.

Sheriff Jim turned to face the door, as he saw his deputy arrive. He said to deputy Barnes, "is there any hombre holding their horses?" "There was an unarmed kid holding three horses, he is now handcuffed to the railing. Did you put these scumbags down?" "No, Wayne saved my bacon, because I knew I was going to die!" Oscar Barnes said, "how could you get them with only one shot?" "Oscar, that was three shots from Wayne's gun."

The tellers were getting up from the floor, opening windows to ventilate the place from the black smoke. The deputy left to get the undertaker and the bank President came up to the Sheriff. "Jim I am sorry you walked into this fracas, I honestly thought you were a goner. And you, Wayne, we will all be forever grateful for your gun handling abilities. Thank You."

Sheriff Smithfield said, "Wayne, you have sand. I have known you for 10 years and never knew you had the handgun gift. Would you escort me to the office for a few minutes." After arriving at his desk, Sheriff Jim started going through wanted posters. He pulled three.

"Wayne, the three you shot were wanted for murder, kidnaping and bank robbery. The two followers each have a bounty of $500 and the leader has a bounty of $1000. Both were wanted dead or alive. With the telegraph, I will have a Western Union voucher for you in 48 hours."

"According to town rules, you are also getting their horses, guns and all their personal belongings." "Sheriff, I cannot accept that, I only did this to save your life and I have no regrets. There was no way I could let three no-goods take the life of our sheriff." "I know and I appreciate that, but take the horses to your uncle and the guns to arm your ranch hands. If they are not needed, Bruce Hawkins at the livery will buy the horses and tack, and Ed's Mercantile will buy the pistols/rifles." "OK I will sell the horses but bring the guns home"

"Now before you leave, let me make you an offer. Hawthorne is going to grow out of control with the RR coming within two months. I am getting along in years at age 55, and I have two green deputies who need guidance. I admit that we need your gun handling expertise. I am willing to train you to take my job and make a lawman out of you. The pay is $100 per month with your room paid in a boarding house and your meals paid at the local diner. You have unlimited ammunition for your practice sessions to maintain your skills. Any arrests of criminals with a price on their heads is your benefit, as well as their horses, guns and personal property."

"I know your uncle and I have followed your upbringing. Sam told me of your interest in the judicial system when you were in school. I will make you a respectable lawman. I will give you the tricks of the trade and help you make your name in this growing community. Go home, think about it, and talk to Sam and Cora. Get back to me."

Before going home, Wayne went to the livery and sold all three horses with their tack and saddles for $140. The saddlebags were included, but not the six boxes of 44-40 new ammo. He went back to the bank to get his payroll cash. He also started a separate bank account in his name and deposited the $140. He then loaded the buckboard with the supplies and headed home–with three Colts and three 1873 rifles.

The ride home was slower than usual. Instead of 45 minutes with a buckboard, it took almost twice as long. Wayne was in a quandary. He had made a commitment to his pa and ma, but saw a way to make his name, and see if ranching was his future. It would take many days of thinking to present a winning argument with Sam and Cora.

***

CHAPTER 2

Changing Careers

After arriving home, Wayne stopped at the barn to unload the hardware, then the bunkhouse to unload cookie's items, and then pulled up to the house. He unloaded the food and dropped the cash payroll on the kitchen table. He then brought in the three Winchester 1873 lever rifles, Colt pistols and the six boxes of 44-40 ammo. The guns went into his room. He then got back on the wagon and went back to the barn. He unharnessed the horses and released them to the corral for some hay. Sam and Cora had noticed the six guns, but decided to not ask questions, since they knew their son would explain when he was ready.

A week went by and Wayne worked the cattle with the other ranch hands. He was noticeably pensive and quiet, but no one would ask him what was troubling him. Finally, one evening after dinner, Wayne spoke up.

"Last week, I killed three men." "We know, George Wilson of the Bar W Ranch next door, stopped two days ago and told us the story." "I had to do it to save our sheriff's life–I could not allow evil men to take the life of a good man. And that is the issue I cannot get out of my mind. With my gun handling skill, I feel I am destined to protect the lives of the innocent and provide justice for the victims."

Sam and Cora listened without interrupting him. "To complicate matters, Sheriff Smithfield offered me a job with the benefit of being trained in the town and county laws. This job would fit with my ideas of protecting people and would also make my name in this community before the RR arrives."

"I feel that being a lawman will be a phase in my life. I know I am destined to be a rancher and I will likely return to the Double S Ranch at some point when it is time for me to settle down. I hope to find a wife and have my own family–lawmen don't fit the family life. Remember, I would only be a half hour away.

"What are your benefits and pay?" "It pays $100 per month with room and board. It is higher than most towns because of the expected activity from the RR, and no one wants a dangerous job. I would have one day off per week but not on weekends. If I arrest a criminal that has a wanted poster, I will be able to accept the reward, get the horses, guns and personal property."

"Are you certain that your gun handling skills will keep you alive?" "There is no 100% guarantee, but with unlimited ammo provided by the town, I will maintain my skills. What I need to learn are the laws and how to function as a lawman. With Sheriff Jim's experience, he will train me and the other two deputies.

Sam added, "we have known for some time that this day would come. Looking back, at a young age you did not tolerate bullies, your zest in learning legal issues when in high school, your infatuation with guns, and learning proper handling techniques, were the signs of the future."

Cora added her feelings, "under the following conditions, that you meet us at church on Sunday's and then join us for lunch at Simms's diner. Plus you come home to dinner at least two nights per month." "And when you come home for dinner, we will have a business meeting. We want you to see where the money is going and what new ranching problems have crept up. We want you to always be current on the status of this ranch—your ranch we might say, heh."

With Sam and Cora approaching their 50's, they felt they were able to manage the ranch for another ten years. Reluctantly, they gave Wayne their blessings. They were only letting him leave on a temporary basis, and knew that he would eventually return to the ranch.

***

When Sheriff Jim saw Wayne arrive, he knew the die was cast. "Well Wayne, are you joining out staff?" "Yes, let's give it a try." Sheriff Jim hands Wayne a Western Union voucher for $2000, and tells Wayne to follow him. "First we are going to the National Bank to deposit this voucher, then we will register you at Rose's Boarding House, Simms' diner, Hawking livery and the paymaster at the town council headquarters.

Back at the office, Wayne took the sheriff's oath and was given his deputy sheriff's badge. He was introduced to the two deputies, Oscar Barnes and Ray Connors. "Now that formalities are over with, let's have an official meeting to go over some basic rules."

1. I am training the three of you because I will retire in 5 years.

2. Wayne is our resident shootist, let's use his skills respectfully.

3. Each man gets one day off per week, but never on weekends.

4. Each man has night duty twice per week. He can sleep in the private bunk in the jail/sheriff's office. I will take one night per week.

5. There are no days off when a cattle drive is in town.

6. No one does private security, you work for the town.

7. Each man gets three books to read, state law, county law and town law. I will hold a weekly class to keep each of you on schedule.

8. Practice regularly at the town range. Ammo is free.

9. No alcohol when on duty.

10. The entire county is our jurisdiction. Know the boundaries and the towns in every square mile.

11. To the victors belong the spoils. Yes, if you arrest a criminal with a price on his head,

the reward is yours as well as their horse, guns and personal property.

12. If you take a wife, you will add $30 to your salary to pay for housing out of the boarding house.

13. The most important—you need to get out and be seen in the town. Consequently, one of us walks the entire town four times a day. Morning as the businesses open, noon, closing time and 11PM each day. It is OK for one deputy to do the north end while the other does the south end.

14. If one or more deputy is sent out of town on county duty, the remaining deputies must cover the town. I will choose the deputy for the outside county jobs.

15. Last—cover your backs—work as teams and rely on each other.

***

CHAPTER 3
Deputy's 1st Month

The first week as a deputy sheriff was an indoctrination week. Sheriff Jim escorted Wayne during his first exposure in making rounds. As they entered Ed's Mercantile, he explained that all deputy sheriffs were expected to walk in all businesses and simply wave.

"If the merchant waves back, then all is well. If he does not wave, there is a problem in the makings. Then you walk out as if all is OK, and wait outside for the customers to leave—and expect a confrontation. We don't want you to ask the merchant what is wrong, for that will place the merchant at risk. If it is a robbery in the makings, the merchant will give the miscreants what they want. You rectify the issue, once the trouble makers exit the business. This is especially true at the bank. All the tellers know to wave to give the all clear sign."

It was good that the first week was slow without fights, robberies, shootings or worse. It gave the three deputies time to start reading the town laws, practice shooting at the range and getting use to keeping coffee on the stove. Since the town paid for meals and boarding, the deputies only had to do their own laundry or arrange an account at Mr. Lings laundry and bath house.

The town council paid to board each sheriff's horse, or to pay for a rental when a horse was needed on outside county activities. Wayne had his own 17 hand Morgan gelding. The town agreement with Hawkins's Livery included hay, oats and an exercising corral. It was up to Wayne to ride him regularly.

It did not take long for Oscar and Ray to realize they could benefit from Wayne's willingness to instruct them in proper gun handling. These handling tricks would be lifesaving in the future. It also allowed the three to get familiar, and know how they could trust each other.

The first class given by Sheriff Jim was on how to fill out an incident report, or how to take a statement from a witness. It was not just a matter of adding a name, date, location and time of day, it also required a detailed description of what transpired when the sheriff arrived on the scene. Witness's statements needed facts, seen or heard, by the individual, not here-say from other people.

Every week day, before the RR arrived, one of the deputies was sent on a day's trip to travel the county roads and introduce themselves to the ranchers and homesteaders. It actually took four weeks for all three deputies to complete their introductions.

During that first week, Wayne went to see the local gunsmith, Omer Harrigan. "Hello Deputy Swanson, what can I do for you?" "First, please call me Wayne. I am looking for a modified 12 gauge double barrel shotgun. I want the barrels cut down to 12 inches with open bores. I also want polished chambers to shuck out spent shotgun shells, and loosen the hinge so the barrels open without resistance. The external hammer springs need to be reduced power so the cocking will be easier and quicker. I would also prefer a pistol grip stock and a single trigger for quick repeat shots. Is this possible?"

"Yes, I will have to order the model that comes with a single trigger and a pistol grip stock. I can do the other modifications." "Great, now I will need a special holster since I have been told that you are a master leather worker as well as a gunsmith. I would like to have a special holster that will fit this shotgun. The holster would fit on my upper back with adjustable belts that go over my shoulder to under my armpits—just like a back pack. The leather should be black to match my revolver holster, and be loose enough for the shotgun to extract easily. Include 5 boxes of buckshot—two in 00 Buck and three in #3 Buck."

"I can do all this. I will include a telegram to my gun supplier, and order the single trigger model. It will come by freight line within two days. I will need four days for the modifications and the holster. You will have it within a week." "The last item is a four round slide to add to my gunbelt for the extra buckshot shells."How much for the entire package including a cleaning kit." "That will be $40 for the single trigger model, $15 for the modifications, $25 dollars for the custom holster, $2.50 for the five boxes of buckshot, 50 cents for the telegram and $2 for freight, the cleaning kit comes with the gun and the black slide is $3. The grand total unfortunately comes to $88." "Not a problem, for a custom job, I expected worse. Here is a bank draft for the amount and thank you so much for the service."

***

During the next month, Wayne learned from his experiences. His traveling of the county revealed the fact that even if he lived in the area all his life, he never realized how many people were in the county. The ranches on the east side of the county included his pa and ma's ranch, and all of their friends. These sections not only had ranches but it had many homesteaders, especially in the northwest to southwest areas. These homesteaders had small cattle herds, large fenced in gardens, chickens and hogs. They basically lived off the land and came to town for food staples, and sell their eggs, fresh vegetables and pork.

Homesteading was a hard way to start, especially if mother nature did not provide decent weather for crops.

Wayne enjoyed his traveling days, he got to meet folks that he would recognize in town. He also got to meet the daughters, who would come to the church socials or the town dances.

The town rounds were a staple of every day activities for a deputy. The morning rounds were quiet. The merchants were opening up and were glad to see that the lawmen were on the job. The midday rounds were busy with the hustle and bustle of people coming to town on business or shopping. The evening rounds were more dangerous and often performed with two deputies, especially in the southern direction where there were two saloons. Whitaker's Saloon was a drinking establishment with private card playing. It was more orderly since the bartender was the owner, Calvin Whitaker. The Silver Queen was a rowdy joint with organized gambling, paid professional card players that covered Faro and Poker. The big wheel was a favorite for quick returns on your money. There was also private card playing. The owner was rarely at the saloon, and expected his armed security team to keep order.

Wayne's favorite was the midday rounds. People were friendly and he continued to learn the names of locals, outside ranchers and homesteaders. One day Wayne had a revelation. He was about to enter Ed's Mercantile, when he looked in the front window. He saw a customer put food staples in his backpack when Ed was not watching. Suddenly the customer turned around and exited the mercantile. Wayne met him at the door.

"Are you sure you want to do this, sir?" "No Deputy Swanson, I don't want to do this, Ed has been fair with me by extending my family credit. Today, my kids are hungry, and I needed more credit. Times are tough with the drought and it doesn't seem to let up. I thought this might be a better alternative, but I was wrong. Is there any way I can reverse my thieving activity?" "Let the customer step out and then let's go in to see Ed." "I am somewhat embarrassed to face Ed." "Nonsense, trust me."

Ed, this gentleman needs our help. He has a backpack full of food and he needs more. He has flour, bacon, sugar and salt. Let's add ten cans of beans, oatmeal, jam, a full ham and ten tins of beef. What is his credit amount up to?" Ed opens the ledger and says, "Mr. Trucot is up to $49.65." "Here is a bank draft for $250. Tomorrow Mr. Trucot will return with his wife and children. Seeing Mr. Trucot's worn out shirt and pants, the family all needs new clothing. Give them all the food they need and extend their credit. Include feed for the horses, chickens and hogs if they have some. Make sure the kids each get a toy and plenty of candy. Until these folks get back on their feet, extend their credit, and when they hit

$50, I will give you a bank draft. Any questions, Mr. Sorenson?" "None whatsoever Wayne." Mr. Trucot was speechless and obviously stunned. Wayne simply said, "you're welcome Mr. Trucot."

After Mr. Trucot left, Ed said, "That is a lot of money to spend on your salary. The word will get around. So to handle this, I think we both have to say nothing to anyone and let this die out. I will tell Mr. Trucot the same thing." "No Ed, I have $2,000 in an account from bank robbery rewards. I can find no better use for that money than in the hands of our residents having hard times. Today, I'll add your name to this benefactor account. Treat anyone that needs help the same way.

A few days later, Omer Harrigan sent word that Wayne's order was ready. Wayne went right over, "I got the good news, my firearm is ready?" "Yes and all is fine." Omer added, "the holster is formed by a double layer of soft leather. There is a firm barrel stop, and the pouch releases the shotgun easily. The fit on the high back with adjustable shoulder/arm straps makes it comfortable. The gun hinge is without resistance and the hammers cock easily. You will love the single trigger, and it has minimal creep. All in all, I believe you will like how this handles in close quarters. Go to the range and try it out. Come back if there is any problem." "Show me how to put the holster on and then I will be off." "Remember to take the shotgun out of the holster before you harness it onto your back, that way the shotgun won't fall out."

***

By the end of the month, Wayne was comfortable with city life and his new job. He had attended several church socials and town dances. He was getting to know the people, his partners and the businesses. One Friday evening a ruckus was reported at Whitaker's Saloon. By the time, Wayne was out of the office on a run, a shot was heard. Wayne pulled out his snubbed shotgun, cocked the hammers and entered the saloon.

"What is going on here?" There was a man standing at a card table and pointing his gun at a player. Calvin was holding his hand up and said, "this fella was accusing one of the card players of cheating. I came over when things got heated up and got shot in the arm." "Mister, put your gun down and we'll settle this." "No way, this scoundrel will get away. He deserves to catch a bullet and I plan to give him one."

Wayne tried a second approach. "Mister, right now you will be charged with aggravated assault. If you shoot this man, you will hang. Use your head, it's not worth your life over a few bucks, heh?" "I can't, if I put my gun down, he will draw on me and likely shoot me."

Wayne saw no solution, he stepped forward and dropped the shotgun's barrel on top of the dude's head. He dropped to the floor like a lead balloon and his gun came out of his hand–still uncocked. "Sorry to have to do that, but I had to save this dude's life. Would some of you gents help me bring him to jail."

"Before we leave, what was the issue that lead to a cheating charge?" One player said, "when we lifted our hidden cards, there were five queens on the table." You three men, pull up your sleeves." All players complied and no cards were seen. Wayne then ordered all hats off. One player had a queen and two kings tucked inside the brim. "Well Sir, you've been had. I am arresting you for inciting a serious confrontation and firearms discharge. You need a few weeks in jail before you leave town."

Calvin Whitaker went to see Doc Sutton to get sutured. Wayne locked up both perpetrators in their own cell. He then took the time to write up the event, and the remainder of the evening was uneventful. In the AM, Sheriff Jim arrived, reviewed Wayne's statement. He then said, "so what did you do wrong, Wayne?" Wayne was at a loss.

"You entered a building knowing that a shot had been fired and you walked up to the perpetrator, leaving men behind you, and without a backup to watch your back. In a situation like this, do your bidding from a safe location with your back to the wall, not to the batwing doors. That is why I like two of you guys to go to a shooting. You need to do your job safely."

Later that day, Sheriff Jim asked Wayne why he had that custom shotgun. Wayne answered, "with my activity at the bank being common knowledge, I feel that anytime I can avoid pulling my Colt Peacemaker, that there is less of a chance someone will die. I guess a sawed-off shotgun is so devastating that it takes an idiot to put up a handgun against it. If I can save a few lives by intimidating a gun holding trouble maker, then it is worth it. Being a lawman is exacting work, but shooting everyone to uphold the law is not the answer." *That day, Sheriff Jim knew that Wayne had the qualities to take over his job.*

A few weeks later, Wayne was doing his midday rounds, when he noticed four horses at the bank. He thought that was a bit unusual, so he walked over to look at the horse brands. He was halfway across the street when three men came out holding bags of money with their guns drawn. Wayne drew his shotgun and yelled, "stop right there and put your hands up. The men looked at Wayne and were weighing their options. "This shotgun will take two of you out at a time. Is it worth dying over money? The three men just dropped their guns and were clearly out of a potential shootout.

Suddenly, there was a gunshot in the bank and the fourth bank robber came out. He immediately pointed his gun at Wayne and fired. Wayne took a bullet in his side and fired one barrel. The bank robber took a full load of #3 buckshot and was hurled backwards through the bank doors. Out of the bank came a teller holding his bleeding shoulder.

The Sheriff arrived with Oscar, and took over. Wayne and the teller were brought to Doc Sutton. Doc said "Wayne, you are lucky. This is a superficial wound, thru and thru, the muscular wall. I will irrigate the wound channel of debris from your shirt, and sterilize the area with alcohol–that will hurt. I will suture the wound as needed and will remove the sutures in 10 days. You will come to my office in 48 hours to change the dressing." "Thanks, Doc, what is your charge?" "$5" Wayne give him a chit for the amount to be paid by the town.

Wayne was out of work the three day minimum for being shot. When he returned, Sheriff Jim told him that those four robbers had a price on their head. The three under arrest had a $250 reward on their heads, the leader who was killed had a $500 reward. Sheriff Jim said, "here is a Western Union voucher for $1250. It will help replenish your account–the one that your have been using up to help people in need. Yes, we all know what you have done for this community." "Well I could not accept the money for personal use, when good people cannot feed their families. It just was not right. Now that you know, I will sell the horses and saddles to Bruce Hawkins at the livery and add the money to the account. I will keep the guns for another project of mine." *Little did the sheriff know that his $2,000 account was down to $350.*

"So what did Wayne do wrong during the robbery?" Oscar and Ray were not sure how to answer. Ray said, "I didn't think he did anything wrong." "So you would also have been shot, but likely had been shot in the chest, and died on the spot, heh! When a crime is in the process, if someone points a cocked handgun at you, shoot him before he shoots you. This is not a game of fairness or luck. It is about upholding the law and stopping criminals, before you get shot or killed. This is a dangerous job, but you can make it safer by setting limits to your bodily threats. Their has to be a line in the sand, if a criminal passes it, then you have to bring the situation to a quick end."

A week later, Sheriff Jim had his weekly class planned. It was time to discuss the town's growth. "Gentlemen, the Monroe Silver Mine just found a rich vein and the mine is booming with new workers and modern equipment. This has pushed the RR. The RR is coming soon because they want the ore freight from the mine. The surveyors are done. The construction crews will be leveling and excavating the trail. Track laying crews will begin. The 40 mile RR spur from the main north/south line at Pueblo will be here in three weeks."

The RR will come from the east. Cattle holding and loading pens will be east of town. The people and freight will transfer at the town depot, and the RR will then continue west for two more miles to the Monroe Mine. There it will drop three open cars and pick up three cars full of silver ore. Everything will then ship east.

This is changing our quiet town. First, the name is changing to Silver Circle, because the town aquifer is twelve feet down in a round circle, and the town is growing because of silver. The council is getting many building permits. We are getting a second construction company, three new saloons, Silvers, Silver King and Gunthers. Other buildings include a ladies house of working girls, several housing apartments, private homes and a second livery. The mercantile is branching out. Ed's will stay as a dry goods store, but Ed will manage a separate hardware store. Another merchant will provide a separate seed and feed store, and a garment store will be started by a statewide chain. We will be getting our own blacksmith and many small service businesses."

Oscar asked, "can the lumber mill handle the demand for construction lumber?" "No, with two construction groups, I suspect lumber will be coming by RR, along with doors, windows and general construction hardware."

Wayne asked, "do we have the manpower to handle this growth?" "Time will tell. Weekends will be busy, loud and difficult to control. The mine workers will be in the saloons on payday, as well as the Cowboys delivering cattle to the RR holding pens. The council has given me the authority to hire as many new deputies as is needed to maintain order and the resident's safety.

Wayne points out, "with the lifting of the town's economy, more money will land in our bank. This will attract a bunch of professional thieves. These are the dangerous kind that have a price on their heads, and often wanted 'Dead or Alive.' The kind that have no choices—if they get arrested they will hang. So they will always take their chances with their guns. This increases our danger level, and the way we respond to a robbery. We have to accept this and become more aggressive shootists if we want to stay alive."

Sheriff Jim adds, "let's spend more time with the wanted posters and share the telegrams from outlying sheriffs. There is a tent city starting south of town. This will become a dangerous zone, and requires two deputies at all times, anywhere south of the courthouse."

Wayne was showing signs of knowing how to stay alive. He had moves that were naturally safe. Most important, it was not just safety tips to protect the deputy, it was also moves to protect the public and victims. His two partners recognized this and gladly gave Wayne the lead. Wayne accepted this because he could rely on Oscar's or Ray's sound backup.

In reality, days on the job were certainly bound to change.

***

CHAPTER 4

Growing Pains

Things quickly started to change, The RR surveyors were done and spent a few days in town—utilizing the diner, hotel and saloons. When they left for their next job, the ground leveling crews arrived and also spent several days in town. Finally the track layers were last to utilize the town's services. By the time they left, the carpentry crews arrived to build the water tower, windmill and RR depot/office.

These RR workers were a lively bunch who liked to celebrate when they were off the job. The tent city was going up with several new saloons with working girls. It was a noisy time, but no one complained. These RR workers were temporary, and tolerated since the RR was coming to town.

Finally the RR came to town. Settlers were arriving by train and heading to the RR office. The RR was selling off land at fifty to seventy cents per acre, depending on the quality of the grassland, water supply and proximity to town. A rancher could pay $320 for a full section of land(640 acres) and raise 250 head of cattle. A homesteader could purchase a quarter section(160 acres) for $80 and could live off the the land with a garden, a few beef, hogs, and chickens—with income from eggs, pork meat, beef and hay.

Each day at 1PM, the RR came to town with its merchant's supplies, lumber and passengers. The deputy sheriffs would meet the train to watch the passengers disembark. They were looking for faces that would match wanted posters, or men that were hard looking, well healed and with their horses in the stock cars. These would match the profile of hired guns or trouble makers. The daily routine would end by changing cars that were full of silver ore and loading stock cars with cattle going east. Passengers were last to board going east to Pueblo where they would change trains to selected locations.

One day on evening rounds, Wayne was in Gunthers Saloon in tent city and noticed a table of card players that looked suspicious. He ran back to the office and went through the wanted posters and finally spotted the one he was looking for. "Ray and Oscar follow me, the Dunwood gang is in tent city at Gunthers. As they ran back, they spread out. Ray went to the rear exit, Wayne went in the front door with Oscar covering his back. "We are too late, the gang left." Wayne steps up to the bartender and asks where the gang might be. "As soon as you stepped out of the tent, they got up and left, rushing out of town on their horses. Were they wanted?" "Yes, but something tells me they will be back."

The next day, Ray did the morning rounds. All was quiet. By 9:30, with all three deputies present, Jim was getting ready for his weekly class on town and county law when a bank clerk rushed into the office. "The bank has been robbed and old man Rumford has been knocked out." "Go get Doc Sutton and we are on our way to the bank."

Wayne confirmed that Mr. Rumford had his head caved in, and Doc Sutton pronounced him dead. The bank tellers described the five robbers and Wayne knew they were describing the Dunwood gang. Wayne went outside to look at the hoof marks and saw one right rear shoe had a forging hammer mark on the right rear shoe tip. That was the only unique hoof marks of all five horses.

The bank president said, "they took $1500 and the bank's survivability is in jeopardy. Are you mounting a posse to go after them?" "It's very dangerous to go after them within the first hour. The Dunwood's gang trademark is to wait for the posse and set up an ambush. These five criminals are murderers. After the ambush, they would be safe to escape and we would have lost some good folks. My department will go after them as soon as we can get supplies to last us a week. We'll get your money and bring them back, dead or alive."

The sheriff and his deputies, gathered at the office to make plans.

Wayne spoke first, "If we don't get this money back and arrest these robbers, it will be a white flag for every crook in our tri-county area that we are a soft town. We owe it to our town to provide a quick justice."

"I agree, the question is how many of you do I send and can safely spare away from town." Wayne says, "send me alone. I'm good at tracking and will not quit till I get them. I may have to pick a few off before I confront the gang face to face. I'm comfortable in arresting them, even if it means a shootout."

Oscar adds, "he's right, Ray and I are not as capable, and you need us here with the way the town is growing." Sheriff Jim adds, "and I know I'm getting too old to go on the trail by myself. Ok, Wayne, but be conservative and don't take any chances. We knew that this criminal activity was likely, which would require one of us on the trail. So at any cost, do the job and come back to us."

Wayne went to get Brownie and rented a packhorse from Bruce. Ed's Mercantile provided his supplies: coffee, bacon, canned beans and beef, biscuits, beef jerky, three canteens, cooking grate, frypan, coffee pot, tin plate/cup, utensils, oats for the horses, bed roll, extra blanket, slicker and a small tent. While Ed was getting everything onto the packhorse panniers, Wayne went to get his firearms, he brought his backpack shotgun and his Winchester 76. He brought several boxes of #3 buckshot, 45/60 rifle ammo, and 44-40 pistol ammo. He also included field glasses, a compass, a warm winter coat and the five wanted posters.

Horace Dunwood had found a perfect ambush spot. After a bend around trees, there were several large boulders. They had hidden their horses, and all five gang members, with their rifles, were waiting for the posse. They waited for an hour and Horace said, "looks like there is no posse on our tails. So there is no reason to stay here. Let's ride east to the next town and beyond. We have a two day ride. Before we ride, we are dividing the money, each of us gets $300. That way if we get separated, everyone has been paid."

Wayne followed the tracks heading east. He quickly came to the ambush site and was glad Sheriff Jim had warned them. He continued at a slow trot while the tracks were clear. He figured the gang was traveling twice as fast as he was for the first day. Then they would feel secure and slow down. Wayne planned to keep his same pace as long as the horses were handling the workload.

That first night, Wayne set up a full camp. He chose a site inside the tree-line at his back, with a good view of any oncoming visitors. He unsaddled both horses and hobbled the packhorse. Brownie would not leave camp without Wayne. The horses had good grass to crop and a stream for water. He started a fire and found some easy firewood around the trees. With a good set of coals, he placed the grate between rocks, heated water for coffee and cooked his canned beef stew.

Since it was a clear autumn night, he did not set up the tent which was reserved for rainy or cold nights. He set up his bedroll and was fast asleep. He depended on Brownie to warn him of visitors or predators. After a good night sleep, a breakfast of coffee, bacon and leftover stew, he saddled the horses, closed camp and was on the trail for day two.

The tracks were still visible and it was clear that they were not trying to camouflage their trail. To Wayne's surprise, the weather cooled off by noon. He was glad that he had brought his winter coat. As he put his winter coat on, he realized that this cold weather was to his advantage.

The Dunwood gang was complaining about the weather turning suddenly cold. Harry Wooten suggested that they should stop by early afternoon to set up camp with a fire for heat. Horace answered, if you had not killed that teller, we might have been safe of the law. Now thanks to you we need to push on. Why did you smash your gun barrel on the side of his head?" "Because no one was responding to your command of filling the bags with money. After I knocked him out, the money was flying out of the drawers, and we were able to get out without firing a single gunshot." "Whatever, but I guess we can quit early, warm up with a fire, and take our chances."

Wayne had figured, that if he stayed on the trail till dark, he might be able to sneak up to their camp. He stopped at a stream with good grass and let the horses crop grass. Because it was so cold, he gave them some oats. They got back on the trail and Wayne's horses were clearly not having any difficulties. He stopped one more time in mid afternoon to again let the horses drink and feed on grass.

An hour later, Wayne suddenly smelled smoke. He had been right, the gang stopped early and were sitting by a rip roaring fire. He then dismounted, tethered his horses and started walking with his high powered rifle—the Winchester 1876. He walked slowly for a half hour till he saw the camp and could make out the five men. He was an estimated 150 yards from camp. He set the rear ladder sight to the 150 yard marking and took aim at the man standing by the fire.

The gun roared and the man standing was thrown five feet backwards and was still. The camp exploded with activity, and the four robbers were trying to see a potential target to shoot with their 1873 rifles. The robbers were blinded by the fire's brightness and were just waiting. Wayne reloaded and took aim at another target of a man kneeling close to the fire. He pulled the trigger and the target shot up and was thrown backwards.

Seeing the results, Horace yells, "that is no regular rifle, he is using some high power rifle and he is going to pick us all off, one at a time. Let's go in the trees, saddle our horses and get out of here, now!"

Wayne suddenly realized that the targets were all gone. He figured they were getting their horses. Thinking they would come back to camp to pick up their supplies, he decided to fire two more rounds into the trees—that would guarantee they would high tail it out without supplies.

As they were ready to leave, Harry said, "we can't leave without the money from our two dead guys." "You are such an idiot. If you go back to the camp, whoever is out there will pick you off. So if you are doing this, leave me your money, since you won't need it where you'll be going." Harry changed his mind and followed the other two gang members with a full gallop out of the area.

Wayne knew that he had dwindled the gang by two outlaws. He then walked back to his horses and rode into camp. The two outlaws had money in their pockets. One had $372 and the other had $339. Wayne separated out $600, to be returned to the town bank, and placed it into his money belt. The remaining $111 went into his pocket. The outlaw's horses were unsaddled and hobbled next to a stream. His horses were similarly prepared for the evening. He then prepared dinner with beans, bacon and coffee. He eventually retired to his bedroll.

In the morning, after taking care of personal business, shaving and having a cold breakfast of beef jerky and cold coffee, he then started to close camp. He collected all the food left by the escaping outlaws, their colts and rifles. Loaded the two dead men onto the saddle and tied their hands and feet to the stirrups. With everything loaded, he headed east to River Bend, a half day's ride away.

Arriving at noon, Wayne went to the sheriff's office. "Good morning, deputy. I have two bodies outside and would like to see the sheriff." The deputy brought him to Sheriff Johnson, "yes young man, what can I do for you?" Opening up his vest to show his badge, he said, "my name is Wayne Swanson, deputy from Silver Circle. I have been on the trail for days going after the Dunwood gang who robbed the bank. I have two robbers outside and need to have them identified."

The sheriff stepped outside, looked at the dead men's faces, and matched them to the wanted posters. "Was there any identification on the bodies?" "Yes, one had his name scratched in the back of his holster as Paul Grumley, and the other had a letter from his sister addressed to Euclide Simpson, but without a return address." "That is good enough for me. I will notify the individuals who posted the rewards and can arrange for a Western Union voucher to arrive in Silver Circle in your name."

"What do you want to do with their horses and guns?" "Sell the horses, saddles and tact. With the money send a telegram to Sheriff Jim in Silver Circle and inform him of current events. Pay the undertaker for a simple burial, Pay for shipping the four guns to Sheriff Jim and keep the rest." "That will give me way too much money since I can get $90 from the livery owner and your requests will not be more than $10."

"That is Ok, the money is yours, I only lay claims to their guns, holsters, and scabbards. I will now go to the bank and arrange for a $600 bank transfer to the bank in Silver Circle. Would you come with me to certify the source of the recovered bank money? "Of course, lets go."

After business was taken cared of, Wayne had a full lunch of fried chicken, mashed potatoes and coffee—paid his 50 cents bill and left the waitress a two bits(25 cents) tip. He then went to the dry goods store to supplement his food supply. He asked the owner, "did you get three men on the run looking for food supplies?" "Yes, a tall guy with long face, white shirt and tall hat crown. They were in a rush, they picked up coffee, tobacco, beans and cooking utensils. The funny thing, all three also left with winter coats. They paid and took off heading north." What is north?" "Brighton, thirty miles into a tough town without law."

Wayne was about to take off when he thought of something and went to see the local blacksmith. "Good day sir, could you make me three -------- ------with a 6 foot ------------. "Of course, it will take me an hour since the parts are already made, I just have to put them together. That will cost you $6 for all three."

Wayne waited and left with his three contraptions. It was late in the afternoon and knew he had 4 hours of riding before dark. That would make him arrive in Brighton early tomorrow morning. Wayne eventually set up a complete camp. He knew the Dunwoods were already in Brighton, and probably drunk at the first saloon they visited.

His horses had good grass and water. He made himself a full hot dinner of ham, fried potatoes, and onions–his recent purchases at River Bend.

Meanwhile in Brighton, at Whilten's Saloon, Horace Dunwood was talking to his two men, Stan Hutchins and Harry Wooten. "That man who took our two guys must have been a lawman. He knew we were wanted, dead or alive, and would fight him. Remember, fighting is the only chance we have. If we are caught alive, we either fight or face the hangman. Now we are relatively safe in this town until we meet with this lawman. Once we spot him, we can kill him and make it out of here without fear of a posse coming after us."

Wayne arrived in town at 3PM. He went to the livery and talked to the owner. "Did you get new boarders last night?" "Yes late last night three men arrived with completely spent horses. I wanted to whip the idiot owners for doing this to their animals. Instead, I charged them double rate of $2 a day per horse." "Does one have a heavy hammer mark on the right rear shoe.? Yes, one has that mark, which I found when I checked their shoes today." "Ok, here is $5. Would you saddle them and make them trail ready with recent oats, water and hay. Keep them in the livery until I send someone saying 'Wayne wants the three horses that are saddled.'" "Be glad to."

Wayne walked his two horses to the hitching rail at Whilten's Saloon. Put his backpack shotgun on, added the sixth round to his Colt and hid his badge under his vest. He walked through the batwing doors, headed to the bar, and ordered a nickel size beer. He slowly started looking at the crowd sitting at card tables. In one corner was Horace's face with two other scruffy looking dudes. Wayne started walking amongst the tables looking for an empty spot to join a game. He found one next to the Dunwood table. "Gentlemen, may I join your game? As he placed his beer on the table, he swiftly drew his shotgun. The men at the table started to panic, as Wayne got up. He opened his vest, turned around and yelled, : "Horace Dunwood, you and your men are under arrest for murder and bank robbery in Silver Circle, Colorado."

Instantaneously, all three outlaws drew their guns. Wayne shot the man to his left who was the first to have his gun drawn. The shotgun blast threw his body against the wall. Wayne dropped his shotgun to his left side and drew his Colt. He then shot at Horace's right hand as he was pointing his gun at Wayne. Horace screamed and dropped his pistol. He grabbed his hand realizing that he had lost two fingers. The third man hesitated. Wayne said, "you're on my right, so you'll have to turn to your left to shoot me. If you start turning, I'll shoot your dead. You would have better odds to escape from me before I get you back to Silver Circle." The man put his gun back in his holster and placed his hands on the table.

Meanwhile, Horace was still screaming out in pain. He swore he would kill Wayne before they got to Silver Circle. Wayne was not listening and yelled out. "Somebody get the Doc" "We don't have one."

Ok, get a clean towel and wrap his hand up. For this dollar, who will go to the livery and say to the owner "Wayne wants the three saddled horses." One fella ran out. "Now for a dollar each, I need two men to help me handcuff these two with their hands in their backs. Then load them on the horses and tie their feet to the stirrups with pigging strings."

After the securing of the two outlaws and the loading of all three on their horses, Horace said, "Good luck in trying to get us to trial. You will slip up and we will put you down." That is when Wayne went in the packhorse panniers and came back with two chains. At one end was a collar that Wayne quickly snapped and padlocked around the two outlaw's necks. The look on Horace's face was mixture of anger and surprise. The other end was secured to the stirrups by padlock. The last items to pack were the three Colts and 1873 rifles with several boxes of 44-40 ammo. Before taking off he went to the bartender and said, "how much for the damage and cleanup." "$20 should take care of it." He knew it was excessive but still handed the bartender a gold double Eagle.

Half hour out of town, on the road to River Bend, Wayne stops the five horse train. He steps to the body and empties his pockets of their content. Then he does the same to Horace and his buddy. He then counts the money. It came to

$989. He placed the $900 in his money belt to return to the bank, and the $89 in his pocket. He had not wanted to expose this money in Brighton where most of the bystanders were likely thieves themselves. Wayne then told Horace and friend, "we are going to travel fairly fast to River Bend, and only stop to rest the horses. If you fall off the horse, you are going to hurt more than die, so hold on or 'tough.'"

The road to River Bend was good and they were covering 8 miles each hour. With two half hour stops for feeding the horses oats, let them drink, and crop grass, they arrived in River Bend in 5 hours.

Wayne went straight to the sheriff's office and walked in to greet Sheriff Johnson. "Good day Deputy Swanson. I wasn't sure if you would head back here." "I got the other three and two are alive outside. Would you identify the dead one?" "You mean you have the remainder of the Dunwood gang?" "Yes." Going outside with the wanted posters, Sheriff Johnson identified the dead robber as Stan Hutchins by wanted poster and a gambling IOU in his pocket–with proper identification. He also verified the living two as Horace Dunwood and Harry Wooten.

"Ok, I will again notify the bank that issued these warrants and send a Western Union voucher to your Silver Circle telegraph office like the last transaction." "Now I owe you some money, I sold those two horses, tact and saddles for $95 and the expenses only cost $10." "No you owe me nothing, matter of fact you can sell Hutchin's horse and gear." "Well, if it's ok with you, I will give it to my deputy who definitely needs a mount upgrade, and I will get Hutchins buried." "Would you jail these two overnight?" "Sure." "I will remove the chains but will leave the neck collars on. Be careful if you take them to the privy, they are murderers. I strongly recommend that you use two deputies and if they try to escape, shoot them immediately. If they want to commit suicide that is their choice. Do not take any chances!"

Wayne brought the four horses to the local livery for oats, hay and water. He paid the $4 and asked that they be brushed down, and saddled in the AM. He then went to the local diner. He had a full meal of roast pork, mashed potatoes, gravy, fresh bread and coffee. He paid his 60 cent bill with a silver dollar to cover the tip. He then went to the hotel and paid $1.50 for a room and included 50 cents for a hot bath. In the morning he brought his gear and had a full 40 cents breakfast of fried potatoes, four eggs, bacon and plenty of coffee. He then headed to the livery for his three riding horses and one pack horse. He then walked to the sheriff's office.

"Good morning deputy, any problems?" "No, the sheriff watched as I took them to the privy, and after he went home for the night, I stayed up all night to guarantee they stayed put. They wanted to use the privy several times, but their requests fell on deaf ears. If you want to watch, I will walk them to the privy before we load them up." "Very good, did they get any food?" "Yes they got a cold roast beef sandwich and water last night–but no breakfast." "Good enough."

After they were loaded, Sheriff Johnson arrived. He said to Wayne, "the weather is turning and we expect a cold rain. Do you have a winter coat and slicker.?" "Yes, but my two passengers don't and that is too bad, heh." "I will telegraph Sheriff Jim, when do you expect to arrive in Silver Circle?" "We will travel all day, rest the horses as needed, and I expect to arrive before dark." As they were about to depart, Wayne added the chains to their neck collars and padlocked them to the stirrups. He then checked their handcuffed hands. After he mounted Brownie, the deputy thanked Wayne for the horse and saddle.

Two hours in the trip, it got cold and it started to rain. Horace yells out, "come on deputy, we are wet and freezing. Let's hole up under the tree cover and start a fire so we can warm up. Wayne who had not spoken a word for two hours finally said, "I don't care a rat's ass if you are uncomfortable. What about Mr. Rumford, killed by you and Wooten. His family will be uncomfortable for many years, thanks to you two scoundrels. You are monsters and need to be eliminated. If it wasn't for the respect of the legal system which I represent, I would slowly string you up to choke to death, and leave your bodies to the predators—that's what you deserve. So SHUT UP and move along!"

The caravan arrive by late afternoon. Wayne pulled up to the sheriff's office and left the two outlaws on their horses. He went inside and was greeted by all three men. "Thank God you made it back, we appreciated the update telegrams especially the one you sent before leaving this morning. Let's go outside and get those killers."

When they got outside their eyes got an overload. Horace and Harry were soaked, shivering, their faces in shock and their bodies leaning over the saddle horn. The real surprise was the handcuffs, neck collars and chains attached to the stirrups. "Well, Wayne, these are two boys that will be happy to lay down in their cells. I suspect we won't hear a peep from them till tomorrow morning." Two days later, Judge Atchison held the trial. The bank tellers and President Miller identified the two robbers. Wayne also testified. They were both found guilty and Judge Atchison sentenced them to hang the next morning.

A few days later, Wayne had a meeting with Ed regarding his benefactor fund. Ed said, when you left, you gave the bank authority for me to make bank drafts to cover homesteader's accounts. Whenever, I gave your money away, the recipients were sworn to keep silent on the subject. It worked, no one ever came to me and asked for your money. Yet your $2000 is gone. Here is the names and addresses of the recipients and the amount they were given. All the recipients know you are their benefactor but they were all told to not come and thank you in public—and it has stayed quiet."

Wayne looked at the list and recognized the names, "that is great Ed, so it looks like we have helped fourteen homesteaders." "Yes, and I have three homesteaders and two small ranchers approaching the $50 limit." "Well Ed, the special account has increased by $3000 as of this morning, from the Dunwood gang rewards. So continue administering the fund as needed."

Wayne went back to the routine of protecting the town. New businesses were setting up. Ed's Mercantile was branching out into three stores. Ed kept dry goods, a new owner took over garments and another started a real hardware. Ed's son started a seed and feed store. Other businesses included: a butcher shop, a tonsorial shop, a blacksmith, a hotel, a newspaper, a well drilling company and a third construction company. The courthouse was enlarged to accommodate the land office, tax department, lawyers and the resident Judge. Doc Sutton employed a new MD out of surgical training and built a small hospital with ten beds, one operating room and two doctor's offices.

Wayne and the deputies were busy housing drunks and breaking up fights. With all the money coming and going by trains, train robberies were getting common. The RR had to add more railroad armed detectives. Fortunately, the Sheriff's department was not responsible for deposits which were regularly transferred, by train, to the head bank in Denver. The shipment costs for cash funds was high because of the train robberies, but it was the price to do business.

With all the money in the bank vault, Wayne proposed a proactive approach to preventing robberies. The bank president agreed and started looking for a resident armed security. Yet, no locals wanted anything to do with this dangerous job. So the city council resolved the issue by allowing the sheriff's department the right to charge $5 for an eight hour business day. This income was above the regular monthly salary. This meant that other businesses would have less security. The merchants accepted this since their daily deposits went into the bank vault.

So for the next month, on a trial basis, a deputy was resident all day in the bank. All the deputies knew that the most dangerous time for a robbery is during the last hour of business. A robbery at that time would not allow a posse to track in pursuit because of darkness. During the day, the deputy had to identify each entry as regular customers or known residents. Any newcomer would raise their hackles. Each deputy was now carrying a back pack snubnose shotgun like Wayne's.

Nothing happened for three weeks, then one late afternoon just before closing, Wayne saw a scruffy individual enter. Wayne knew that this was a scout so he turned his back to hide his badge, and pretended to be a customer looking at banking brochures. The scout left without doing any banking. That is when Wayne went into action. All the tellers and customers were moved into the president's office and the vault was locked. Wayne placed his back against the boardwalk wall next to the front door but hidden by a tall grandfather clock.

Suddenly, four armed men with face masks ran into the bank. They were yelling a mixture of orders when they all went silent. There was no one in the bank. Wayne surprised all four, "put your hands up or get ready to die." The leader of the gang said, "that is not going to happen. We are four against your toy shotgun and"................ Wayne's shotgun roared once, and the leader was blown away against the teller's barred windows. Wayne moved the shotgun to his left hand, drew his pistol and said, "you three are looking at jail time if you are not wanted for murder. What is your decision, jail or death?" "I am not dying today and I'll take jail time. Come on guys, join me, we are not murderers."

Their trial was delayed four days because the Judge was ill. Sheriff Jim gave Wayne an assignment. "This morning, George Wilson of the Bar W Ranch came to file a complaint against his neighboring rancher, Stuart Boswell of the Box B Ranch. Apparently these two ranchers have large spreads of eight sections each. Wilson's ranch has two good streams and even several wells with windmills. The Box B has only one large stream with two branches that is showing signs of drying up in this drought. Boswell wants to buy a section with a good stream from Wilson, but George is not selling. George has offered to pipe free water from three of his wells through pipes to the Box B Ranch holding tanks, as long as Boswell pays for the pipes and tanks. Boswell refuses, and is beginning to threaten George Wilson. Would you go over there and talk to both of them, they are your parent's friends."

Since he had four days before the trial, he decided to visit his family's neighbors. Wayne arrived at the Double S Ranch and visited with his parents. After dinner, Wayne had his usual business meeting with his dad. Over the past years, these meetings and review of income and expenses kept Wayne up to date. The family ranch was doing well in all aspects.

Before bedtime, they got to discuss the feud going on between the Boswells and Wilsons. Sam repeated what Sheriff Jim had said. He summarized by saying that Stuart needed to accept George's generous offer and stop being a demanding bully."

In the morning, after breakfast, Wayne headed to the Bar W Ranch.

The access road branched into a Y with the Bar W Ranch sign on the right and the Box B Ranch sign on the left. Wayne arrived at the Wilsons and got the same story from Mr. Wilson plus some more news. "For the past two nights, we have had cattle shot dead. The first night it was ten, last night it was 27. What's it going to be tonight?" "You suspect the Boswell ranch hands are following Boswell's orders?" "Yes." "Well I am heading to the Box B Ranch, and I will make myself very clear about your offer, and the shooting of your cattle. I will then return and report to you." "Thank you, Wayne."

Arriving at the Box B, Stuart was sitting on the porch. Wayne asked permission to set down. Stuart said, "Ok Wayne, I knew you would show up sooner or later." "Well things are getting out of hand, George is losing cattle nightly. Would you know anything about that, sir?" "None of my doing. Just want to buy a section of his land that is overrun with water." "Well he doesn't want to sell, so why aren't you taking his offer of free piped in water?" "No, I want the land to solve my problem permanently." "Well this is your only warning, stop shooting his cattle and stop threatening him. The next time I come back will be to arrest you and your culpable ranch hands. Then where will you be—in jail. Not too smart, heh?"

Wayne stopped at the Wilsons. He told them of the threat of jail time if the shooting or threats continued. "Let me know what happens. I hope he accepts your offer." "As much as I would like an agreeable solution, I don't think he'll accept it."

Wayne went back to town and within a few days, the trial was held. All three robbers had no priors, and so were sentenced to 2 years in the tri-county penitentiary in Pueblo. After a few days, the three prisoners were transferred to Pueblo by train, and Wayne was the chosen escort.

Little did Wayne know that the return train trip to Silver Circle would change his life forever.

***

CHAPTER 5

Amanda

The two hour train ride to Pueblo was uneventful. The three convicted men were handcuffed to their seat. Upon arriving at the Pueblo station, the train was boarded by two County Penitentiary guards who took over custody of the prisoners, and walked them to the prison barred wagon for transfer to their two year home. Wayne was surprised by two of the prisoners, who thanked him for not shooting them during the robbery, and speaking on their behalf during the trial. Wayne filed this behavior into his memory banks.

The next train to Silver Circle was tomorrow at 10AM for the usual 1PM daily arrival. Wayne used his sheriff's department chits and bought a $11 ticket for tomorrow. To spend the night, he used another chit to pay for the RR hotel/restaurant, room, dinner, breakfast, and a hot bath. The second chit came to $6 including the waitress's tip.

Wayne went to his room and the first thing he did was take the bath. He then dressed in clean clothes and headed to the hotel restaurant. Wayne sat down and ordered the daily special: roast beef with mashed potatoes, fresh carrots, sourdough rolls and coffee. While he was waiting for his order, he noticed a young lady eating alone at her own table. She was tall, slim, well endowed, and with short blonde hair. She was wearing a very nice dress without jewelry. He tried not to stare at her but found himself taking subtle peeks. He may have been wrong, but he thought she was looking in his direction—several times.

The lady finished her meal and went upstairs to her room. He wondered why a young lady was traveling alone in such a violent country. His thoughts changed when he got his meal. He was pleased with his food and thoroughly enjoyed his dinner. He then retired to his room and found himself reading a novel about the life of a bounty hunter in Texas. He was enthralled with its content, and found himself reading under a lamp into the late evening. He finally went to sleep and consequently got up late, just in time to get breakfast before the lunch menu came out.

By 9 he arrived at the train station. The young lady was at the ticket office and asked for a ticket to Silver Circle. When she sat at a bench, Wayne had some kind of drive to introduce himself. As if out of his control he said, "hello ma'am. I'm deputy Wayne Swanson from Silver Circle and I wondered if I may sit on your bench?"

The lady answered with a smile, "certainly, I will feel safe sitting next to a lawman. My name is Amanda Currier." "Nice to meet you, I could not help noticing your unusual hair style since most women wear their hair long. I like it, and it gives you a unique feature. Where are you from?"

"I'm from Denver. I'm a student in a modern progressive teaching institution that encourages individuality–my hair style has become part of my persona." "Really, what do you mean by a modern and progressive teacher?" "A modern teacher teaches by classes, not the old single room method for all students. I would change the school into an early education 1–4, and intermediate group 5–7 and an advanced group of 8–10. *Suddenly the train whistle blasted and the conductor yelled "all aboard!"* "Amanda, I would like to know more, and I wonder if we could sit together in the train to continue our conversation?" "Why not, sitting next to a sheriff can be interesting since we have the same destination."

There were 10 passengers boarding. Wayne carried Amanda's travel bag and chose two benches that faced each other. "So the big question is why you are heading to Silver Circle?" "My uncle notified me of some interesting facts about Silver Circle. This town is growing fast and the school attendance may be up to 70 students within one year. The council is progressive and wants to separate the classes. They are willing to convert the school into three classes. They want a teacher that can teach the advanced group and they will provide teacher's aides for the other classes–all under the head teacher's supervision. This system is what I am after."

"Wow, that would fit your training. So who is your uncle?" "George and Sally Wilson." "Unreal!" "Why?" "The Wilson's ranch is close to my parents ranch, the Double S, and they are both large ranches of 8 sections. Actually, I was investigating the Wilson's complaint that the other neighbor, the Boswell's Box B Ranch was trying to push your uncle into selling a section rich in water. I hope to have settled the issue to everyone's benefit."

"So do you know the financial remuneration?" "No, do you?" "Well historically, they pay a schoolmarm +- $30–$40 a month and includes year round room and board at a local boarding house. I also happen to know that the school is open in two seasons. The long season is November 1 to April 1. The short season is June 1 to September 1. The school is closed April and May for the ranch roundups. It's also closed September and October for harvests and cattle drives to market."

"Wow, that is good information to know. If I get the job, my uncle and aunt want me to live with them." "In that case, the council will offer you a higher salary to compensate their room and board savings. You will also have to travel six miles to work. Can you ride a horse?" "Yes, and I will ride to school wearing riding pants. I will change at school into a more appropriate dress."

"I don't mean to be out of line, but do you plan to marry?' "I know that historically a schoolmarm has been a spinster. I want to marry and share my life with a man, and yes, I want to have children!" "Wow, that is going to be a shock to the busy bodies with their higher than thou attitudes. Fortunately these stuck-up women are not on the council and have no control in the hiring. Actually, these city bible thumpers don't have any children in school, and are just trouble makers. Again, still being on thin ice, do you have a man in your life?" "That is real thin ice, but no, I am a 19 year old single woman." "Do you?" "No, and touche."

"When is your interview with the council and how long are you visiting your aunt and uncle?" "My appointment is tomorrow afternoon at 4PM. I plan to stay two weeks if I get the job. I want to get to know the town and as many of its people. Then I return to Denver for my last year of training to get my teaching certificate."

"So if I may be forward, can I give you as a reference along with my aunt and uncle?" "Oh yes. I have lived all my life in the area and have been a deputy sheriff for two years. I know the council quite well. By the way, it includes Ed Sorenson of the Mercantile, mayor William Hawthorne, and the bank president Nathaniel Miller. I have a special arrangement with Ed, and I will talk with him in the morning. Stand by your beliefs, your offer, and your willingness to fight for your new method of teaching, and I suspect you will win the council."

"Now that you know my life's history, please tell me about you." Wayne went through his formative years with Sam and Cora, his adoption, his ten years of schooling, and his training as a ranch cowboy and business manager. He finally discussed his career change into law enforcement. Amanda asked, "why law enforcement when you are the only heir to your parents ranch?" "Because I believe that people need protection, the victims need justice, and the criminals need to be stopped."

"Those are honorable virtues, but being a deputy sheriff is a very dangerous profession." "Yes, but if you are cautious, follow rules of safety and self preservation, it can be a long career." "Do you have special skills that give you an edge over criminals?" "I am better than average in gun handling skills, and I am gifted with intuition in predicting human behavior."

"Enough about me. If you get this job, how do you propose to meet men. Men generally feel intimidated with teachers because of their higher education. The local men are mostly ranchers, cowboys or homesteaders. To make it worse, a church social or town dance is not the place for a teacher to join the social networks. Remember the social witches will crucify you." "Yes, I realize that this will be a problem, and I do not want to be a permanent single woman. So do you have any suggestions?" "Yes, talk to men. Other than your good looks, your best asset is your head. You are a smart person and you have something to share with any man other than higher education."

During their discussion, Wayne noticed that the train had slowed to an alarming speed on the train's climb to a high elevation. This could allow outlaws to board the train. Despite his awareness of a potential problem, he continued to talk intently with Amanda. Suddenly, a man opened the door to the passenger car. His gun was drawn and he yells, "this is a robbery, put your cash in this bag." When no one was responding to his command, he grabs Amanda by the neck and places his cocked gun to her head. Amanda was petrified and scared to death. The bag was going around and getting filled with large amounts of cash. All of a sudden, a shot ran out in another car. To Wayne, it sounded like a shotgun blast. The armed robber looked surprised and was panicking. He yells to Wayne, "you're the last, out with your cash." "Wayne answers, "I can't do that."

As Wayne removes his hammer loop, he opens his vest and shows the sheriff's badge. The robber naturally takes his gun off Amanda's head and turns it toward Wayne. Amanda heard a loud shot and the gun smoke filled her face. She knew that Wayne was dead when she heard the thud of a body hitting the floor. As the smoke cleared, Amanda saw the robber on the floor and Wayne was getting up. He said, "you are safe now, and I have to go to check out that gun blast. I suspect this dude had a partner."

Wayne starts heading towards the blast. The next car was an empty passenger car. The next one was a closed freight car. Wayne knocked, and introduced himself as a lawman. The RR detective opens the door. The RR crewman was standing next to the safe and the detective was holding a shotgun next to a body on the floor. He said, "this dude had the surprise of his life when he saw the shotgun. I didn't even hesitate, I let him have both barrels." "Yes, I see the results, heh. When we stop in Silver Circle, his partner needs to be picked up in the first passenger car—he is missing the back of his head."

Wayne rushed back to the passenger car. Someone had pulled the dead body away and covered it with a tarp. A lady was trying to console

Amanda. Amanda was still standing, trembling, white as a sheet, and obviously in a state of shock. Wayne said, "Amanda, it's over, you are safe." She looked at Wayne and said, "I knew my life was coming to an end before I had lived. Then you made him move his gun off my head and turn it to you when you showed your badge. That moment, I realized you were sacrificing your life to save mine. The gunshot convinced me that you were dead, especially when I heard the body fall to the floor, and I never saw you draw your gun."

"Mandy, I was never in danger. I had to pull his cocked gun off your head. With my gun handling skill, I knew I would shoot him before his brain told him to pull the trigger and shoot me. It is what I do. I am a natural talent with guns, supported by years of practice."

Amanda sat down, she was again speechless and suddenly erupted with heart breaking crying. Wayne sat next to her, turned toward her and simply held her. Amanda turned, put her hands around his neck and cried on his shoulder for a long time. After she regained control, they continued to hold each other. They both felt that an unexplainable bond being formed. Out of this horror, something good was being created.

Once they separated, Wayne said, "we will be arriving shortly. Amanda, you are a smart and strong person. You're going to walk off this train and greet your family as if nothing happened. Tomorrow you will go to your interview with all your faculties at top performance. You'll convince the council that they need you. Then you'll spend two weeks convincing the people of this town that you have something great to offer their kids. Then go back and finish your degree."

"During the week, I'll come to you and teach you how to shoot a rifle and a pistol. Since I know you'll be living here, you need to defend yourself, especially when you ride solo six miles twice a day."

Amanda finally spoke, "that's a large order. What about what I want?" "What do you want, Amanda?" "During my two weeks, will you come and visit–actually call on me!" Wayne responded by slowly leaning over and softly kissing her. She did not pull back, she actually prolonged the kiss. As they separated, Amanda said, "oh my, what is happening?" "If it feels right, it's right, Mandy!"

***

CHAPTER 6
Call on Mandy

The next day, Wayne awoke knowing that he had experienced an epiphany during a dream. Realizing he had two weeks to spend with Mandy, Wayne asked for a private meeting with Sheriff Jim. Wayne started the meeting by saying, "I'm very much involved with George Wilson's niece. She is applying for the teaching position and I suspect she will get the job. So I would like some extra time off in the next two weeks so I can call on Mandy. Also, I'm giving you a two week's notice, I am quitting the deputy sheriff's job."

"Why?" "I just realized that I have a calling. It's not enough to go after criminals after the fact, when there are too many victims and ruined lives. I want to be proactive and rid this tri-county area of killers and the like. I can't do this by staying in my county jurisdiction. I need to be able to travel anywhere the criminals go, and I have to do this as a bounty hunter."

"I have a strong feeling that Mandy will get the teaching job, and I assume that I will get her blessing in this endeavor. This year is my chance to make our community more secure before I settle down with Mandy, on my family farm. I really feel strong that the dregs of humanity need to be eliminated–I just hate to see good people getting hurt by evil monsters."

Sheriff Jim was quiet and pensive. He eventually says, "I have known for some time that this day would come. Your time frame has been accelerated, and if Mandy goes along with your calling, let me tell you what you are up against. As a bounty hunter, you work alone. Don't expect much help from the law. Once the word gets out that you are on a crusade, things might change. Then the most you can get from the local law is a list of recent crimes, and an identification by the local law of your arrests and dead bodies. This will allow you to claim the reward money."

"Remember, a respectable bounty hunter brings in at least 60% of his captives alive. Those that are dead should show a front entrance, not drygulching and shot in the back. For these reasons, this is a very dangerous profession. The real issue is whether Mandy can live with this."

"I agree, and I will broach the subject soon, assuming she gets the job."

"What are you planning to do with the extensive reward monies if you are successful and return alive?" "I plan to telegraph my vouchers to Stan Bulow, our telegrapher. I will pay him to deposit the vouchers into my benefactor account, which Ed Sorenson manages. I will sell their horses, tact and guns to the local livery and gun shops. This will finance my travels. My hope is to build this benefactor account to a point where the interest will cover the necessary disbursements to help people in need. I'm not planning to get rich with this crusade."

Sheriff Jim summarized, "Well Wayne this is truly a honorable mission. When I saw you come off the train holding hands with Mandy, I knew the writing was on the wall. I've been preparing for this day. I have three good candidates to replace you, and the council has given me permission to hire them."

"What I need from you the next two weeks is to train the new guys. This will give you several days off and weekends to spend with Mandy. I need your expertise in gun handling and safe enforcement techniques. The knowledge they gain from you in the next two weeks will follow them for years. It's the only way I can risk their lives doing this dangerous job." "OK, If Mandy gets the job, we have a deal." "What about Mandy living with this way of life for a year?" "If she can't see my need, then it may be a provincial sign that our lives together wasn't meant to be. My gut feeling is that she will come around."

"Do you want me to talk to the council before Mandy's 4PM interview?" "No, If this happens, it must be because of Mandy's merit. Since I have a special arrangement with Ed, I will sound him out. I am curious where this idea of an alternative teaching system comes from."

It was a slow day, Wayne filled out a report on the attempted train robbery. As he finished, the telegraph messenger walked into the office and handed Wayne two papers. He gave the messenger a 10 cent tip. Wayne read the telegram: *thank you for aborting a robbery and likely saving the lives of our passengers. Enclosed is a RR voucher that covers the reward on this criminal.* Wayne walked to Miller's bank and deposited $500 to his benefactor account.

Wayne then went to see Ed at the Mercantile. There were no customers, so Wayne broached the subject. "Who's idea was it to hire a modern progressive teacher and change our schooling system. "It was me. The only way to teach 70 students in a growing city, where the attendance is expected upwards, is to get away from the one room schoolhouse and the traditional schoolmarm." "Hey, you are preaching to the choir. I'm all in favor of changing with the times." "In short, I will not be asking questions at the interview, Mandy has to convince President Miller and Mayor Hawthorne for us to advance our schooling methods."

"Now the real reason I am here. My life will be changing in the next year." Wayne went through the entire scenario of being a bounty hunter for a year, building the benefactor account, and then with a perpetuating benefactor account, settling down as a rancher married to a professional teacher. Ed added, "I'm not a strong religious type, but this appears to be providence at work. I'm proud to be part of the solution. It will happen, Wayne. Trust me!"

***

Sitting on the Sheriff's porch, Wayne saw Mandy arrive, on a Bar W Ranch horse, at the courthouse by 4PM. She was well dressed in riding pants, a conservative blouse, Cowboy boots and hat—not the schoolmarm dress and look. Wayne waited patiently, but by 6PM he was about to jump out of his skin. He was making coffee for the third time when the front door exploded open. Mandy was holding a sheet of paper and jumped into Wayne's arms. She whispered, "It's going to happen Wayne." "Sit down and tell me how it went."

"I gave a half hour presentation of what progressive schooling involved and what I had to offer. The mayor and the bank president fired away with one question after another. Ed Sorenson never asked any questions but listened intently with a frequent smile. The mayor got bold and asked if I planned to marry. I said yes, and Ed broke silence and said, 'good for you.' Mr Miller then followed by asking if I planned to have children. I said, of course if I am so blessed. Again Ed said, 'wonderful, I can see the town biddies throw up on that one.'"

"The mayor got down to specifics, 'historically the schoolmarm taught basic reading, arithmetic, writing, and spelling in the lower grades. In the higher grades the schoolmarm added history, geography and proper public manners. How do you propose to arrange the grades.

"To simplify, Grades 1–4 will have the basics plus writing, reading, spelling and early arithmetic. Grades 5–7 would be a progression of the previous grades, plus history and geography. Manners and family values will be emphasized through all the grades. The biggest change is grades 8–10."

The mayor said, "tell me what you would add to these advanced grades." "World and American history, civics, science of the times, geometry/map reading, business accounting, composition and personal hygiene."

President Miller said, "how do you propose to cover all three classes?" Assuming the school structure is enlarged and changed from one room to three rooms, it is impossible for one person to cover all three classrooms. I would need teacher's aides under my supervision."

"And that is when the council started to talk and summarize."

1. Ed said, "the butcher's wife has a one year post 10th grade partial teaching certificate and could handle grades 5–7. Our gunsmith's wife has a 10th year certificate and could handle grades 1–4. They both are looking for work."

2. President Miller said, "let's do the math. Two teacher's aides at $30 per month each. The head teacher salary of $60 per month. We have no room and board to pay year round at $40 per month since Miss Currier will be living with George and Sally Wilson, and the teacher's aides already have husbands and living arrangements. That comes to $120 per month times twelve. Our tax base is increasing every day with the influx of people. We can afford to do this!"

3. Mayor Hawthorne said, "let's vote." The vote was unanimously in favor of the changes. The mayor added, "Miss Currier, are you ready to sign a contract starting one year from today." "I said, yes sir." Mandy handed the paper to Wayne and said, "here it is."

***

As Ray arrived to take the evening duty, Wayne and Mandy walked hand in hand to Simms Diner. They placed their celebratory order of steaks, baked potatoes, string beans and coffee. A dessert of bread pudding capped off the meal. They held hands till their meals arrived. Wayne said, this means, I have two weeks to woo you and win your heart." Mandy said, "that won't be too difficult, since I'm already on the way." They kissed and were totally oblivious of their surroundings until the waitress arrived with their steaks. The steaks were fantastic and after dinner, Wayne left a dollar to cover the 80 cent meals and tip.

They rode to the Bar W Ranch, and George and Sally were on the porch. Sally asked, "how did the interview go?" "Very well, I have a contract." "Oh that is wonderful, we look forward having you with us next year." They all went to the living room and visited for a while. Mandy went over some sections of the interview, especially when the council was told I plan to marry and have children. The Wilsons were stunned and started laughing when they envisioned President Miller's reaction. Wayne asked George if he had heard anything from Stuart Boswell? "No, we have heard nothing, but with the drought worsening, we expect another offer from the Box B Ranch." The Wilsons finally retired and gave the young couple some privacy.

With two eager participants, kissing became wild. Fondling was more aggressive and wandering hands were finding new places. Mandy was wanting more and Wayne was willing. Suddenly, Wayne moved away and said, "Mandy, we both want each other, and if we don't stop, we won't be able to stop. I'm so comfortable with you and I want it to grow even more. Now I'm going back to town and hope I don't end up walking my horse back. Right now the saddle is not the most comfortable seat in town. Mandy could see his problem and just smiled. She said, "now whose fault is that?" They kissed and planned to meet tomorrow night to practice shooting. Wayne even said he would come every night during the next two weeks, but without an explanation.

The next morning was spent on intensive gun handling. Wayne showed them how to do a quick draw. He said, "don't grab your guns grip with a hard hand squeeze. Use your middle and fourth finger to lift the gun out of the holster as you pull the hammer back with your thumb. Once the gun is pointing downrange, apply a death grip to the gun before pointing the gun at the target and firing." The boys practiced this maneuver for two hours and were on their way to mastering it. More practice would smooth the draw and get the gun on target quicker.

After lunch, Wayne gave his first class on town rules and laws. The last demonstration was how to safely handcuff a suspect when you were alone without a backup. That impressed the students, even Oscar and Ray. By 4PM, Wayne went to the town dump and picked up two old rusted buckets for the evening shooting practice. Wayne arrived at the Bar W Ranch for dinner. Mandy was on the porch waiting. He had one foot on the ground and Mandy was kissing him. Wayne said, "I see you missed me as much as I missed you."

After dinner, Mandy admitted that Uncle George had spent several hours today, going over the Peacemaker pistol and 1873 rifle. She was ready for the practice session.

Wayne put one rusted bucket at 5 yards for the pistol and 100 yards for the rifle. He watched Mandy load and shoot. She hit the buckets repeatedly and handled the guns safely. That is when he said, "now put those guns away. Here is what you will need. Next year you will be traveling 6 miles to school twice a day, and often in the dark. This is what you need on your body for self defense. This is a Webley Bulldog, it shoots the same 44 caliber ammo as the Peacemaker or the 1873 rifle. It fits in a shoulder holster or in your purse. It is smaller and will fit in your hand. Unlike the Peacemaker, this one is double action. You don't have to pull the hammer back, just pull the trigger. Mandy tried the trigger and was pleased with the ease of firing. He then showed her how to load it. She then fired the pistol several times and learned up close self defense firing when a man is in her face. He had her empty the five shots standing one foot away from a tree—to simulate a personal attack. If you ever have to pull this gun out, remember this. You have already decided that your life is in danger, and you are pulling this gun out to kill the man threatening you. Never hesitate, the attacker wishes you harm or death. If you don't kill him, he will rape and kill you. He then proceeds to tie the shoulder holster to Mandy, he found himself touching some female curves that were in the way, but they managed to accomplish the feat. The final item of the practice was the next gun he had brought.

This is a 41 caliber Remington derringer. The gun fits in your pocket. He showed her how to load it and fire by pulling the the hammer back for each shot. This is also a self defense gun made for close quarters. She fired it several times at a bucket up to ten feet. This is the gun you rely on when your Bulldog is not on your person."

Mandy adds. "I am finally comfortable with guns. I hope I never have to use one." "But if you need one, it better be on your body."

Wayne adds, "and if you do use one, as the law arrives at the scene, you simply say, I feared for my life, I knew he was going to kill me. If you repeat it several times, the lawman will get the idea that this was self defense, heh."

After the shooting, they went in the living room for some private time. Mandy said, "it appears you are preparing me for my presence in this violent land." "Yes, I am. Am I pushing you too fast?" She bent over and planted a very passionate kiss. She then said, "is there any doubt?" Wayne just said, "I'm falling in love with you." Mandy said, "I'm also getting there." As Wayne was leaving, Mandy said she had an arranged meeting with the two potential teacher's aides in the morning, and would be done by lunch. They agreed to meet at Simms Diner by 1PM.

***

The next morning, as Mandy was in town for her meetings, Stuart Boswell came to see the Wilsons. "I will pay $1500 for that adjoining section with a stream. This is my last offer and it's over twice what it's worth." George said, "this doesn't make sense. I'm willing to give you the water free of charge. All you need to do is to buy the pipes and tanks which would cost you less than $200. Take it or leave it, this is also my last offer. Sorry it has come to this, between neighbors."

Boswell turned to leave, "you are going to regret this!" He went straight to town and stopped at the telegraph office. "Mr. Bulow send this telegram immediately–To Milton Demers, Grand Hotel, Pueblo CO,------Need your services STOP Your fee is confirmed STOP Bring three men STOP Come today by train STOP Immediately proceed to Box B Ranch-------- from Stuart Boswell, Silver Circle, CO. He paid the 90 cent fee and left.

That same morning, Wayne purchased three double barrel shotguns with the sawed off barrels and each with a backpack holster. The local gunsmith, Omer Harrigan, had ordered them days ago and had made the modifications. His friend, Dan Evans, had fabricated the modified holsters. His total cost was $100. The three new deputies had already had a Colt and 1873 rifle upgrade from his confiscated outlaw supply.

He took the students to the range and showed them how to draw and cock the shotgun hammers. They shot them and saw the result of #4 and double aught buckshot. They also practiced their new quick draw technique.

Lunch was a get together with Mandy. Wayne had waited for Mandy on the diner's porch. When she arrived they kissed passionately, and walked into the diner holding hands. The diner was full. The patrons all had a rubber neck spasm and clearly read the significance of the couple's demeanor. As the pair sat down, Wayne said, "our entrance will spread through the town within hours." Mandy said, "It's about time don't you think."

They ordered beef stew and coffee. Mandy said, "the two meetings went very well. These two ladies are polite and smart. They are both enthused with this new schooling method. Both even volunteered to do the job free of charge. I told them that the council would offer them $30 a month, and both would go see the mayor today. It will be great to see a team of Gemler, Harrigan and Currier. *Wayne thought, Swanson, not Currier!* As Mandy was about to leave, Wayne saw that she had her Webley in the shoulder holster.

That afternoon, Wayne demonstrated how a deputy should enter a dangerous saloon after gunshots were heard. "If you are alone, enter with your cocked shotgun drawn. Immediately get your back to the wall next to the batwing doors. You will be able to view the entire room and no one will be behind you. Never leave your back exposed if you are alone. If necessary, have some of the patrons or bartender cuff the suspects. If you have a backup partner, he will do the same, so you can move forward where the problem exists.

By 4PM, Wayne was on his way to the Wilsons. Tonight he would present his plans for the coming year.

That same day, Sheriff Jim was scheduled to meet the 1PM train from Pueblo. Sheriff Jim noticed four men gathering on the platform. Two were very well healed with low lying Colts tied to their legs. That is when he paid more attention: The leader was over six feet, had a scar on his left cheek, and was well dressed in black. The second healed man was a short skinny fella that acted cocky with a smart aleck look. He had a distinctive flat top hat with a silver concho loaded hat band. The third was a 300 pound hairy fella that looked like a bear with a full beard. He wore his Colt in a cross draw because of his protuberant belly. The fourth one was a little old man that just looked scruffy with a shirt full of tobacco juice.

He watched them and wondered what they were doing in town. When their horses were brought from the stock car, they headed east out of town. Sheriff Jim went back to his office and went through the wanted posters. He found one, the leader of the gang–Milton Demers wanted dead or alive for murder and kidnaping. The reward was $1000.

Sheriff Jim went to the telegraph and sent a telegram to the Sheriff's department in Denver and Pueblo. He asked for any information on this outlaw and his gang. With the fees paid, Stan said he would send a messenger with the response as soon as they arrived.

Within a half hour, a telegram arrived from Denver. Sheriff Jim summarized it to Oscar and Ray. "Basically it said that the US Marshall service had been after them for one year. This gang moved frequently. They moved by train and usually hired out to perform violent crimes, and disappeared right after their depredations. They were well known for kidnaping and torturing. These were known as very dangerous men and all lawmen were advised not to engage them. All lawmen should notify the US Marshall office in Denver. The latest intelligence was that they left Denver a week ago and headed south by train. Two US Marshals will soon be en route to Pueblo, and likely to Silver Circle thereafter."

The second response came in from Pueblo. Sheriff Jim summarized it. "The Sheriff's department had no idea this Demer's gang was in town. They also advised we wait for the US Marshals."

Sheriff Jim then said, "it appears they left town. They could be headed to our ranchers to cause their mayhem. Let's start a communication relay. Oscar you head east, and Ray to go west. Notify the first ranch of this gang's arrival and to take precautions against strangers. Ask each ranch to send a rider to the next ranch to repeat the warning, and to continue the relays for at least ten miles either direction. Let's hope that this works and saves lives."

Meanwhile, the Demers gang arrived at the Box B Ranch. Stuart met with them and said, "I want to buy a section of land from my neighbor, George Wilson, and he won't sell. I want you to jump them after lunch tomorrow when the ranch hands are back in the fields. Punch out his wife Sally to keep her out of the fracas. Restrain his niece and beat George. If he won't sign, beat him again and even torture him. If he still won't sell, kidnap his niece and head north through Wilson's land, and then cross-country to Hyde Center some 40 miles away. I will leave a message at the telegraph with directions under the code names, To Blackie from the Boss. If you have a tail, head north again to Millers Crossing and I will leave directions again at the telegraph office with the same code names. Now here is half your pay of $1000. The other half is when you return the niece alive at White City, which is a town 40 miles west of here, and southwest of Hyde Center and or Millers Crossing. Remember, she must be alive, but I cannot control in what condition. Now, get out of here before the ranch hands return for dinner. Do not go to town where you can be recognized. Set up camp close to the Wilsons Bar W Ranch, but not close enough for them to see your camp fire."

An hour after the Demers gang left, a rider came in from the Bar W Ranch, informing Boswell of the Demers gang being in the area. Stuart decided to send a rider east to continue the relay. He could not afford the risk of terminating the relay without incriminating himself.

By 4PM, Oscar and Ray were getting back from starting the relays. They informed Wayne of the Demers information. He then headed out to meet Mandy for dinner and an important discussion.

The dinner conversation centered on the communication relay. George was pleased with Sheriff Jim's decision to start this warning system. Wayne added as much information he could about this gang. After dinner, Wayne and Mandy went for a walk. They found a private spot and expressed their feelings with a passionate moment.

Wayne then started, "Mandy, the days are so long when I don't see you all day. I miss being with you, talking with you, and sharing the every day activities. You will be leaving in a week and I'm having trouble accepting how I can be without you for so long." "Mandy said, I have never had a man in my life, and never even wondered what life would be like with one. Now I met you and I'm a sick love bird. All I think about is you, and I realize I need your help coping this next year when we will be apart. When I signed that contract, I promised to finish my training and be certified in the new system. So I have to go back."

"While you are in school, my life will change. I have resigned my deputy's position effective the day you leave for Denver. For the next year I will become a bounty hunter." Mandy was shocked and brought her hand to her mouth. Wayne said, "my dear love, hear me out. I feel a calling. There is so much crime and victims are suffering needlessly. I need to be proactive and rid our homes of these evil men before they cause more mayhem. As a bounty hunter, I would not have a limited jurisdiction like lawmen. I would go where the outlaws are. I need to stop these monsters before they cause pain to good people."

"The other reason I need to do this is to build my benefactor fund." "What is that?" "It's a bank account that allows Ed to help the people in financial need. The funds come from reward monies from wanted posters, as well as the sale of their horses and guns. The fund has disbursed some $4000 and still has a balance of $3000. With the drought we are experiencing, the need will go up. My goal is to build this fund to a point where it will be self sustaining. The interest will go into disbursements as needed, but the principal will not change."

Mandy says, "so you are a paladin, heh." "What is a paladin?" "From Medieval times, paladins were a class of warriors who supported a cause, were devoted to kindness, honor, and ridding the world of evil. You are this type and it's a calling as you suggested. But, despite it being an honorable mission, it is a very dangerous one."

"Well, I guess I am a paladin. Evil men do evil things, the devil doesn't control them, God doesn't stop them, but men like a paladin or a bounty hunter needs to stop them. Sheriff Jim calls my year on the trail a crusade. I need to do this, I can't stand seeing dead victims after the fact."

"Selfishly, I'm afraid to lose you. How dangerous is this?" "I trust my gun handling skills in dealing with three outlaws. For gangs of four or more, I would have to eliminate them down to three. These outlaws are usually wanted dead or alive and will fight to avoid arrest because an arrest means hanging. Drygulching is a serious issue, but I have a strong intuition for this type of shooting. Basically, I know I can do this and return alive. What I need is your support. I need you to say, go get those bastards."

"Wayne you have my heart and I will always support you in all your endeavors. It is just that I am scared. Let me think on this for a while. Trust me. We will talk again about this tomorrow."

The next day, Wayne was still training his new deputies, They started the day by practicing at the range. Wayne noticed that they had all the proper techniques in gun handling and simply needed more practice. He also was running out of safety tips in handling dangerous suspects. So today he discussed how to handle a fistfight or brawl. "When called to stop a fight or brawl, don't physically jump in the ring thinking you can bring the fight to an end. The participants will pull you into the melee. So the answer is to stand in the sideline and watch. When a fighter pulls a knife or gun, stop the fight by firing a round in the floor or at the sky if outside. If a fighter is down and out, or giving up, the other fighter must stop, and it is up to you to stop him. Basically you are not trained to physically fight it out with these brawlers. Be there to prevent a fatal event, and know when enough is enough. I also recommend that you attend a brawl with a backup partner. The brawlers have so much adrenaline that you may have to knock them out to subdue them. That is when a partner coming from behind can coldcock the fighter since his attention is on you. With the mine employees, you are going to have drinking brawls. So plan on it. That's it for today."

As he was getting Brownie at the livery, a rider at full gallop came into town and headed to the sheriff's office. Wayne rode to the office and heard, "I'm a hand at the Bar W Ranch. When we came in from the range, the foreman went to report to Mr. Wilson. He found Mrs. Wilson barely conscious with a face injury, and Mr. Wilson unconscious. He had been beaten and tortured." "What about their niece?" "She was no where to be found." The Wilsons are being brought to the Sutton hospital by wagon."

Wayne said to Sheriff Jim, "I'm going after them and will bring Mandy back." Wayne ran to Ed's store and asked him to pull his traveling gear out of storage, and stock it with food for a week. He then rushed to the livery. Bruce had surmised that Wayne would need Brownie and a strong pack horse with a pack saddle. He had both ready. Wayne thanked him and rushed back to the mercantile. He attached his two panniers and loaded his gear and food. He then went back to the office to pick up his field glasses, compass, Winchester 76, his 1873 rifle and his sawed off shotgun. He loaded ammo for all four guns.

As he left the office, he said, "I'm off, I'll stop to talk with George when I meet up with the wagon." "God speed and bring Mandy back."

Five minutes later he met the wagon. He saw George's bleeding left hand and asked what transpired? "Four men jumped us in mid afternoon. One from the rear kitchen entrance, one from the living room window, and two from the front door. We had no chance to get to our guns. They punched Sally in the face and knocked her out. A huge man restrained Amanda and they beat me up. After breaking several ribs and my left arm, they wanted me to sign a bill of sale for the section of land Boswell wanted. When I refused they smashed my left hand, pulled out three fingernails and then cut off those three fingers. When I refused again, the leader said that I would get my niece back after I sold the land to Boswell. I then saw Amanda scratch the face of the bear holding her. She was then restrained with her hands tied behind her back. The last thing I remember is when the outlaw leader kicked me in the head, and everything went black."

"Ok George, whatever you do, don't sell. I'll bring Mandy back and we will deal with Boswell later. George last words before the wagon started to move was, "fireplace, third brick from floor, on right. Remove the brick, there is $20,000. Bring back Mandy alive and it's yours." "Not necessary, she will come back alive and I'm going to marry her."

Wayne rode away, he was on a personal mission to rescue the first and only love of his life. The kidnappers had no idea what they were up against.

***

CHAPTER 7

Mandy's Rescue

Wayne's first stop was the Bar W Ranch. He was greeted by the foreman, Brett Hanson. He said, "we tracked the kidnappers to the end of the ranch. We headed north, three miles, to the east/west fence. They had cut the fence and continued north cross country towards Hyde Center. Because it was dark and couldn't follow the tracks, we had to come back. I assume you are going after them and I'm willing to go with you. Better still, let me take a couple of cowboys and we will bring her back. This could have a horrifying ending." "Thanks, but this is my job. I can do this, and I want to do it alone. If she is dead, I will follow the killers to the end of the earth to satisfy justice and my revenge."

"Wayne added, what I need is a change of clothes for Mandy." Wayne went in Mandy's bedroom and gathered the clothes. A complete change of clothes, a winter coat, a rain duster and some personal care items. Brett added, "you can gain three miles tonight by following the fence line between the Wilson and Boswell properties. That will bring you to the cut fence and you can camp there for the night." "Great, and I will repair the cut fence. Would you tell Sheriff Jim that I will send him a telegram when I arrive in Hyde Center?" "Sure will, and good luck."

It took Wayne two hours to get to the end of the ranch's three miles. It was pitch dark and besides following the fence-line at a safe distance, he had to watch for trees and prairie dog holes. When he finally got to the border, he repaired the fence and decided to make dinner. Wayne figured that the kidnappers were far enough ahead to not see the camp fire. He watered the horses at the nearby stream, and hobbled the pack horse. Brownie would not walk away. The horses were unsaddled and allowed to feed in the tall grass. He started a fire and boiled water for coffee. He warmed up a can of beans and had biscuits provided by Ed. He retired to his bedroll and slept in fits till pre dawn, when he got up to get ready. He set out as soon as the tracks were visible.

Meanwhile, Milton was talking to his men, "we can afford to make camp. There is no one on our back-trail. That Bar W Ranch posse turned back as soon as it got dark. We are 15 miles from that east/west border line. We will be up early and get to Hyde Center where we will have a telegram waiting from the boss." "What do we do with the hostage?" "Give her some water and tie her hands behind her, tie her feet and rope her neck to a tree. Don't give her any food, we are short of supplies." "Do I give her a blanket, it's going to be cool tonight." "You only have one blanket, so if she gets a blanket, it's yours."

Mandy had heard them and knew she would be tied up till morning. She said, "I have to pee." Bear said, I will take her to the bushes. He placed a rope around her neck and followed her to a tree. She insisted he turn around while she did her business. When they returned to camp she was tied up, with no chance for escape.

In the early morning, after everyone had taken care of their business, they rode off at a full trot to Hyde Center. They skipped breakfast except for some water and beef jerky. They allowed their hostage to ride without restraints, but warned her that if she tried to escape, they would tie her feet to the stirrups and her hands to the saddle horn.

Wayne knew he was 40 miles to Hyde Center. However, he had no intelligence that this was their destination. So, that meant he had two long days of tracking to stay on their trail. Wayne had stopped several times when the tracks were clear. He finally found a shoe mark that identified them as the criminals he was chasing. That shoe feature was a wider pattern, made custom to fit a misshapen hoof. It was also the deepest hoof marks, presumed from the huge dude that looked like a bear. Wayne stopped for lunch, watered the horses, gave them some oats, and let them crop some grass for a half hour before getting back on the trail.

The Demers gang were riding their horses hard. Mandy was having trouble keeping the pace. Bear had to pull on her horse's reins to make her horse keep up. Mandy was in pain. She was getting chaffed from the saddle and would not give these scoundrels the benefit of knowing her problem. By noon, they arrived five miles from town. Milton told his boys to make camp, start a fire, cook the remainder of the beans, and make the last of the coffee. When Mandy got down from her horse, she could not walk. Milton said, "so that is why you had so much trouble keeping up today, you have saddle sores." Everyone broke out in laughter and offered to rub the "bo-bo."

After lunch, Milton rode into town. He headed to the telegraph office and asked for a telegram in the name of Blackie. He read.

> Have a dangerous tail STOP
> Continue to Miller Crossing STOP.
> Will contact you before arrival with
> further instructions. The Boss

Milton was not happy, their plan had been to hold up in camp near Hyde Center until the telegram said that the bill of sale was signed. Then they could head southwest to White City and collect their $1000 for a live hostage—even if damaged. Now the run was to continue. Milton went to the dry goods store to buy supplies. He bought canned beans, corned beef, bacon, ham, crackers, canned peaches and coffee. He also bought stogies for smoking and chewing tobacco for the scruffy one.

Demers's gang was not pleased. Demers said, "we have no choice, we cannot afford to confront a lawman on this escapade. Let's have a full lunch and we can make the 30 miles before dark. We will camp some 5 miles from Miller Crossing."

By evening, Wayne had made up time because of the terrain that allowed deep hoof marks, and also because this gang was not even trying to hide their trail. He arrived in Hyde Center by business closing time. He went directly to the telegraph office and said to the telegrapher, "sir, I am a deputy sheriff from Silver Circle. I am after kidnappers that may have been in this office today. Have you received a telegram from Silver Circle regarding some strange and possible nefarious activity?"

"I am sorry sir, but by law I cannot divulge that information." As Wayne places a $20 gold double eagle on the counter. The telegrapher stared at two weeks worth of income. "Well sheriff, maybe we can make an exception for lawmen." As he pulled the double eagle, he said, "yes there was a message to someone called Blackie." "What did it say, as Wayne pulls out another double eagle and holds it at eye level. "Well, it appears that I made a copy." There was a mutual transfer of items over the counter.

After reading the copy. Wayne said, "would you relay this emergency message to Sheriff Smithfield in Silver Circle."

> Cannot proceed any further STOP Have had accident when horse hit a dog hole STOP Have a broken arm and bad back injury STOP Will be laid up 10 days STOP Ask US Marshall service to take over STOP Inform appropriate persons. Wayne

Be glad to, that's a long message of 37 words for 74 cents. Wayne paid and the telegrapher sent the message. The telegrapher then said, "that's a bad arm break you have, deputy. Get those bastards. It sounds like you just fooled them into your trap. Good luck."

Meanwhile, Sheriff Jim asks Oscar, "do you know which saloon the Box B Ranch hands frequent?" "Yes, it's the Silver Queen." "Ok, go there and pass this message loud and clear to the bar tender. Then after leaving, hide in an alley. If a rider, comes out and heads east, we'll know that the message will get to Boswell."

Oscar came back 15 minutes later and said, "it worked, message delivered." "Good, I will tell George at the Sutton hospital the proper message, so he doesn't believe the rumors we started."

Meanwhile, Wayne laid out his plans. He had two hours left of daylight and knew the kidnappers had 4 hours ahead of him. He decided to take a chance that the kidnappers would head to the next telegraph office as ordered–Miller Crossing. Wayne would push his horses and not bother with tracking. He figured that they would camp a few miles out of Miller Crossing, and send a messenger to check on a telegram from Boswell.

The full moon was out and thanks to his compass, Wayne made the decision to keep riding all night. By dawn, Wayne started to smell camp smoke. He proceeded slowly until he spotted the camp fire. He tethered the horses, and walked with his Winchester 76 towards the camp. He got within 100 yards, camouflaged by the trees surrounding the camp. He heard the gang leader give his orders. "Reese and I will be going into town to check for orders from the boss. If we still have a tail, we will pick up supplies and be back here pronto with instructions. If we lose our tail, we will stay in town a few days before returning to camp. We will eventually arrive with supplies and head south west to White City where we meet with the boss and collect our $1000. You two will stay here and watch our hostage until we return."

Wayne watched two riders pull out of camp. He figured it would take them an hour to get to the telegrapher. With the fake message he had created, he knew that those two riders would head to the nearest saloon/whore house for at least a few days, and then one more day just to sober up. So Wayne figured Bear and Scruffy, as he called them, had two hours before realizing that they were going to be extended hostage sitters. Wayne decided to wait the two hours out and then start looking for a plan to overtake the camp. He made himself a comfortable spot, and set up a gun rest that centered his 100 yard sight on the center of the camp—and waited. His only question was why Mandy was not sitting or standing.

Bear and Scruffy were getting irritated when the boss did not show up within two hours. He said, "we are doomed to babysit this cutie for the next several days while Milt and Reese are drinking and whoring. We were told we had to bring her back alive, but not necessarily in perfect condition. I think we should have fun. Let's tie her in four points, spread her legs, and cut off her clothes. I'll go first and you can watch."

Mandy had not been able to sit or stand and had to relieve herself in place. When she heard them talk, she knew she was going to get raped or killed. When she saw Bear naked and hobbling in place she screamed in horror.

Wayne heard their plans and was up with his rifle pointed at camp. He saw Mandy tied down and stripped naked. Then Bear dropped his gunbelt and pants. As he was hobbling between Mandy's legs, he heard Mandy scream. Wayne had Bear in his sights and pulled the trigger.

Bear was hit in center mass. The bullet entered his breast bone, went through his heart and exited with several pieces of his spine. The 300 pound monster was lifted up into the air, pushed backward several feet, and fell into a puff of dust. Scruffy was shocked at the massive gun shot and it's result on Bear. He ran to get his rifle and shot at the smoke generated by Wayne's shot. Wayne didn't even flinch as he heard the lead flying by. He aimed at Scruffy hurriedly and pulled the trigger. Scruffy was hit in the neck, his spine was torn out and his head nearly fell off his body–hanging by a thread of skin as his body fell backwards.

Mandy stopped screaming and was frozen in time as she lay there naked and spread eagle. She saw a man approaching and was certain that her fate was again sealed, as she expected another evil person to finish the other scoundrel's attempt. She kept looking but because of the brightness of the fire, she could not identify the man. She saw him walk into camp and grabbed a bedroll. He then walked to Mandy and covered her with the bedroll. He then knelt down and brought his face to Mandy. Mandy broke out crying loudly and tried to talk. Wayne said, "Mandy you are safe and your ordeal is over. So stop blubbering and listen to me." Mandy went silent. "It's one thing to call on you at the Wilsons some 5 miles from town, but this three day cross country riding is for the birds. "To resolve this, **will you marry me**?"

"Mandy started tearing up with tears of love and said, YES and I understand. They kissed for a long time. Wayne said, "let me cut your restraints and you can explain what you 'understand.'"

Mandy said, "every minute of the last three days was spent thinking about the fact that I may never see you again. I also realized what a victim must feel when losing a loved one, abused, raped or taken hostage. If there is no guardian angel, these victims are lost. There is no doubt that your type is the person to bring victims to safety or provide justice for their loss. I swear to you, that as your wife, I will support your endeavors and will champion you on your crusade. You are going to be my Paladin husband."

Wayne was so happy with the outcome. He had his Mandy and would spend his life loving and protecting her. Wayne then said, "let's get you up." Mandy with help got her chest off the ground, and then yelled out in pain. "Wayne, I can't get up, I have blisters on my bum and have saddle sores down my legs. My private areas are on fire." "Turn on your side and I will look to see how extensive your burns are." As she turned sideways, Wayne lifted the bedroll and saw her bum, private areas and inner thighs completely covered with raw weeping red areas. Blisters had broken and there was dead skin everywhere.

Wayne said, "I have to wash your backside and then I can apply some antiseptic ointment. This salve will provide some relief, prevent infection and help you heal. Tonight we are leaving your backside exposed to air. We will try to travel in the AM."

Wayne went to the stream, came back with two soaked towels and 5 canteens full of water. He gingerly wet her skin and started cleaning the areas. When he got to the private areas, he warned Mandy and proceeded cautiously. Eventually the areas were cleansed and he started applying the ointment. Mandy immediately felt some relief even if her modesty had gone down the tubes, at least she was exposed to her fiancé.

Wayne built up the fire and started to prepare dinner. Mandy admitted that all she had for the past three days was water. Wayne prepared coffee, canned corned beef, canned carrots and potatoes. With crackers on the side and canned peaches for dessert, the meal was complete. Mandy did well to feed herself while laying on her left side. She was amazed that Wayne had brought some clothes, She managed to dress her upper half with a blouse but wondered how Wayne would manage to get her to travel in the morning.

That night Wayne explained. "We need to try traveling by morning." He explained how he had tricked Milton and Reese to stay in Miller Crossing for a few days. He then explained, "these bodies will start smelling by morning and will attract predators. I won't bury them because I want the two remaining outlaws to see what their fate may be. Plus, if my deception failed, we again need to be gone from this camp."

Before nightfall fell, Wayne went to get his two horses. He brought them to camp, removed their saddle, brushed them and watered them at the stream. He gave them oats and hobbled the packhorse in an area of good grass. He then did the same with the two outlaws's horses. Brownie was not hobbled. The last thing he did was go through the dead bodies pockets and their saddle bags. The saddle bags had dirty clothes, which he threw in the fire, and several boxes of 44 ammo. Their pockets had a total of $500 which was their partial payment. He pocketed the money. They each had receipts for livery charges, with their names. This was an ID he needed for the reward money. Finally, he collected their Colts, holsters, and rifles. Preparations for sleep were simple, he placed Mandy on a clean bedroll and covered her with a blanket. He kissed her and joined her on his own bedroll with a blanket. Before they fell asleep, they held hands, and Mandy knew she was rescued from this kidnaping and a potential life of loneliness as a single female.

The next morning, Wayne greeted Mandy with a passionate kiss. Breakfast had to wait for Mandy to go to the privy/bushes. Wayne helped her get up and she was able to walk with her legs spread out. She made it out of camp and was able to squat. After returning to camp she elected to have breakfast while standing. Wayne had prepared coffee, bacon, biscuits, and oatmeal. They then discussed how she could possibly ride a horse. Wayne said, "lets reapply some ointment with a thin coat, then put your underwear with leggings. These will act as bandages. I will tie a bedroll to your saddle and extend it for your thighs. We will double the bedroll for your seat. In addition, I will shorten your stirrups, to allow you to place some pressure on your feet/legs and relieve the pressure on your bum. You won't have to climb in the saddle, I will lift you and place you where you need to be. Let's try it for a few hours, at least if we can't go further, we will be out of this camp." After the horses were saddled, and the food and gear picked up, Wayne tied a trail rope off his saddle to two horses and Mandy was free to ride her horse herself.

The sixty mile journey to Silver Circle had begun, with all it's perils.

***

CHAPTER 8
Going Home

Mandy had managed to keep riding for two hours, thanks to her ability to periodically push her bum off the padded saddle. They had been traveling at a walk and an occasional slow trot, but had only covered an estimated eight miles. Suddenly, Mandy says, "Wayne, I can no longer lift my bum off the padded saddle, and the pain of sitting on the saddle is unbearable." "Ok, that's it for today." Wayne got off his horse and was about to lift Mandy off her's when Mandy screamed in horror. Wayne turned around and said, "not to worry Mandy, these are Cheyenne Indians and we are on their reservation. If they wanted us harm, we would have been dead a long time ago."

Wayne addressed the apparent leader or chief of the six member band, "Do you speak English?" "Yes, we speak the white man's tongue." "What brings you to visit us?" "We have been following these four men. They are bad men and have not treated your woman kindly. We saw you killed two with the big and loud rifle to rescue your woman. We know your woman is in pain caused by the white man's leather seat.

I have sent a warrior to our medicine woman. Here is an herb that will heal your woman over one night. Apply it with this horse brush now, at sleep time, and morning–let it dry. She will be able to ride by tomorrow. The other two bad men are still in the white man's town drinking your fire water. Rest in camp today and tonight without fear of attack."

"Why are you helping us?" "Because, we see that you are a good person, and represent your law with your star. We respect an honorable person, even if you are white." "How do we repay you?' "Not necessary." "Well, you gave us a gift, and I wish to give you one in return." "That is acceptable." Wayne walks to his pack horse and mentions that the warriors look lean. The chief says, "with the buffalo gone, game is scarce and getting too far for our bow and arrows."

Wayne takes out the two outlaw rifles and one Colt/holster. He hands the warriors the rifles and the chief the Colt. He adds four boxes of 44 ammo. In addition, he releases the trail rope and walks one of the outlaw's horse. He gives the chief the reins and says, "I know you have no use for a white man's horse, but you can trade the horse and saddle at the Indian Trading Post for food–to help your people."

"In return for helping us, we would like to help you to capture or kill those two other bad men." "I am grateful, but you cannot. If you help kill a white man, you will be punished by the US Army." "That is true, but we can warn you and no one will know. If you keep looking at the sky, when you see three smoke clouds, the bad men have left the white man's town. When you see two smoke clouds, it is time to stop, choose a camp you can defend, and fight for your freedom." "Such a warning will be greatly appreciated." "Good, we go in peace and be successful."

Camp was set up after the horses were watered, unsaddled, and brought to some good grass. Mandy then asked, "are we to use this potion from the medicine woman?" "Oh most certainly, I have more trust in this ancient herb than this salve you are plastered with. Let's remove the salve and apply this herb instead."

Mandy knew the routine. She stood in place, removed her britches, and slid off her underwear.

She stood in front of Wayne, naked from her blouse down and said, "I never envisioned, in my entire life, any man ever doing what you have done and what you are again about to do." Wayne answered, "Mandy, modesty between us will no longer be paramount because we will be lovers for life."

Mandy turned around, spread her legs and Wayne started to gently wipe off the salve. He hesitated as he approached the very private areas. Mandy felt his hesitation and said, "it's Ok, do it. Those areas are the most sensitive when sitting in the saddle." When the skin was clean, he applied one third of the bottle to all inflamed areas, especially the very private areas.

Because Mandy had to let the potion air dry, Mandy was walking around camp half naked. Wayne took the opportunity to give her some privacy. He went to the stream and with a bar of lye soap, cleaned the ointment off her two pairs of underwear. He then stretched them out on sticks next to the fire. He went back to the stream and rinsed the ointment off her riding skirts and also stretched them out next to the fire.

Wayne looked at the potion which was taking longer to dry than he wished. To give Mandy more privacy, he volunteered to go hunting to see if he could get some rabbits or grouse for dinner. He brought his shotgun with bird shot. Within a half hour, Mandy heard and recognized Wayne's shotgun blast at least three times. Wayne had walked in to an area rich in grouse and shot three. He field dressed the birds, wrapped three grouse breasts and six small drumsticks/thighs in a game pouch, and went back to camp.

On arrival, Wayne told Mandy to dress up with her loose riding skirt and save the underwear as dressings for riding tomorrow. With dinner already planned, Wayne made some coffee and a luncheon snack of beef jerky and crackers. After lunch, Mandy still had to stand but noticed that the burning and pain was drastically lessening.

With the afternoon ahead, Mandy decided to broach a very personal subject. Mandy stepped in Wayne's arms, kissed him and said, "Wayne, when do you want to get married?" "It depends on how big a wedding you want." Mandy said, "I want my uncle and aunt, my mom and my college roommate." "Ok, and I want Sheriff Jim, Oscar, Ray, Ed and my mom and dad." "So a small wedding. It will take one day to get your mom/roommate here by train." "Yes." "Then any day you choose is fine with me as long as we get married before you leave for Denver."

"That is what we need to talk about. It is not going to be easy for me to get married and then leave for nine months to finish my degree. The only time off from school is three weeks at Christmas. Marriage also provides other problems. A married student cannot live in the campus dorms. That means, I will need to live at home with my mom. The biggest issue, is pregnancy. In these times, our school board just accepted married students, but pregnancy still means an automatic expulsion. There are rumors that this pregnancy issue will be eliminated this year, but is still in effect this school year. And last, how do we consummate our marriage without the chance of getting pregnant?"

Wayne had been listening attentively. He said, "So we have four roadblocks to our union. They are: a nine month long distance marriage, arranging transportation to and from school to your mom, avoiding pregnancy and consummating our marriage. Is that all?" "Yes, I love you so much, and I want you to find a solution, because I am marrying you as soon as we get back home."

"Well, lets resolve each problem individually, We are not going to have a long distance marriage. I have already made plans with the district US Marshall's office in Denver. As a bounty hunter, I would go after the criminals that are out of their jurisdiction or offer special problems. That means that I will be in Denver at least once a month or more." "Wow, that is very good news my darling."

"Now for the transportation, I will arrange a taxi service of rain covered buggies. They will pick you up at home at a specified time and return you home at another specified time. I will pay for this service since I see it as a secure way for my wife to travel in a large city. Also, the drivers are armed and their track record is excellent." "How do you know of this service?" "Sheriff Jim was on business in Denver a year ago and he told me he had used the service and was pleased with it. Besides, you will be armed with your Webley and derringer."

"Now about pregnancy and consummating our marriage. Unfortunately the only absolute way to avoid pregnancy is abstinence of intercourse. I can wait another six months if you can. I love you so much and I want you for our lives. I cannot risk for you to be thrown out of your dream of teaching because you are pregnant." "Why did you say six months since the school year is nine months?" "Because, if we consummate our marriage at Christmas, you would not show by May 1st–your graduation, heh." "Yes, yes, and yes. I guess I am so full of lustful desires for you that I'm not thinking straight."

Wayne adds, "let's not forget that as a married couple, we can practice some very personal intimacy. We can pleasure ourselves as husband and wife, without any chance of pregnancy. If you agree, we need to treat our union as one without restrictions, and we can experience ecstacy with our loving." "Oh yes, and anytime you're ready, as she jumps in Wayne's arms and they passionately kiss."

Wayne adds, "there is no problem we cannot solve if we respect and trust each other without reservation. So now, I'm hungry, lets prepare our chicken dinner with crackers and coffee.

As he was setting the grouse meat on sticks, he noticed that Mandy was walking with her legs touching and was sitting on a padded stump without grimacing. The small drumsticks/thighs were cooked first and they ate while the breast meat finished cooking. They both appreciated the change in menu. They finished with the last can of peaches.

After dinner, they decided to retire early in hopes of getting on the road by daybreak. Wayne reminded Mandy that they had to apply the second potion before bedtime. Mandy stripped and assumed the position. Wayne noticed that she was already showing signs of healing.

After the drying process, they laid down and started to naturally grope each other. When Mandy noted that Wayne was getting into a sorry state, she said, "Wayne let's stop. I know you are stimulated, and I am as well, but I'm still too chafed to physically respond." They kissed and rolled over to sleep—without question. Mandy was able to sleep on her back for the first time in days.

In the AM, Mandy got up and went to the bushes by herself. After she got back, she undressed, turned around, bent over, separated her legs and said, "I'm ready for my last treatment." Wayne obliged and finished the bottle. After the potion dried, she got dressed and said, "the next time you see me naked, it's going to be with passion, heh?"

They picked up camp and Wayne was about to pad Mandy's saddle when she stepped up and boarded her horse. She then snuggled her bottom in the saddle and said, "thanks to the Cheyenne, I am ready to ride. How far is home?" "Not sure, but I am planning a three day trip to keep you from getting saddle sores again."

They traveled at a walk and a slow trot. By noon, they had covered ten miles in tough cross country areas. The horses needed a rest. They were watered, given oats and allowed to crop some grass. Since the noon break was for the horses, they had a cold lunch of left over bacon, biscuits and water. Mandy looked pensive so Wayne asked her what was wrong. "I'm spending all my energy just to stay on the horse and follow you. I'm not looking at the sky like you are, which is why I worry."

"Stop worrying. You should never worry about a situation until it becomes a problem, I don't think we missed the sign. But to reassure you we will take precautions tonight."

They traveled another ten miles and stopped to make camp in early afternoon when they found some cover, water and decent grass. Other than the routine in setting up a full camp, Wayne took his reel cord and set up a perimeter between trees. The string was taut and hanging six inches above the ground. The tin cans Wayne had been collecting were put to good use. They were tied into a bunch and looped over to a branch, and then secured to the perimeter cord. Anyone tripping on the cord would scramble the tin cans and ring out to wake the dead.

They then prepared dinner. It was getting cool so Mandy went around getting extra firewood. For dinner they made coffee and they finally had the smoked ham which had been reserved till approaching the end of the trip home. The smoke meat had preserved well. Mandy pealed some potatoes, and fried them in the frypan with bacon grease. They added the ham and feasted.

After dinner Mandy asked, "you said we were 40–45 miles to home. Do you think we could push our horses and get home by dark."

"Yes we could, but I don't think that is wise. These men will be seeking revenge. If we don't stop them now, we will have to face them at home and we'll get drygulched." "What is drygulched?" "Shot in the back when least expected." "Ok, so what are you expecting tomorrow?" "I expect we will get a morning sign of three smoke clouds, and a late day sign of a double smoke cloud. We will keep looking for that double smoke cloud, and we may even set up camp early if the right location pops up."

"So now, let's get some sleep, we will be riding by early dawn. They laid out near the fire in their bedroll and with the extra blanket on top. Wayne had his shotgun and Colt next to him and Mandy had her Colt handy as well.

In the morning, the routine again started. Go to the bushes, pack up gear in the panniers, saddle the horses, have a breakfast of fried ham and crackers, put out the fire and change the water in the canteens. Mandy had to ask, "why do you change the water every time we stop and find running water?" "Water tends to go stale which can cause diarrhea. More important, metal canteens impart a metallic taste to the water, which I can't stand." "As I expected, that was a good answer." "Ok, let's get on the road."

They had been riding for three hours when a clear sign appeared–three smoke clouds. Wayne said, "let's stop to rest the horses and have a snack." The horses were watered, given a full portion of oats, and brought to good grass to crop. While they were waiting for the horses, they had a snack of leftover cold ham. Wayne noticed that Mandy was getting anxious and fidgety. He decided to make Mandy think of something other than the future fight.

"Mandy, why do horses blow every time we stop to rest them?" "I don't know, it's one of those things we know happens, and everyone takes it for granted." "Well there are two reasons, one is to clear their nasal passages of mucous. Since they cannot breathe through their mouths like we can, they have to clean their noses once they are not moving. The other reason is because of their demand for oxygen. A horse on the run needs more oxygen than at rest. So they inhale more than they exhale and so they blow up their chests. That is also why their cinches get tight when running. Once a horse stops, they no longer need the extra air in their chests, and so they blow–to decompress their chests and clean their nasal passage."

"Boy I'm getting to know you real good. I knew you would not ask a question without having the answer on the tip of your tongue. By the way, that was kind of you, for reading my mind."

"As far as my anxiety and apparent pensiveness, I haven't been myself since I met you on the train. Aunt Sally said that I was smitten with you. She said that smitten people don't act like themselves. They try to be what the other person wants. Wayne, I want to be your partner, friend and lover. I don't want to put on airs."

"Mandy, I am also suffering from this need to be like you. I also want a partner, friend and lover that I can trust. I know I have found the woman of my life. Once this kidnaping ordeal is finished, we can relax and live a normal life." "And you won't have to apply that Indian potion ever again, heh."

Meanwhile, Milt and Reese were finally sobering up. They picked up supplies plus stogies, chewing tobacco and two bottles of whiskey for Bear and Scruffy. As they arrived, they saw human body parts and bones–strewed all over camp. Milt exploded. "That tail has our hostage and $500 of our money. If we don't kill that bastard and get our hostage back, we will be losing $1500." Reese added, "that bounty hunter or lawman can't have gotten far, with a hostage that was covered in severe saddle sores. There is only one way out of this country, that's on horseback." "That's right. If we push our horses, we can catch up with them by nightfall. We could sneak up on them in their bedrolls and solve our problem." "Great, let's do it."

Wayne and Mandy were getting on the trail when Wayne said, "We will start looking for a safe camp area for tonight. As soon as we find it, we will stop even if we haven't seen the next cloud warning.

They were on the trail for six hours when Wayne stopped. "Look at the open area with an L-shaped defensible backdrop of large pine trees. There is good grass and a small pond to water the horses. Let's break and set up camp."

Mandy was getting use to the camp setting routine. She started the fire and prepared the food to be cooked for dinner. She boiled water and added coffee. Wayne took care of the horses, but this time brought them a hundred yards from the camp—potentially safe from the expected shooting.

Just as they were enjoying a hot cup of coffee, Mandy spotted the double smoke cloud. "Well, just as expected, we will have visitors by nightfall. Let's get extra firewood, we want them to see our fire from afar."

They enjoyed cooking the last meal of ham, canned carrots and crackers. Afterwards, they laid out the security cord. Set up six inches above the ground and wound around trees. The jangle of tin cans was again set up off a branch. Wayne said, "as soon as one trips on the cord, the tin cans will be our warning bell."

They then filled their bedroll with the extra blankets and bedrolls, to make it look like they were asleep in their bedrolls. They then set off to the pine trees, made themselves a seat of pine boughs. Wayne gave Mandy the same directions. "I am setting you behind the protection of this large pine tree with a rifle. You don't start shooting unless I'm incapacitated. I need to function without fear of you getting hit. Ok?' "Yes, I will follow your orders, as you knew I would."

With everything in place, they put on their winter coats and sat on their benches. Wayne was armed with his sawed off shotgun and his Winchester 76 rifle. He had added the sixth round to his and Mandy's Colt, and started their vigil.

Wayne expected Brownie to warn them of visitors, but the two outlaws left their horses out of range. Thanks to a full moon, Wayne saw the two men walk in from almost 100 yards. They were only ten yards from the camp fire when the lead man tripped on the cord and activated the jangling tin cans. As he tripped, he fell to his knees and accidentally fired the cocked pistol. The second man started firing at the apparent figures in the bedrolls.

Wayne yelled out, "stop plugging holes in my bedrolls, you dumb idiots. Now drop your guns, I have you covered with a double barrel shotgun loaded with #3 buckshot. If you point your guns in my direction, I will let go both barrels, and you won't be identifiable."

Wayne saw both men hesitate. They only heard his voice and did not know where he was. Wayne added, "now you scoundrels will be found guilty of kidnaping, and may get a prison sentence if you have a good lawyer. You may even get lucky and escape from me before we get to Silver Circle. If you don't surrender, you will both die. Make up your mind, before I make it for you."

They saw they had no choice. They both dropped their guns, put their hands over their heads, and said, "Ok, we give up." Wayne signaled Mandy to follow with her rifle. They walked up to the kidnapers and Wayne popped each one in the back of the head with the butt of his uncocked shotgun. He then dragged each one to the fire. He tied their feet and hands together with pigging strings. He then walked to the panniers and came back with a contraption that Mandy didn't recognize. Wayne said, "we won't have to worry about these two animals. This is a steel collar which is padlocked to this chain. The end of the chain is wrapped around a tree and locked on itself with another padlock. When they wake up, they will have a four foot span to move about—just like a wild animal. Mandy looked it over and said, "and we will be able to sleep in peace tonight."

Wayne made a fresh pot of coffee and they waited for the monsters to wake up. The look on Milton's face when he realized he was tethered to a tree was worth a thousand words. You could see that the notion of escaping them was no longer even a remote possibility. Reese was slow to wake up, so Mandy threw a bucket of water in his face with sudden results. Again, Reese could not believe he was tied like the madman that he was. Mandy looked at both of them, spit in their faces, and grabbed a two inch thick piece of firewood. She walked up to Milt and smashed the piece of firewood into his mouth. Teeth were flying all over the place. Reese was laughing at Milt, when Mandy did a back swing and caught Reese in the face–more teeth were spit out. Mandy's revenge was still not adequate, she took the piece of firewood and slammed it into the kidnapper's crotches. Both men started vomiting. Mandy then said, "don't give them any food or water. They can relieve themselves in their pants." "Ok, and remind me never to cross you."

Later Wayne added, "this is the way it's going to be tomorrow. First of all, if your old crimes involved the death of a victim, then you are wanted dead or alive. Which means, I could shoot you and bring you back laying on your saddle. I'm a lawman and I won't do that. However, I will sit you on your horse, tie your hands behind your back, secure the horse's reins to your saddle, and lock your chain to a stirrup.

If you fall off your horse, you will experience some torturing pain as I let your horse drag you to your death. Remember, we don't give a rat's ass about you, your comfort or your survival."

That evening, Wayne and Mandy had a mixture of all their leftovers. They only kept bacon, coffee, potatoes and one can of beans for breakfast. They boiled the potatoes that night so they could have them in the morning for fried potatoes. For lunch they kept the leftover smoked ham and crackers. For a traveling snack, they had plenty of beef jerky. They didn't keep any food for dinner tomorrow night. They would be in Silver Circle by mid afternoon.

As Wayne and Mandy got in their bedrolls, Reese yells out, "hey, I've got to relieve myself!" Wayne yells back, "shut up, one more word and I will use my fence repair tool to crush your tongue."

During the night, the Demers boys had visitors. They never heard or saw the Cheyenne warriors. They brought several snakes and left them out of the leather bags, near the prisoners. Suddenly, there were piercing screams of terror in the camp. Mandy sat up, saw Wayne walk toward the tied animals. Reese screamed in pain as he suffered a vicious bite to his arm. Milton was trying to kick the snakes away as Wayne picked up one of the snakes by the tail and threw it at Milton. Milton screamed even louder as the snake bit him on a nipple.

Mandy finally said, "are they going to die from the bites?" "No, these idiots don't recognize that these black snakes are not venomous. They bite with excruciating pain, and the bite hurts for half a day. They won't sleep for the rest of the night–such a shame, heh."

In the morning, the temperature had plummeted–it was cold. Unusual this time of year but known to happen. Wayne and Mandy put on their winter jackets and took out their gloves. Mandy prepared their last breakfast while Wayne saddled all the horses. While they prepared to have their breakfast, smart ass Milt said, "hey, we are hungry, how about sharing some of that bacon?" Wayne said to Mandy, "would you hand me my fence mending tool?" "Wayne why would you want to get blood on the pliers? Let me give them some bacon." Mandy stands, grabs the frypan and tosses the hot grease at their prisoners. She got some splatter on their arms and faces. They both screamed out again, but never said another word.

Suddenly, the screaming captives attracted some activity in the forest. Three Indians appeared, and the chief was recognized. The chief says, "I came to thank you for your generous gifts and wanted to introduce you to my two sons. It is time that they meet a good whitey." Mandy surprised the chief and said, "would you like some coffee, beans and bacon?" To Wayne's surprise, the chief said, "It would not be good to say no, my sons need to learn your ways, yes we will join you." While Mandy was now really pulling out all the leftovers, Wayne was seen adding the last of the oats to all the horses. The chief said, "you are good to your horses and to your woman." Mandy smiled and realized that she was at least as important as a horse to this chief.

They all ate quietly, and the two warriors said, "thank you." Wayne got up, went to the pack horse pannier and came back to the camp. He hands each of the sons a rifle and two boxes of bullets. The chief says, "why, you have already been generous." "A thank you for the double smoke cloud and the snakes." The chief nodded with a smile, turned to leave and said, "we like your animal collars, and go in peace. Remember to be good to woman, it goes a long ways. I am called Chief Blue Sky, and we will likely meet again. We will tell our people that your name is Iron Man, what it means, and what you have done for us."

He then changed the kidnappers restrained hands to their backs. He walked each one to their horse, and padlocked their chain to one stirrup. He helped each one to sit on their horses. He then tells them, "we're riding straight through to Silver Circle, stopping only to rest and water our horses. It might be a bit cold today, but you'll be in a warm jail cell by tonight–unless you fall off your horse."

They rode in silence for three hours. When they found a good creek and good grass, they made their first stop. Mandy stepped down and ran to the bushes with privacy papers to do her business. Wayne brought the horses to drink and let them crop some grass. Milt and Reese were left in the saddle, but their horses were hobbled.

During the rest, Wayne and Mandy enjoyed some jerky and fresh water. Mandy looked at the feeding horses and said, "do horses actually sleep standing up?" Wayne said, "they certainly do. Horses like many large animals don't sleep laying down because it takes too long to get up, and they are targets for predators. Horses, can lock their knees and remain stable while sleeping. That is why you see them sleeping in their barn stalls. Besides, stalls are too narrow for a horse to lay down. Horses sleep 2–5 hours each night. Occasionally, a horse will be seeing laying down in a secure pasture. That is when they get into a deep sleep for a few minutes."

After the break, Wayne said, "it looks like we may get some cold rain today. So lets add our rain dusters over our winter coats till the weather improves. After a half hour of grazing time, they got back on the trail. Suddenly, a wind blown cold rain came blasting from the north. Wayne and Mandy were well protected, but the two kidnappers looked like frozen rats. They kept pushing till it was time to rest, water and feed the horses. Reese said, "come on deputy, we are freezing and wet, let's stop. We need cover and some heat." Wayne said nothing but grabbed a dry willow stick. He walked over to Reese, and let him have three good switches across the face and shoulders. "I told you to shut up. You must have a pea brain, because you don't seem to learn."

Wayne and Mandy had their leftover smoked ham and crackers, under cover of a huge pine tree. When it was time to leave again, Wayne said, "this is our last leg, in about an hour we should fall on the road west of town.

When they found the road, Mandy finally realized that their ordeal was over. As they entered town, people were waving and cheering from the boardwalks. Mandy commented, "this is a welcoming gauntlet." "Yes because these are hard working good folks." As they arrived at the sheriff's office, they were greeted by Sheriff Jim, and Ed. Ed gave them a hug and said to Wayne, "I have good news, we will talk this week." Sheriff Jim gave Wayne a big hug and Wayne noticed a tear. "God am I glad you and Mandy are back alive. This has been a very long ten days." As Wayne was walking into the office to take care of business, Mandy asked Ed where her aunt an uncle were. Ed says, "they were both badly injured and tortured, but I hear they have stabilized. You'll find them in Sutton Hospital. Mandy gets on her horse and says to Wayne, "when you're done here, meet me at Sutton Hospital."

And so the kidnaping ordeal was in the past. Expecting a normal life was wishful thinking for these two dynamos.

***

CHAPTER 9
The Wedding

Mandy arrived at Sutton Hospital at a full canter. She jumped off her horse, wrapped the reins around the railing, and ran up the steps of the hospital. Without knocking, she entered the lobby. A nurse in full uniform saw this tall woman in a full length duster, winter coat, a sidearm, cowboy hat and boots. All she could think was, here was a woman with a powerful and determined presence. The nurse said, "may I help you?" "Mandy said, "I wish to see George and Sally Wilson." The nurse said, "oh my goodness, you must be Amanda, the kidnaped niece!" "Yes, may I see my uncle and aunt." "Why, of course, follow me."

When she saw them seemingly comfortable sitting in a rocker, they got up and hugged their niece. Sally said, "you are back and safe, we thought we lost you, but Wayne came through." "Yes, Aunt Sally, he is a Paladin. Uncle George then hugged her and everyone cried tears of joy. It was then that Wayne appeared in the doorway. George stepped forward and said, "thank you for bringing her back, and don't forget that third fireplace brick, it's yours." "Not necessary Mr. Wilson, we are getting married."

George explained that Sally was recovering from a severe concussion and he had to have surgery on his amputated fingers. Had his arm put in a cast. The major problem was that he had broken ribs that lacerated a lung. He had to have a tube placed in his chest for a week to drain the blood. They were very grateful for the surgical skills of the young Doctor Sutton.

Mandy said, "what is your cost for 10 days and several surgeries?" "We will be released in two days. The care has been marvelous. Our bill is $92. We are making a $500 donation so Dr. Sutton can order some new and modern equipment.

George asked Wayne what will happen with Stuart Bostwell. "As we speak, Sheriff Jim is trying to work a deal with Milt Demers and Reese Holloway. We'll know more tomorrow when the prosecutor gets involved with a deal. I will let you know because you and Mandy should be able to put a claim for damages if Bostwell is found guilty."

The next morning at the Wilson's ranch house, plans were being laid out for the next four days leading to the wedding. Mandy would pick up Aunt Sally at the hospital by buggy, and go to the new Madison's Garments. On the way, they would stop at Western Union and send an invitation to Mandy's mom and roommate. Wayne had business at the sheriff's office, Ed's Mercantile, and had to buy a suit at Madison's Garment. Together, they would choose wedding bands and make arrangements with Father Mahler at St. Helens.

They both left together, Wayne on Brownie and Mandy in the ranch buggy. Mandy picked Sally up, sent the two telegrams and went to look for a wedding dress. Sally chose several designs. The choices were extensive, just as expected in Denver. After trying five dresses, the last one was perfect. The fit was natural and did not need modifications. It was a white flared dress with half sleeves and a closed neckline. It had a veil for catholic church requirements, but it did not have a trane. With a white pair of gloves, the total bill was $29.

Mandy and Sally continued shopping for other clothes they needed. Mandy needed conservative dresses for school. She also needed riding skirts and matching blouses. Sally needed an elegant outfit for the wedding and other everyday dresses. After personal items were chosen, they both headed to Simms diner. They had a lunch favorite: vegetable soup and hard boiled egg sandwiches. The eggs were local, and with the train, vegetable produce was a regular delivery. After lunch, Mandy brought Sally back at the hospital. She visited with her aunt and uncle for a while. When she presumed that Wayne would be done with the sheriff and Ed, she decided to join him at Madisons to help him pick out a suit.

When Mandy walked in Madisons, she saw Wayne staring at six suits on display. Mandy walked up to him and pointed at a blue pin striped tweed suit with a white shirt. She said to the clerk, "Wayne is 6 feet 2 inches and weighs 200 pounds. Do you have this one in large/long coat and 38 inch waist by 36 inch leg?" The clerk left, shuffled the clothes and came back with the exact sizes. Mandy says, "great, try this one on with a large white shirt. Come out with your boots on, once you're dressed."

Mandy and the clerk waited patiently. There was a lot of scurrying, moaning, and cussing behind the changing room curtain. Finally, Wayne stepped out. Mandy tried to hide her smile and said, "well how does it feel?" "Feels great." The clerk rubs his hand against the material, looks carefully and says, "folks that is a perfect fit without the need for alterations—a rather rare find."

Wayne says, "I like it, how does it look on me?" "Ravishing, if you don't go change, I will join you in the changing room and. . . . . . .!

The clerk interjected, "well while you are changing, I will prepare you bill, heh." The suit, shirt and tie cost him $19.

The next thing they did was stop at Aronsons Jewelry and chose matching wedding bands with the size fitted to their fingers. That cost them $20.

With their errands done, they went to Simms diner. Wayne had not had lunch yet. He ordered a pork sandwich with coffee, and Mandy had a glass of lemonade. Mandy said, "Tell me about your visit with Sheriff Jim and Ed."

Wayne started, "when I arrived at the office, Sheriff hands me Western Union vouchers for the reward money on those four kidnappers and hired guns." He then hands Mandy the four vouchers. Mandy takes them and reads, "My God, Wayne, these are $500 each!" "Yes, and after lunch we are going to the bank and start a private account in both our names. This is not to be deposited in the benefactor account. These vouchers represent a personal matter involving the both of us."

He then says, that the prosecutor was with the two prisoners. Suddenly, the prosecutor comes out of the jail room and says, "I have a tentative deal with Demers and Holloway. They will implicate Stuart Bostwell as the organizer of this kidnaping in exchange for a 15 year sentence in the county jail. It is a good deal for them, and they have to wave their right to a trial. They both realized that a trial would have found them guilty of kidnaping and risked being hung. I have to see Judge Atchison to get this plea deal approved, and I suspect that he will go with it, since it guarantees the incarceration or hanging of Bostwell."

Mandy adds, "I didn't know that such plea deals were legal, but I like it since it brings Bostwell to justice. Now what did Ed want?" "Well that was a pleasant surprise. It appears that there was a gold strike in the homesteading ranches west of town. One homesteader used dynamite to dig for a water source. He didn't find water, instead he found a gold vein. The area became a race to buy land to dig for gold. Land was selling at $5 per acre instead of the usual $1 per acre. Speculators were buying a quarter section of land(160 acres) and buying dynamite by the case. No other strikes were ever found. The lucky landowner sold the strike to McNeer Mining for a rumored $200,000. No one knew who the lucky fella was.

With this background, Ed adds, "now this is where you come into the picture. One day, Mr Trucot comes to my store, You may remember him as the first recipient of your benefactor account. Well to get to the chase, he hands me a bank draft made out in your name. He adds, 'tell Deputy Swanson, thanks for helping those in need.'" Ed hands Wayne the receipt of the bank draft deposited in the benefactor account.

Wayne hands the receipt to Mandy, she looks at it and says. "Wayne, this can't be right, it's a receipt for $25,000. You can't accept this!" "You're right, I can't accept it for personal use, it's for the benefit of good people in need, and it will be spent that way."

After lunch, they went to Miller's Bank. A clerk asked, "how may I help you today?" "We wish to open a joint bank account and make a deposit." The clerk opened a drawer and came out with the appropriate papers. He said, "Wayne sign here, here, and here, Wayne signed. When it came to Mandy, Wayne said, "sign as Amanda Swanson. After signing, the clerk noticed a smile from ear to ear on Mandy's face.

Wayne and Mandy were preparing to leave with all their purchases in the buggy. Sheriff Jim interrupts them and says, "Oscar just saw Stuart Bostwell and two ranch hands riding through town. They came from White City as Demers had predicted. The judge just issued a warrant for Bostwell's arrest. I thought that as your last official duty as a deputy sheriff, you may want to serve the warrant for personal satisfaction."

"Yes, I will serve it as a badge wearing deputy, but I will bring him back as a private citizen." "That sounds good to me. Wayne."

"Mandy, I will meet you at the Wilson's home in a few hours." "Ok, and send him my regards, heh!" Mandy took off and Wayne headed to the Box B Ranch. As he arrived, he stepped down without being asked. Stepped on the porch and banged on the door. Bostwell yelled out to stop pounding on the door. As he stepped out, he said, "what in hell are you doing here, get off my property." Wayne responded with, "as a legal messenger of Judge Atchison, I am serving you this arrest warrant." Bostwell starts to read the warrant as Wayne places his deputy badge in his pocket.

Bostwell lifts his eyes off the paper and says, "this is crap, my attorney"–that is when Wayne landed a perfect punch to Bostwell's nose. Bostwell was pushed back several steps with a look of total disbelief, Wayne planted another punch and flattened his nose. The warrant went flying. The next punch pushed Bostwell through the door and several teeth and blood went airborne. The next punch to the eyes flattened Bostwell to the floor. Wayne's anger was still peaking. He kicked him in the ribs three times till he heard ribs cracking. Then he picked him off the floor, held him by his left hand, and pummeled him with two more rights.

Bostwell collapsed to the floor and was moaning. Wayne leaned down and said close to his face, "this hurt is from Mandy." He steps up and swings his boot at full force into his crotch. Bostwell threw up and screamed the sound of the damned. Wayne then dragged him to the porch, and pushed him off the porch as he rolled in horse manure.

The sounds of a beating brought the ranch hands to the house. Wayne said, "anyone of you want a dose of the same?" No one spoke or moved. "Then hitch up a wagon so I can bring this animal to jail." "Don't you mean the carriage?" "No, the buckboard, I want him to enjoy the bouncing ride to town."

The buckboard arrived, Wayne picked up Bostwell and unceremoniously threw him in the wagon. Bostwell went into a fetal position, holding his crotch, and resumed his moaning and crying. As Wayne was leaving he said, "you boys better pack and head to the Courthouse. Apply for your last month's wages and a severance pay. This animal is never returning, and the ranch will be confiscated."

"The ride to town was at a good clip. Bostwell was seen bleeding from his mouth and nose, while crutching at his ribs and crotch. Finally he yelled out, "stop this wagon and shoot me." "I doubt it, that would be more than you deserve–you'll likely get a public neck stretching." As Wayne encouraged the horses to increase their trotting speed.

When they got to the sheriff's office, Sheriff Jim came out to check out the package delivery. He said, "I see he resisted?" Wayne added, "well he kept walking into the main entrance door smashing his face. Then as he ran out of the house, he accidentally landed his crotch on the hitching rail. When he yelled out in pain, he startled my horse who kicked him in the ribs. But I managed to get him here in one piece. Maybe we better have Doc Sutton see to his stupid accidents, heh?" "Maybe in a few days once he stabilizes."

After depositing Bostwell to the floor of a cell, directly across from Demers and Holloway, Wayne was heading to the Wilsons. As he passed the telegraph office, he decided to send a good news note and a wedding invitation to his mom and dad. He added that he needed a best man. After he paid, for the telegram, Stan Bulow said, "Wayne, Miss Currier got some bad news an hour ago, and I immediately sent a messenger to deliver it. I think you better intercept the messenger and deliver it yourself."

Wayne took off at a full gallop, He met up with the messenger a mile from the ranch. He told the messenger that he would deliver the telegram at Mr. Bulow's suggestion. He gave the messenger a dollar which quickly made up the messenger's mind that this was proper. Wayne read the telegram and quickly realized he would have been better off not knowing.

He proceeded to the Wilson's home. Mandy was sitting on the porch waiting for him. He stepped down and said, "you have a telegram from Denver." Mandy starts reading:

> To Amanda Currier, c/o the Bar W Ranch, Silver Circle, CO.
>
> Bad news STOP Mom is terminally ill with heart failure STOP Need to come to St. Mary's Hospital ASAP Send train arrival time.
>
> From Kathy Somerset, Smith School, Denver CO

Mandy hands the telegram to Wayne with tears in her eyes. He says, "I know, I am so sorry. It is 11AM and the train leaves at 1PM. Let's pack a travel bag and our Webley Bulldogs. We head to town, leave our horses with Bruce at the livery, and send a telegram to Kathy. We will be in Denver by morning and will meet her at the hospital." They closed the house and were on their horses within fifteen minutes. By 12:45, their errands done, they were waiting to board the train.

The long ride was slower than usual because of many cars loaded with ore and cattle. Wayne and Mandy were both silent and held hands the entire trip. They slept on and off because of the stops for water and coal. When they finally arrived in Pueblo, they changed to the passenger over night Express directly to Denver. They finally traveled the 140 miles and arrived by morning. After arrival, they took a buggy taxi to St. Mary's Hospital.

As they entered the lobby, Kathy jumped in Mandy's arms and they cried themselves dry. Eventually they separated and Mandy said, "Kathy, this is my loving husband to be, Wayne Swanson. After introductions were done, Kathy said, "Amanda, your mom's doctor said that her heart is failing fast and she is not expected to live past today. Let me bring you to your mom, she is waiting for you."

Mandy was escorted to the room labeled Mrs. Delia Currier. Kathy encouraged her to enter the room alone. Her mom was sleeping but the footsteps woke her up. She smiled at Mandy and with open arms greeted her daughter. They both cried until the tears stopped flowing. It was Delia who suggested that they clear up family matters and business before they can enjoy each other's company.

Delia began. "A week ago, I changed the name on my house deed to you. The taxes are paid for the next year. My bank account has had your name added, and my balance is $22,500, thanks to your father. My funeral arrangement and head stone have been paid for at Penrose Morticians and funeral parlor. My will gives you all my personal possessions. Whatever legal papers you need are in the house safe, and you know the combination. The only bill left for you to pay is my Doctor and hospital bill. Be generous, they have all been good to me."

"If you choose to sell the family home/two acres, the bank has evaluated it at $4750 because there is room to add a barn/carriage house. Last, I have paid your tuition for your last school year. I presume you will live at home instead of boarding at school, but that is your choice. Now that this formal business is completed, I want to meet the man that swept you away–this is something I never expected."

Mandy got up, went to get Wayne and made introductions. Wayne politely kissed her mom on the cheek. Wayne volunteered the first words and said, "Thank you for giving me your daughter that I love so much. I will protect her, support her and do my best to make her happy." "Well Amanda, you are one lucky girl."

Kathy joined them for a short time. Wayne and Mandy never left her side. Delia wanted to know what their short and long term plans were. Delia summarized their plans by saying, "so it sounds like nine months of schooling while you act as a bounty hunting Paladin. Then you move to Silver Circle where Amanda will teach and you will take over the management of my brother's ranching empire!" "Yes, but as expected, there will be a few twists and turns to get there, but we will deal with them together."

They visited several hours until Delia got exhausted. She asked Mandy her last question. "Are you happy?" "Oh yes, mom. Plus, feel reassured that I am in good hands." Delia fell asleep and two hours later passed away peaceably in her sleep.

Later that evening, the three of them were in the Currier home. While Mandy was taking a bath, Wayne took the opportunity to make Kathy a business proposal. "Mandy will be living at home during the school year. Were you to cancel your room and board contract at school, you could live here free of charge. I will provide your food and any other needs, as well as a buggy taxi service with a rain bonnet. They will pick you up mornings to get to school, and will bring you back home at night–plus any other time you have need of the service. Mandy will pay for everything else, and I will give you a monthly stipend of $30 for personal use."

Kathy was flummoxed but managed to answer, "Oh my, I would love to live the year out with Amanda, The room and board savings is more than the tuition. I have run out of money, and without any living parents, I was going to go to the bank for a loan to finish my degree." "There is no need for a bank loan, I will pay your tuition under the 'other needs' category, and we will start a joint bank account in both your names to serve as an emergency and day to day fund."

That is beyond generous, what do you get out of this?" "Mandy needs your support and friendship to get through this grieving period, plus I will be on the bounty hunting circuit for the next nine months. The two of you as a team also adds extra security—a plus. The both of you have spent a lifetime in school, and you are both only nine months from completion. I want both of you to finish your schooling without financial or security issues." Kathy thanked Wayne and graciously accepted his incredible offer. Wayne added, "our deal depends on Mandy accepting it."

The next day a quiet funeral was held. Delia's life long teaching associates, neighbors and other close friends were present. After the Catholic mass and burial. The three of them again gathered in the Currier home. Mandy was subdued and pensive all day. Eventually Wayne told Mandy of his offer to Kathy. Mandy was so happy with the arrangements that it relieved some of the painful grief she was experiencing. Suddenly, Mandy finally spoke. "Wayne, let's go home.

Kathy you have the run of the house, and I promised my mother's final request —that I would not allow her passing to delay our wedding. Time to go home, the wedding is in four days and school starts in ten days."

"I think that is a wise decision. Tomorrow morning, go to the bank with Kathy and transfer $1000 into a joint account. Kathy will draw enough cash to pay for her train tickets to the wedding and back, plus keep some cash for traveling emergencies—especially important when traveling alone. Also, Kathy, when you are in Silver Circle, we'll show you how to shoot your own Webley Bulldog for your self defense." Kathy adds, "what is that?" As Mandy opens her purse and pulls out her Webley—Kathy smiled and said, "yes, it's about time I learned." Wayne volunteered that in the morning he would go to a buggy taxi company and set up a contract for the girls.

By 9AM Wayne was at Carl's Taxi. He was greeted by an older chap who by his name tag was the owner. He said, "what can I do for you sir?" "I wish to arrange for a 9 month taxi service for my wife. It entails two rides per day M–F, from 17 Spring St. to Smith school on Liberty street, plus any other excursions that come up."

"For this type of service, each trip is charged by the traveling time. The charge is placed in the driver's ledger. The accountant keeps a tab going, and when the deposit is used up, the passenger has to make a new deposit with me—not the driver.

With the two locations you gave me, I suspect the daily charge would be in the vicinity of 80 cents per day." "Well in that case, I will give you a deposit of $200 and you can start your service on September first."

"For any other needs of transportation, your wife only needs to walk one block to your nearest sub station and board a taxi. All she needs to do is give the driver your contract number and the fare will appear on the master ledger. This system works great and we have rare complaints. We've been in business for twenty years because of our service and honesty."

Wayne and Mandy were at the train station by 11AM. They hugged Kathy and boarded the train with a smile. They were headed home. After the train departed, Kathy went to Western Union and sent three telegrams—to Sheriff Jim, the Wilsons at Sutton Hospital, and Wayne's mom and dad. It read:

> Will arrive Silver Circle tomorrow at 1PM. STOP Mandy's mom has passed. STOP Coming home to wed. STOP Love you all. STOP From: Wayne and Mandy

***

Sheriff Jim was waiting at the RR depot. He greeted Wayne and Mandy and extended his sympathies. He then said, "Mandy, the Wilson's were just discharged from the hospital and are waiting for you by the street. Their foreman, Brett Hanson, came down to pick them up with the ranch buggy. I brought your horse, and you can trail him behind the buggy. Wayne needs to do some closing and exiting tasks before he leaves my service. Yet he will be at the Bar W Ranch before dinner time." Mandy kissed Wayne and walked to the waiting buggy, kissed her uncle and aunt, and headed to the ranch.

Wayne says, "now what tasks are left for me, since you already have my badge." "Edna Ferguson is in Sutton Hospital. She has been beaten to a hair of her life. She's been comatose for 5 days, has several broken ribs, belt marks over most of her back, and a broken/crushed hand. Floyd has been beating her for years, he is just an angry drunk. Now the problem is that Edna has finally had enough and wants to press charges. This means that according to ancient laws still on the books, a husband can beat his wife to maintain marital stability. The judge cannot sentence him to a long incarceration, since that means that his wife will not have his financial support, and wouldn't be much better off. The judge can send him to my jail for 30 days, but that means that Edna will get another beating when he gets out of jail."

"The way the system is, it's a loose-loose situation. The only solution is for Edna to be granted a divorce on the grounds of excessive abuse." "Yes, but it also must include a financial settlement for Edna to restart her life–fortunately there are no children involved. Now, I can go and arrest him, but what we need is to forcibly convince him to a divorce and monetary settlement–which as sheriff, I cannot do. Edna now prefers this solution over pressing charges."

"Got it, I will persuade him to do the right thing. Mandy calls me a Paladin, and I am beginning to think she's right. Edna is a victim that was dealt a bad hand, and she is stuck knowing that her hand will not improve. We will help her, and give her a second chance at life." "Just remember, Floyd is a fist fighter and loves to brawl. You have to disable that right fist or you won't have a chance."

Wayne arrived at Ferguson's ranch an hour later. He stepped off his horse and knocked at the door. A gruffy voice, yelled out, "what do you want?" Wayne answered, "the Wilsons want to invite Edna to a quilting party." "The door opens, Floyd was holding his head from a recent drunk and added, "She's not here, she went to visit her sister in White City." "Hello Mr. Ferguson, as Wayne extends his hand to shake hello, Floyd responded naturally, but Wayne did not shake. Instead he grabbed Floyd's right wrist with his left hand, and used his right hand to extend two fingers some 90 degrees upwards. Floyd eyes popped open and he screamed bloody hell. Wayne immediately added, Oh I'm sorry but my hand slipped. Floyd knew that he was in trouble when his third finger got hyper extended and found his face bouncing off the wall. Wayne continued to swing him into the door frame, along with several elbow slams to his kidney. Floyd was going from one wall to another with no chance to fight back with his right fist in an unnatural and painful position. Then, Wayne punched him in the nose and teeth came flying out, eventually he collapsed to the floor. Wayne then stepped on his left hand

and heard bones cracking. Floyd was screaming, moaning and begging Wayne to stop.

Floyd you have to be the most stupid son of a bitch to ever walk the face of the earth. Edna was a cook, house keeper, laundress, milked your cow, and took care of the barn animals to include mucking their stalls, when you were on one of your drunks. And how did you repay her—by beating her and raping her. Wayne was still angry and kicked him in the side chest till ribs broke. Floyd said, "what do you want from me?"

Wayne said, "I want you to come to the courthouse tomorrow. I want you to sign voluntary divorce papers. Since you have enslaved her for ten years, what you call marriage, I think you owe her a salary of $1 per day. That is 365 days per year, times ten years, comes to $3650. Now if you don't show up by noon, I will be coming back tomorrow. Your left hand will also have three fingers pointing at the ceiling and the beating will continue. I will break one leg at the knee by tearing all the ligaments, and you'll never walk again. You'll be in bed for a month, and we'll have to bring the judge to you so you can sign the divorce and settlement papers. Seems like a waste, don't it to you." "Yes, I'll be there, as long as you stay away from me."

As Wayne was leaving, he decided to give Floyd some mercy. He stepped to him, grabbed his right hand and slowly brought the fingers downward–slow to increase the agony. Floyd was dancing, crying and ranting. Wayne added, "heh, I had to bring them back, otherwise you wouldn't be able to sign the papers tomorrow!"

Wayne made his was to town to report to the sheriff. "Well did you convince him to do the right thing?" "I think so, he wasn't the most cheerful person when I left, but we will know by noon tomorrow. He will be seeing Judge Atchison, and you will have to pick up a settlement for Edna, and open a bank account for her." "What do I expect for a deposit?" "A $3650 bank draft." "Wow, out of the generosity of a grateful heart." "No, out of fear of more justifiable retribution."

Sheriff Jim changed the subject and said, "I want to bring you up to snuff on the Bostwell issue. Judge Atchison has had several meetings with Bostwell. I heard him on his first visit when he said to Bostwell, "You are a real pea brain. With your doings, you are going to hang!" "For shock effect, the judge walked out of the office. Bostwell cried all afternoon."

The next day, the judge had a very long meeting with Bostwell, and walked out of the cell area with a handful of papers. "Stuart Bostwell agreed to the following conditions:

1. You will be paid $100 per day to rescue Mandy—or $1000.

2. The ranch hands will be paid their last month's wages and a severance pay of $250 each.

3. A financial settlement to Mandy and the Wilsons. The 1000 cattle will be sold at $22 per head. The $22000 plus a bank account balance of $12000 will give a retribution fund of $34000. Or $17000 each.

4. The ranch consisting of 8 sections, the ranch house, barn, bunkhouse, and several corrals, will go to auction and will be bought by the highest bidder."

"In return, Bostwell will waive his right to a trial. He understood that if found guilty at trial, he would have been hung. His sentence will be 20 years minimum in the state penitentiary. For a 58 year old man, that is a death sentence." "Yes, and like a life sentence, those prisoners are called 'the walking dead.'"

***

The next three days were spent enjoying everyday life before the big day. Mandy was serving the Wilsons as much as they would let her. Wayne was closing his room at the boarding house in town. Two traveling crates were brought to the ranch for Wayne and Mandy to start packing what was destined to be needed in the next nine months. Mandy's stuff was basically her clothing since everything was in her home on Spring Street. Wayne's stuff was his guns: Colt Peacemaker, Win 1873 rifle, Win 1876, his new sharps in 45-90 caliber with a ladder sight and a new 8X Malcolm telescope for long range. He also packed his sawed off shotgun with a backpack holster. He had a good supply of ammo for each gun. He also loaded several changes of clothes and finally loaded his cooking supplies, and pack animal panniers.

Once Wayne's boarding house room was closed, Wayne moved into the mandatory third bedroom at the Wilson Ranch–the bedroom at the other end of the house. The Wilsons were early to retire, and this gave them some welcomed private time.

They enjoyed being alone for the evening. They talked about how they would deal with the next nine months, especially how to hold their desires for marital intimacy. Things always led to passionate kissing and to fondling. When the fondling extended to under the undergarments, the heat of their desires started to rise. They always stepped back, and knew that this behavior would be expanded to their marital consummation on their wedding night. Being left high and dry was a sacrifice for both of them–fortunately, the wedding was now two days away.

Kathy arrived by train the next day at 1PM. They had arrived early to pick her up, because they were picking up a special order at Harrigans Gunshop–a Webley Bulldog in 44 caliber. It included a shoulder holster but like Mandy it would be carried in her purse or a pocket.

They greeted her at the train depot, and loaded her travel bags in the buggy. On their way home, the two ladies talked continuously. They had a lot to catch up with–after all they had been apart only a couple of days! Arriving at the Wilson's home, Kathy's stuff was moved into a cot in Mandy's room and lunch followed. After a long discussion again with the Wilson's, Kathy was finally free for a gun instruction course.

"Kathy, this is a double action 44 handgun. He explained that this gun should never be pulled out unless it was to shoot someone who was threatening her life. He explained the difference in single and double action, how to load it and how to fire it." Kathy picked up quickly, and was firing successfully at a one foot target at eight feet. She then learned how to do a double tap (two quick shots) through her purse for a killer at her throat. Mandy was watching the entire lesson and admitted that the double tap was new and most important.

Once Wayne was satisfied that Kathy was competent in handling and shooting her Bulldog, he approached the issue of home security beyond wearing their Bulldog. A shotgun is the best home security, anyone looking down the double barrels would freeze on the spot. Kathy was shown how to load, cock and fire. The first shot set Kathy back two feet. He had her continue to load, cock and fire till she could fire two consecutive shots and hold her ground. Mandy also practiced this technique as well.

The last part of the course was familiarity with the 1873 rifle and a Colt Peacemaker. He showed her how to load a rifle, cycle the lever and drop the hammer on a live round. She fired it a few times. He taught her the same with the Colt pistol, including firing it. He made it clear that he wanted her to rely on her Bulldog and the shotgun. Kathy asked where she could get a house shotgun, and Mandy said she was bringing one with shells, to stay in their house. Kathy finally said, "can Mandy join me and shoot our Bulldog for practice?" "Yes, and here is another two boxes. I will set up one foot targets at four, eight, and twelve feet. That is the reliable accurate range for you ladies."

"Remember one parting thought. If you ever have to shoot someone in self defense, when the police arrive, repeat the same words over and over again—I feared for my life, he was going to kill me and I fired in self defense." Wayne stepped aside and watched the two ladies from afar. He was satisfied with their performance.

That afternoon a telegram arrived from Sam and Cora Swanson. Mom and Dad were arriving tomorrow by train at 1PM. Wayne and Mandy were there to greet them. As they stepped on the RR platform Wayne hugged his mom and dad and said, "I would like to present you with my future bride, the woman who stole my heart, Amanda Currier, known to us from now on as Mandy. Cora hugged her and said, "welcome to our family, Mandy. Sorry for the loss of your mom. I want to hear all about you, so let's go to lunch at Simms and we can talk."

While waiting for their order, Mandy went through her childhood, years at school and her mom's funeral. She then went through a history of current events in the past three weeks in Silver Circle. Wayne added the ten day kidnaping and the planned nine months ahead. He told them about Mandy's last nine months in school and his spending those nine months acting as a bounty hunter–to build up his benefactor fund. Mandy added, "Wayne has a calling, he is a true paladin and I am proud of him. I also know he will be back to me after the nine month ordeal."

Lunch arrived and only small talk continued. After lunch, Wayne ordered a dessert of fresh oatmeal cookies and plenty of coffee. Sam took over. "Well, we are certain that the nine months will safely come to an end. What happens after that?" Wayne said, "we come back to Silver Circle, Mandy becomes the town head teacher and I become my father-in-law's general Bar W Ranch manager. Mr. Wilson wants to retire and will prepare me to purchase the ranch."

Cora adds, "so you're planning to make Silver Circle your home as well as the Bar W Ranch?" "Yes, for two years, I have been a deputy sheriff in this town. I have made many friends and business acquaintances. Basically, I have made my name in this town and I love it here. Mandy's only living family is George and Sally Wilson. They look at Mandy as their only child. Plus Mandy has landed a well paid modern teaching job in a progressive school. She will be only six miles to work."

Cora held up her hands to stop Wayne. She looked at Sam and said, "you have my blessing Sam, please take over and share our wishes." Sam hesitated, put down his coffee and started, "we have been made a generous offer by our foreman. He is marrying a widow with three kids and wishes to buy our ranch. He has approval, at Miller's Bank in town, for a 100% loan to buy the ranch. Apparently, Mr. Miller said that the financial accounting showed that any buyer could make the loan payments. Plus Mr. Miller said that he owed you so many favors that this would be a drop in the bucket as pay back. So we can have a big nest egg to build a new home."

Cora then took over. "Wayne, you are our life, and now you give us a daughter-in-law, and maybe some grandchildren. We have been away from you three years, even if we were only six miles away and would see you once a week. We now want to be involved with your family and ranch on a daily basis."

Sam took over, "living six miles west of town puts us twelve miles to the east side Bar W Ranch. Twelve miles is too far. We are buying three acres from George and will build our new small house with a small barn, chicken coop, and garden."

Mandy just could not believe her ears. She added, "I cannot believe that Uncle George kept this from us. That is the best wedding present we could ever get." Wayne simply added, "you have just solved my only hesitation to living at the Bar W Ranch—not having you close by. Thank you, this is better than the day you adopted me—almost."

Sam then added, "we will be staying at the hotel till after the wedding. We will be seeing Rafferty's Construction to lay out plans for a two bedroom home with running cold, hot water, water closet and a septic tank We need to contract for a new well and windmill. We will also spend many hours with Ed's furniture catalogs to choose the furnishings. We also have to order a hot water coal fired boiler, cook stove and several heating coal stoves. We will be shopping and organizing things during the next two days before the wedding. Plus, we would like to get together again for lunch and or dinner."

The next morning Mandy and Sally had prepared a large breakfast of bacon, fried potatoes, eggs over easy, toasted home made bread and coffee. After the grand meal, the ladies were picking up dishes, while Wayne started a business meeting with George—for all to hear. "I have been informed by Sheriff Jim that, for a long prison sentence, a tentative settlement deal has been reached with Bostwell. The settlement after emptying his bank account and the sale of the cattle will be $17,000 each for Mandy and you. You both need to file a claim for damages against him. The county will confiscate the ranch and sell it at public auction.

"This is where you come in George. The land encompasses eight sections—that is 640 acres times eight equals 5120 acres. At the current market rate of $1 per acre and $1000 for the house, bunkhouse and barn, the market value will be in the range of $6,000. You can probably get it for much less during a drought, assuming few ranchers bid for it."

George thought of this and said, "why would I want it, I certainly don't need it?" "To grow hay for harvesting and sale. The Bar W Ranch has more water than needed. We can fence off hundreds of acres in the southern section of bottom land, and keep the northern section for grazing cattle as well as using all of the Box B land for cattle. We can develop an irrigation system to promote the growth of hay. We would cultivate the land and seed it with timothy and other local grasses. The hay would be stored in a warehouse for local and wholesale distribution. The ranchers will be able to grow their herds without the fear of lacking feed during a drought or a bad winter."

"What would you need for harvesting equipment?" "It so happens that companies like McCormick, Deering and John Deere have developed modern agricultural equipment. They include plows, harrows, seeders, hay cutters, windrow rakes, hay loaders and now a new one horse hay baler."

"This would require the construction of a new barn to store the equipment and a large storage shed for the hay." "Yes, Mandy and I have the money to pay for the Box B Ranch, the equipment and new buildings. This would be our new source of income, and you can continue ranching and even grow your herd."

Sally spoke up and said, "it appears we are all on the same page. Now is the time to tell them of our plans. Go ahead George." "Ok, I will buy the Box B and deed it to you. Sally and I know that Mandy will eventually inherit this ranch. We feel that this should occur sooner than later. We will deed this ranch to the both of you after the wedding. We will build a small house/barn next to your parents and next to the main ranch house. We are ready to retire as soon as you both return from Denver. We will be able to live off the interest of our bank account. But like your dad, I will also work for you to keep busy."

Mandy added, "wow, you are obviously ahead of our planning. Are you sure this is what you want?" Sally added, "oh yes, this is a win-win situation for us. And if you're blessed with children, I will take care of your kids so Mandy can continue teaching."

Wayne reflected on this news and finally said, "Mandy and I are certainly blessed. I thought we had an innovative idea, but you were way ahead of our plan. We are so thankful to have you as our second parents." Wayne shook their hands and Mandy hugged them with a firm expression of love and appreciation.

***

The last two days were spent preparing for the wedding and reception. The wedding would be held Saturday at 11AM. Father Mahler offered the parish hall for the reception. Cora and Sally went to Ed and selected the decorations. They hired Simms Diner to cater a hot meal for one hundred invited guests. Sam and George were assigned the job of hand delivering the invitations. Cora and Sally decorated the hall for the event. The invited guests included, Sheriff Jim, Oscar, Ray, Ed,

President Miller, Mayor Hawthorne, gunsmith Harrigan, telegrapher Bulow, butcher Gemler, sadler Evans, foreman Hanson, Judge Atchison, both Doc Sutton, livery man Hawkins, the RR agent, the land office agent, the courthouse clerk, the prosecutor, all the bank clerks, all the Bar W ranch hands and the Wilsons neighboring ranchers. Adding all their wives,guests and the wedding party came up to 106 people.

Wayne and Mandy were left out of the work load. Wayne added, "so much for the small wedding you had wanted, heh." "I know, but this is a big event for our families and our friends. So let's it proceed as they wish. All we have to do is to show up as the celebrants. This is their day as well as ours."

The wedding day arrived. Wayne was to be dressed and out of the house by 8AM. He went to the office and was escorted by Sheriff Jim to Simms for breakfast. Fortunately, they lingered to pass the time. By 10AM, he was headed to the church. He met his dad, his best man, and they met with Father Mahler who was good at cooling down the groom. The church filled with the invited guests. A few minutes before the entrance of the bride, the last two guests, Sally and Cora, were escorted to a front pew. Wayne and his dad were then escorted to the front of the church.

Mandy's preparation started after Wayne left the house. Her routine included a bath, a hair setting session, finding something old, new and blue. She was ahead of schedule and did not want to dress with the wedding gown, so George was sent to the porch to wait while Mandy walked around the house in her undergarments. Once she put the dress on, the carriage was brought from the barn to the porch. The entire wedding party boarded and were on their way, driven by Brett Hanson, the ranch foreman.

The wedding party was at the church door when a signal was sent to the organist. As the doors opened, she started playing the Bridal Chorus by Richard Wagner—also known as the wedding march or "here comes the bride." Mandy was walked down the isle by Uncle George who was wearing a proud smile. Mandy was beaming with joy in her white wedding dress. Following Mandy was her bridesmaid, Kathy, dressed in a light blue dress.

As Mandy was approaching Wayne, their eyes met and they both realized that the ultimate moment of their lives had arrived. They faced each other and held hands as Father Mahler made his introductory remarks. When it came to the vows, Father had to cough to get their attention.

> "Do you Wayne Swanson take Amanda Currier for your wedded wife, to. . . . . .Yes And do you Amanda Currier take Wayne Swanson for your wedded husband, to . . . . .Yes"

The rings were placed on their fingers. "By the powers invested in me by the Catholic Church and the state of Colorado, I thee wed. I pronounce you man and wife. You may kiss the bride."

Father Mahler they says, "Ladies and gentlemen, I present you Mr. and Mrs. Wayne Swanson. *Enthusiastic applause followed.* Father Mahler reminded the guests that they were welcome to a reception and dinner in the parish hall. The married couple walked back down the isle followed by Kathy, the Wilsons and the Swansons.

The reception was a two hour event of individual congratulations and comradery. It was a gathering of friends and business associates.

Everyone knew each other and it made for pleasant conversations. At 1PM, dinner was announced. A buffet line was started. There were choices of rolls, pickles, hot carrots, hot peas, boiled potatoes, beef stew or meat loaf. Dessert was a choice of wedding cake or bread pudding. Coffee, tea or lemonade also included.

The newlywed's dinner was interrupted with the traditional ringing of silverware on glass. They complied with the tradition but Wayne interjected with, "if it were a small wedding as you wished, we wouldn't have to deal with this kissing game." Mandy's answer was to give Wayne an unsolicited kiss for all to see. She added, this is the best way to stop the ringing. The crowd will now think that we want to continue kissing, so they will try to deny us by not ringing the glasses, heh."

The afternoon was spent dancing to the local town band. Wayne and Mandy started the first dance with a traditional slow wedding dance. People joined to fill the dance floor. The band played for two hours and a grand party was had by all. At 4PM the band played the closing song, the Anniversary Waltz. For the next hour, Wayne and Mandy said their farewell goodbyes to all the guests, and thanked them for their gifts and attendance. Sam and Cora were moving in with the Wilsons, while Wayne and Mandy moved into the hotel bridal suite. Kathy would wait at the Wilsons for Mandy since school started in five days.

Arriving at the bridal suite, Wayne locked the door. They started kissing and fondling and knew that they could finally bring the urges and desires to a culmination. Wayne said, "I want to bring you slowly to a peak of desire." He started to undress Mandy, off came the dress followed by her undergarments. Mandy proceeded to undress Wayne as well and they were both naked at the same time. Mandy saw Wayne in full stimulation for the first time. They laid down and continued unrestricted fondling till neither could hold back. They touched each other and both had a frenetic and explosive release of total ecstasy.

After their recovery from reaching nirvana, Wayne said, "In our bedroom our nakedness will be our clothing decorum. We can enjoy our naked mutual voyeurism. Also our love making will be to pleasure each other, because it will not just be animal rutting."

Mandy added, "with our aggressive fondling, I may no longer be intact." "That does not matter, it has been the beginning of our marriage consummation, which we will finalize at Christmas." "If I've not been misled, I've been told that men cannot repeat their intimacy until a few days." "I don't think so, let me prove them wrong", as Wayne made advances that convinced Mandy otherwise.

For the next two days, they would go to Simms for their meals. Thereafter, they spent their time in the bridal suite. They enjoyed bathing together in the double bathtub with hot water. Their lovemaking was of a continuous nature. They finally satisfied their desires, and decided to go back to the Wilson's home.

They finished packing and prepared for their train trip, with Kathy, back to Denver. It was time to start their new life as a married couple, a senior student, and as a paladin bounty hunter. Neither fully realized the great events waiting for them.

***

CHAPTER 10

DENVER

The day after the wedding, Kathy changed her mind and decided not to wait for Mandy to return to Denver. She needed to move her belongings from the school dormitory, before the beginning of school. Plus she wanted to get familiar with the house at 17 Spring Street before Mandy and Wayne returned from their honeymoon.

After their three day honeymoon, Wayne and Mandy finished packing. Somehow they filled that extra large crate with stuff. The good thing was that they carried a light travel bag of personal items for the train ride to Denver, including Wayne's Colt and both their Webleys. On the day of departure, the foreman and one cowboy brought the traveling crate to the RR depot. Mandy and Wayne said their emotional goodbyes, and George drove them to the RR in his buggy. Trailing the buggy were Wayne's two gelding horses, Brownie and the reliable second horse, Blackie, with a pack saddle. Either horse would follow the other without a trailing rope.

At the train depot, they arranged for passage to Denver. Wayne paid for two adults, two horses, and one crate. The cost from Silver Circle to Pueblo was $9(7 cents a mile/person plus two horses and one crate). The train arrived at 1PM on schedule, it was 2PM before the incoming freight and horses were unloaded. It took another hour for the train to reload the horses and freight, to unhook three open freight cars, and exchange them for three loaded cars with silver ore. They finally got underway by 3PM. The trip was usually two hours, but with the silver ore, the ground speed was reduced to +-15 mph for a 40 mile trip.

Once they arrived in Pueblo, they had a choice of two trains to Denver. The first choice was the 8AM standard passenger train that stops at ten or more stations to take on passengers. That train would take all day to travel the 120 miles to Denver. It also required an overnight stay in the RR Hotel. The second choice was the Overnight Express. This was a direct trip to Denver with two stops to take on water and coal. Departure was midnight and arrival was early morning.

They decided to take the Overnight Express. At 5PM they sent a telegraph to Kathy informing her of their morning arrival. They again paid for the same tickets, at a cost of $19(7 cents a mile per person plus 2 horses and a large crate to cover 130 miles). Departing on time, this was a good travel time since some passengers slept all the way to Denver.

Once settled in their seats, Mandy asked, "how fast does a train go. Wayne answered, "It depends on many variables: temperature, weather conditions, day or night, or flat/hilly land. Plus the number of passenger, freight, cattle, and ore cars. Taking all these plus others, a train will travel between 15 to 40 mph. To compare, a good horse can usually travel, on average, 40 miles in a very long day, dawn to dusk." "Ok, now explain how two trains can meet head on when there is only one rail track?" "One train is switched off the main track, onto a side track, for holding until the other train passes. The holding train is then switched back to the main rail and resumes traveling."

Many of the passengers were asleep but Wayne and Mandy were still talking. Mandy changed the subject to wedding gifts. Despite the fact that times were hard with the drought, everyone managed to give something. Mandy said, "I received conservative schoolmarm dresses, riding skirts and blouses, riding rain gear, and educational tools for the final school year. My most frequent gifts were student aids for the coming year in Silver Circle. Ed gave me a whopping 40 books of McGuffey's Primer—grades 1-6. A progressive book to teach kids how to read." Wayne finally asked, "what did Doc Sutton Jr. give you anyways?" "That was a new Hoosier Belt." "What is that for?" "Female item, never you mind."

Wayne then went over some of his gifts. "Sheriff Jim gave me several Bounty Hunter novels. Bruce Hawkins gave me handmade handcuffs. President Miller gave me topo maps of northern Colorado and southern Wyoming. Oscar and Ray gave me a box of 45-60 for the Win 76, and a box of 45–90 for the Sharps. One rancher going through hard times gave me a bag of pigging strings. Butcher Gemler gave me a bag of beef jerky. Gunsmith Harrigan gave me a bottle of sperm whale gun oil, and a dismantling tool so I can add +-10% more powder to my 45-60 loads. The extra powder would convert it to a 45–70 hot load for extra distances. Ed gave me a new hand held 'telescope' that extends from eight inches to two feet. It has a zoom lens that increases the magnification of distant objects– great for spying on a camp or picking up on riders at 500 yards or more."

Having exhausted the gift subject, Wayne said, "since we're heading to Denver, tell me what you know about the city." Mandy said, "well since I've lived there all my life, let's see what I remember of the local history. Denver is still in the Victorian era. The economists say that the modernization period is still a decade away. Currently, it's called the mile high city because the elevation is 5280 ft. above sea level. From now on, let me cover the history by dates."

"In 1850's, it was a frontier town serving local mines, gambling saloons and ranches. In 1861, it was incorporated as Denver City and became the county seat. In 1863, Western Union established their regional terminus. In 1870, the population was 5,000 and the Denver Pacific RR was built as a 100 mile spur to Cheyenne WY., to connect with the Transcontinental RR. In 1872, we had the first horse drawn rail carriage through the city. In 1876 Colorado became a state. It is also the Centennial year and the year your Winchester 76 was designed."

"Finally we arrive to the 1880's. The population is now 35,000 and the rail carriage was expanded throughout the city. This is the decade of corruption. Crime bosses are in cahoots with lawmen and politicians. Major improvements include gas street lamps. Gas is now at its peak. The system, compared to coal oil lamps, is clean and rids the air of smoke and soot. It is now being installed in large buildings such as Daniels and Fischer Department Store and public places. Some high end districts, to include homes and businesses, have gas lamps. And this, in 1881, is where we are."

"What is the next improvement to come to Denver?" "It appears that electricity is just around the corner. There is talk of installing electric arc street lights, but the big controversial one is the development of electric rail street cars with an overhead power source. Eventually, every business and home will have electric lights as a starter."

Shortly thereafter they arrived at the first water/coal stop at Colorado Springs. On the next leg of the trip they started reading. Mandy was reading a primer for the advanced science course, and Wayne started reading a bounty hunter dime novel. They read for about one hour, until the clanking of the wheels against the rail joints pushed them into a deep sleep. They slept through the second water/coal stop at Castle Rock, and continued sleeping until the conductor announced they were on the outskirts of Denver.

It was 8AM when they stepped onto the platform and met Kathy who was waiting for them. They arranged for the large crate to be delivered at 17 Spring St., and commandeered a buggy taxi with Brownie and Blackie on a trailing rope. After the driver added the entry in his ledger, they disembarked and Wayne realized that he had made a big mistake–17 Spring St. did not have a barn for his two horses. Wayne walked his horses some three blocks to the nearest livery. He would rectify this deficiency today.

By 10AM all three were sitting in the living room. Wayne said, "you gals have three more days before school starts. Today is shot and we need to rest from the wedding and the train trip. I need to visit a construction company to get a barn built, and Mandy needs to unpack her crate of stuff. Before I leave, I will unpack all my guns and my things." Mandy asks, "What would you like to do tomorrow, Wayne?" "I would like to get on a rail carriage, take a guided tour of the city and have lunch in a big famous hotel restaurant." Kathy chimes in, "I've lived in this city all my life and I've never done that." "Can I come too?" "Of course, and I know that this will be a wonderful day for all of us, heh!"

Mandy then adds, "the next day we have school registration and an introduction to our senior year course schedule." "Ok, that day, I will have a meeting with Captain William Ennis of the US Marshall Service.

The third day will be preparation day for everyone."

After lunch of a cold roast beef sandwich and coffee, Wayne walked one block to the nearest telegraph office and ordered a buggy taxi. The driver quickly brought Wayne to the Preston Construction Company. The driver entered the trip, charged to Currier, into his ledger. Wayne entered the office and was greeted by an elderly white haired man. Wayne said, "are you Mr. Preston?" "Yes, how may I help you?"

"I would like to have a one story barn built at 17 Spring Street. To include four horse stalls, a tack room, a work bench, an area to house a buggy, hay bales and a corral to exercise the horses. Would also want a water supply by underground piping from the house." "Is the construction site ready with a flat area?" "Yes." "Did you want a wood floor?" "Yes." Mr. Preston designs a rough blueprint, and Wayne says, "that is perfect."

Mr. Preston says, "that will be $400, and we can start in one week." "Seems a bit high, but I'll take it." "The rate may appear high because this is city rates." "How much to start tomorrow?" Wayne slips a double eagle on the counter. The owner looks at the $20 coin and motions to add another. Wayne adds a second, then a third, and a fourth. Mr. Preston pockets the $80 and says, "I'll have an eight man team on the job tomorrow. In two days, it will be completed. Notify this feed store by telegraph, and order some bales of hay and oats for delivery by the second day, late afternoon." Wayne hands the owner a bank draft to pay in full. They shake hands and Wayne leaves with a smile on his face.

On his way home in a buggy taxi, Wayne schedules a 10AM pickup to the city terminal for the horse drawn rail carriage. That afternoon, everyone was relaxing and reading. The girls were reading their school curriculum for the year, as

Wayne was reading his bounty hunter novel. After a fine dinner of a pork roast and fresh vegetables, they visited and planned their day in the city. Kathy retired early to her upstairs bedroom, to give the newlyweds some privacy. The newlyweds never hesitated as they walked to their first floor bedroom to enjoy some marital intimacy.

The next morning at 6AM, several wagons arrived with lumber and accessories needed to build the barn. They unloaded the wagons and left the site, as the eight man team arrived with all their tools by 7AM. Wayne spent some time with the foreman going over the construction site and the corral. He also showed them where the house water intake was, to tap the pipes for the barn. Wayne reviewed the official blueprints and approved them.

By 10AM, the buggy taxi arrived and the three tourists left for a tour. On departure, Wayne noted that the pipes were already buried, the floor was completed, and one wall was being put together on the floor before lifting into place. He also noted how the team was working well together. The two features that impressed him was the fact that the foreman was working along with his men, and one burly man, with massive arms, was efficiently doing most of the lumber sawing.

They arrived at the carriage terminal and Wayne scheduled a six hour guided tour, a stop for shopping, and one for lunch at a famous hotel. The rail route was a straight line through the business section and it included a few private mansions. The guide was a comedic well informed individual with many anecdotal stories.

As they approached the Tabor Grand Opera House, the passengers were welcomed to enter the massive structure under construction. Everyone was limited to a roped off section in the lobby. The view of the theater was amazing. The next stop was Union Station, also under construction. They were again limited to a restricted area, but they were able to view the grand station in the making.

They then arrived in the business district. The streets were lined with massive multistory brick and wooden buildings. Every bit of real estate was utilized. The guide pointed out that there were no outside privies. Every building had public water closets. The buildings that were impressive included: the courthouse, department stores, stock exchanges, hotels, restaurants and saloons.

By lunchtime, they were dropped off at a series of hotels with restaurants on the first floor.

As they walked about, Wayne said, "let's go in this one with a ragtime piano player." As they entered, Mandy said, "look at the beautiful Victorian design." The piano player was pounding the ivories with a lively rendition, without following a music sheet. They were seated and they looked at the menu. Mandy said, "look at the prices, did you bring enough money to cover the bill?' "We are good, and I am having their specialty, prime rib with the fixings." The ladies did the same, and both enjoyed a glass of red wine–Wayne had a beer.

While they were waiting for their meal, Wayne said, "look about and you will see three clientele. One is the business people or professionals with their suits, and some with their wives dressed in Victorian gowns. Another group are the 'dandy' that work in the city, and last, the group of well dressed Cowboys wearing their Colts, some with their conservatively dressed escorts." Kathy added, "I especially noticed the Cowboys, I guess this is still a western city, where wearing guns is still the norm. I suspect that all the men in suits are wearing a Webley in a shoulder harness, as well."

Their meal arrived and they all enjoyed the great taste of the beef. For dessert they had apple pie a la mode, with coffee and tea. When the guide announced boarding in fifteen minutes, Wayne looked at the bill and placed $25 on the table, along with a $5 tip. Mandy just smiled and Kathy said, "thank you."

The tour continued and the next stop was the shopping district. The ladies went to the garment stores, they needed more clothes for all occasions. Wayne went to a gun shop. As Wayne entered, he was amazed at the selection of modern weapons. Since he had a current arsenal and did not see anything new, he moved to the accessory section.

The first thing he saw was black powder cleaning solutions in a durable metal flask. This was ideal for on the trail, when one was in a dry camp, to clean guns without using up precious water in canteens. He picked up several flasks. The next thing he picked up was a quality leather clip-on bullet pouch with 20 shell holders that could hold shotgun shells, 45-70, 45-90, and even loose 44-40 ammo. The advantage was the clip that fits on the front of the gunbelt, and the fact that the centerfire/shotgun ammo was kept separate from the loose 44-40 ammo. This would be good for bringing ammo to an outlaw camp with the potential for a gunfight. The ammo would always be on the gunbelt, in case one had to change shooting locations.

The next item was the newly developed local padlocks. They were one third the size and one third the weight, and all with the same key. He picked up six of them. To his surprise, the new chains were smaller, lighter but the same strength. He took three 6-footers. The new padlocks would attach the chains to the neck collars. Another item was the water proof covers for panniers and scabbards. The last item was a new small farrier tool that would pull out old anchoring nails, install new ones and could even cut and repair barb wire. This tool would replace two heavy tools—a hammer and fence mending pliers. Before heading to the cashier, he picked up two boxes of ammo for each gun he owned. This ammo would stay in Mandy's house as a backup supply. At the cashier, all items were placed in a strong burlap bag. Wayne paid the $16 charge, and headed back to the carriage.

He waited for the girls. They arrived just in time to board the carriage. With a smile ear to ear, they each had a large bag full of clothes.

Kathy said, "I really feel bad that you are paying for this, and every time I mention it, Mandy hits me!" "Good."

Fortunately there were extra empty seats to hold all the customer's shopping bags. The remainder of the tour didn't have any more stops. We went through the upper class mansions. The well known owners were foreign to us. Wayne said, "I wonder if we'll ever be that well off?" Mandy answered, "we are now better off, we have each other, heh!"

The next day the girls went to school for registration, and the introductory day to cover the curriculum of the year. Mandy brought several bank drafts to pay for the year's two tuitions, required textbooks, and cafeteria lunch passes. She also had $100 in cash to pay for miscellaneous unplanned purchases. Their buggy taxi arrived promptly at 8AM to start their seasonal contract.

Wayne had the day to himself, and decided to take a buggy ride to the US Marshall's Office. After he arrived, he introduced himself to the receiving clerk as Wayne Swanson from Silver Circle. The clerk stood up, shook his hand, and said, "I am proud to finally meet you, sir. Captain William Ennis has been waiting for you for a week since he received a letter from Sheriff Jim Smithfield. Let me check with the Captain."

The Captain came out of his office, shook Wayne's hand and welcomed him into the office. "Mr. Swanson, what can I do for you?" Well first, please call me Wayne, Mr. Swanson is my dad." "Very well, then please call me Captain to maintain some office decorum." "Thank you." "Some time ago, Jim Smithfield was in town on business and came to see me. He told me of this deputy sheriff that had unbelievable shooting, tracking and common sense skills. I thought he was recommending you for a position on the US Marshall Service. He surprised me when he said that you would likely spend some time as a bounty hunter. After a long visit, we left it at that. Then a week ago I got a letter from Jim explaining your proposed nine month crusade to rid our state of violent criminals. The financial gain would be to build your benefactor fund, which he explained. To make a long story short, I'm so pleased that you are here. So, what can I do for you?"

"The reason I'm here is to find out if you have an individual or gang that is causing depredations, and are escaping your deputies for whatever reason?" "Yes, The Jackson gang of six bank robbers and murderers are raising havoc with communities between Denver and Cheyenne, WY. They have already hit banks close to Denver in Loveland, Johnstown, and Windsor. They have since moved north to the banks in Norfolk and Carr. We think the next towns to be hit are Livermore and Virginia Dale, which are on a major route, and Buckeye which requires a cross country escape. If they hold their pattern, hitting the closest town first, that means to me that Virginia Dale is next."

"If they hit these last three, do you think they will restart the pattern or move on somewhere else?" "I think they would hit three banks west of Cheyenne in Tie Hiding, Butte, and Buford. Then they would move on to terrorize another unsuspecting community."

"Why is this gang on the top of your list, they seem to be bank robbers?" "No, they are murderers. They kill for fun. During each bank robbery they always shoot some clerk or customer. Then on their way out of town they shoot at bystanders, to include women and lawmen. Each robbery results in the loss of a half dozen decent and innocent people. To complicate matters, they always hit the bank at closing when the vault is open. They always steal $1500 to $3000, and they escape when there is only an hour before dark, preventing tracking. They also travel all night on the well traveled roads heading north. In the morning they move to cross country."

"So why is it that your deputies have not been able to catch these scoundrels?" "By the time we receive a telegram of the event, and the fact that local law lost their tracks, we are several days late to pick up their tracks. In addition, they always head across the state line to Wyoming, which by law is out of our jurisdiction. Wyoming has a small Marshall Service for a large unpopulated territory, and they have not been able to even find their camp. In addition, Wyoming is in turmoil with fighting between cattle ranchers and sheep ranchers, as well as coal miners fighting with Chinese workers. Wyoming Marshalls will not catch this gang and we haven't been successful."

"Ok, I will take the job." "Now remember, we never had this meeting, and if you get into legal trouble, we never heard of you." "Understood, what I needed was this information. After this ordeal, I hope I can return here to find out about another bounty hunting job." "Looking forward to our next imaginary meeting. Good luck and be careful, here are the six wanted posters–dead or alive. Don't hesitate to pick some of these murderers off to dwindle their numbers. Also, the five banks and towns that have been hit have placed rewards, dead or alive, of $1800 for each town. That means a total reward of $9,000." "The danger always matches the reward, heh?"

After the meeting, Wayne decided to make a detour to a well known agricultural equipment dealer. He had the floor manager guide him through the extensive assortment of new machines. He saw plows, harrows, seeders, manure spreaders, hay cutters, rakes, hay loaders, reapers, threshers, fanning mills, and the new one horse powered bailer. The guide provided extensive explanations how each machine worked. He got prices for each implement, and left with brochures. He pointed out that his interests were for next year, and that he would be back to get firm prices for a package of several implements by April 1 1882.

Wayne finally got home by 3PM. Shortly thereafter, the girls arrived, obviously happy with their day per the smiles they displayed. Mandy said, "This was a well organized day. After the registration and settling financial issues, they presented a fantastic preview of the courses that would be taught. We will be learning applied geometry to include surveying and map reading. The science course includes a new modern lab and will cover subjects such as physics, chemistry and metallurgy. A new course is business accounting which will include private ledger entries to balance the books, as well as personal banking, and an introduction to becoming a bank teller. One minor course includes legal documents such as deeds, property tax, and bank drafts/vouchers. The last two minor courses include writing composition, and personal hygiene for women." "What is this personal hygiene all about?" "Again, don't ask!"

"Ok, well it sounds like you're preparing the kids for ranching or town work?" "Actually, we are preparing 10th grade graduates for two futures. The first is a business profession, instead of manual labor. This includes managing a ranch, working in a bank, legal assistants, and or starting your own business." The second is to prepare them for an academic profession or a technical trade in a post highschool college."

"So how was your meeting with Captain Ennis?" Wayne summarized the meeting and told Mandy he would be going after the Jackson gang of six miscreants. He did not cover the violent aspects he may potentially encounter. He did mention he would be leaving in two days by train to Fort Collins and then travel north by horse some thirty miles to Virginia Dale and possibly beyond.

By 4PM, they went to see how the barn construction was coming along. The foreman was loading left over lumber and tools in the wagons. They were done. They inspected the exterior and interior features. The water was flowing by a turn of a faucet. There was a location behind the barn for a manure pile and a nice corral was finished. Wayne signed off the final inspection, and gave the foreman a tip of $90–$20 for the foreman, and $10 for each of the seven men. Wayne heard cheers and many thank you, as the wagon departed. He then noticed that hay and oats had already been delivered. After dinner, he and Mandy would go to the livery and bring back his two horses.

The last day off was prep day for everyone. As the girls were choosing their clothes and books, Wayne went to the train depot. He bought a ticket for Fort Collins and two tags for his horses. The train left at 8AM and Wayne planned to be there by 7AM to board the horses in the stock car. When he returned, he told Mandy, "today we load the saddlebags and panniers to be ready for an early morning departure." One pannier was loaded with a neck collar, the new padlock and chain, cooking grate, frypan, coffee pot, tin eating utensils and cups. The other pannier had two neck collars/chains/padlocks, and mostly food: coffee, bacon, canned beans and beef, onions, oatmeal, sugar, salt, crackers, and beef jerky. Both panniers were topped with bags of horse oats, a spade and a hatchet–distributed to balance the pannier weights.

The extra large saddlebags were next. One side held the field glasses, telescope, compass, reel of cord and ammo boxes. The other side had a spare pistol plus clothing. This included: spare pants, shirts, socks, underwear, one blanket, one rain duster, a flask of medicinal alcohol, and a sewing kit.

Four guns were placed in scabbards, including a specially made scabbard for the sawed off shotgun. These included, a Win. 1873, Win. 1876, a Sharps with a Malcolm scope, and his specialized shotgun. Other items included his bedroll and a tarp, both to be tied to the back of the saddle.

That night they enjoyed and pleasured themselves several times.

Mandy finally said, "I won't worry, I promise. You are on a job and I will see you when you return. I've finally learned that worry will not improve our situation." "In regards to our situation, realize that the moments in time spent with you, and our restricted love making, are temporary situations. Our lives are about to change for the best."

Kissing started again. Wayne tried to be gentle but Mandy would have none of it. After being totally spent, Mandy said, "well there is no doubt now. I'm certain that I'm no longer intact!" "Mandy, to me you will always be intact. That is part of love."

In the morning, everyone was up by 5AM. Kathy made a full breakfast of eggs, bacon, biscuits and coffee. Mandy and Wayne saddled the horses, loaded the panniers, saddlebags and guns/scabbards. They added the new accessory items Wayne had purchase, but had forgotten to pack. By 6AM Wayne said his goodbyes, and reminded Mandy that he would be back before his next job. He also said that he would keep her up to date with regular short telegrams, when next to a telegraph office. He then rode off for the half hour ride to the RR station.

Both knew that this was the beginning of a temporary period that would be the foundation for their future.

***

CHAPTER 11

The Chase

Wayne's trip to Fort Collins was uneventful. Arriving at 1PM, Wayne had a quick lunch at a local diner and then headed for Virginia Dale. It was a good road and, with fresh horses, he suspected he would cover the thirty miles before the bank closed.

Meanwhile, the six member Jackson gang arrived in town. Five of them entered the bank and proceeded to rob them. They emptied all the drawers of the paper currency, while the leader, Floyd Jackson, escorted the head clerk to the vault. When he refused to unlock the vault, one of the men killed a clerk with a knife. After the vault was emptied, the gang leader shot the head clerk. The gang then departed and raced through town, shooting at town's people, and wounding the elderly sheriff.

Wayne arrived and noticed a paucity of people on the boardwalks. When he arrived at the bank, he found a gathering of upset individuals.

Wayne stopped next to a deputy and asked him what was going on. The deputy said, "the bank has been robbed by the Jackson gang, two clerks were murdered. Several bystanders and the sheriff have been wounded." The bank's president added, "we have been cleaned out of $3000 and will have to close our doors." Looking at the deputy, Wayne says, "don't organize a posse this close to nightfall because you won't be able to track them. Plus, you'll likely ride into an ambush and be massacred. I'll give chase and if I'm lucky, I'll bring back some of your money before dark. This is what I do." After introducing himself, the deputy didn't even hesitate when he found out he was the bounty hunter, Wayne Swanson, that an anonymous telegram had informed their office of his imminent arrival.

Wayne left his pack horse tied to the hitching rail, and took off on Brownie with his shotgun and Winchester 76. Half an hour on the trail, Wayne had a premonition. He saw a left bend in the road with large pine trees on his left, and large boulders on the right of the bend. This was a perfect site for an ambush as he would make the turn in the road. He stepped down, tethered Brownie to a tree, and started walking with his shotgun in his backpack holster and his rifle in hand.

As he was slowly walking, he was watching the boulders through the pine trees. Suddenly, he spotted a row of men waiting with their rifles in hand. Wayne continued walking while hiding behind the trees. Eventually, he positioned himself to the outlaws right at a distance of only fifteen yards. He placed his rifle down, pulled out his sawed off shotgun, pulled the two mule ear external hammers and yelled. "I have you covered with a shotgun, put your hands up, now!"

The gang members never hesitated, they all turned to the right, and started shooting at Wayne. He was well protected behind a massive pine tree. When he heard someone yell, "stop shooting, you're wasting ammo shooting at a tree." Wayne stepped out and fired both barrels at the outlaws. He saw two men drop to the ground. Meanwhile, the leader ordered his men to get to their horses and get out of there.

Wayne reloaded and ran directly to the road. He saw the four men reenter the road. They were about thirty five yards and beyond the kill range for a shotgun. Wayne decided to cause some of them serious pain, as he aimed high and let go both barrels. The impact of a #3 buckshot caused two of the rear outlaws to bend to their horses neck. Wayne knew that they would be hurting and likely head to Tie Harding, some fifteen miles northwest, to find a doctor.

Wayne scavenged the two dead bodies. They both had their share of the loot, $500 each. That $1000 went into his saddlebags. The remainder of the pocket cash, $82, went into his own pocket. The outlaw's saddlebags had some 44-40 ammo which he confiscated. The two dead men were then straddled on their horses' saddles. Their feet and wrists were tied to stirrups with pigging strings.

The caravan moved back to town. Wayne was leading the two outlaw horses on a trailing rope. As they arrived in town, they headed to the bank where several town's people were still circling the bandaged sheriff and the bank president. Wayne stepped off Brownie, and handed $1000 to a grateful president. Then he introduced himself to the sheriff. "Would you identify these two so I can claim the reward?" After the outlaw's faces matched the wanted posters, the sheriff said, "I'll wire the organizations that put up the reward, and get you a Western Union voucher for each one." "Ok, I'll make a deal with you, sell the two horses and saddles, and keep the money. In return, send a bank transfer for the vouchers to my bank account in Silver Circle. Pay for their burial and hold the guns for me till I return with the other gang members."

The sheriff objected that he was getting too much money. Wayne added, "I'm paying you for your honesty, and there is no real price for an honest service." "How do you know that I'm honest?" "Because a certain US Marshall captain told me so."

As he picked up his pack horse, he said to the bank president, "I'll bring back your money, so don't close the bank." "If you bring back the $2000, I'll give you a $500 reward." "Deal, but give the money to the dead clerk's families, heh."

Meanwhile, the Jackson gang escaped the crazy bounty hunter at a full gallop. When their horses were spent, they stopped to rest them. The two carrying buckshot pellets were moaning. Floyd looked at their backs and said, "great, we need to get to Tie Harding. The local doc will need to cut those pellets out or you'll die from infection. So let's get there and then head east to our camp near Buford. We can travel all night since we'll be on the main road except for three miles."

As Wayne got on the trail, he only had an hour of daylight before he stopped to set up camp. He figured that the gang was already in Tie Harding getting pellets plucked out–as he smiled to himself. It had been a long day, and Wayne felt safe to set up a full camp and cook a hot meal. With the horses, unsaddled, watered and both feeding on grass, Wayne finished dinner and had a restful undisturbed sleep.

The next morning, feeling alert, he started thinking about a way to find this gang, without spending days tracking and risking being drygulched. It finally came to him. Wayne would head cross country from now on and aim for Buford. He figured that this gang's camp would be close to Buford, giving them access to a store for whiskey and supplies. Having a camp close to Buford would also allow this gang to slip into Cheyenne, some twenty miles away by road. There they could disappear, by mixing with other miscreants, for days. Cheyenne would be where they got their entertainment spending their loot on whiskey, whores and cards.

Since it would be too difficult to find them in the many Cheyenne saloons, Wayne knew he would have to capture them in their camp near Buford. To accomplish this, he would have to be in Buford awaiting their arrival at the local mercantile.

He arrived in Buford by 11AM. As he was riding through, he noted the minimally essential businesses that outlaws needed: a mercantile for clothing, food and ammo, a livery with a farrier, feed store, and one or more saloons. For Wayne's needs, it had a small hotel and a diner. The lack of a sheriff and a telegraph office was ideal for this gang of outlaws.

The hotel was nothing fancy. The locking rooms included a bed, chair and a small table. There was a privy outside. The rooms were $1 a day and 50 cents for a hot bath. The diner was adjacent to the hotel and both their porches faced the mercantile. The horses were left at the livery, hay and oats included, and the rifles and panniers were locked up in the man's private quarters in the livery. The total cost was $2 a day.

Wayne moved in the hotel with his shotgun, pistol and a clean set of clothes. After a great dinner, a bath and a full night sleep, Wayne started day one of his vigil. After breakfast at the diner, his first order of business was at the mercantile. The owner's name was Willy Endicot. "Sir, I'm looking for some killer bank robbers that may occasionally visit your store." Willy looked at the four posters and said, "yes, these two come by once a week to buy smokes, whiskey and food supplies. They are not pleasant but don't give me trouble and they pay cash. They are overdue this week." "Great, the day they come, would you step outside after they leave and simply wave at me. I will be on the porch across the street." "Be glad to, sir."

For two days, Wayne sat on the porches and watched every customer entering the mercantile. None matched the posters. Wayne read two bounty hunter novels. The third morning, Wayne was having an extra cup of coffee on the diner's porch. Suddenly, two scruffy types showed up at Willy's store. One horse was badly limping. After stepping down, it's rider, with a bushy black mustache, looked at his horse's hoof and said something to his partner.

After they entered the store, Wayne ran to the horses and noted that the limping horse had thrown a shoe. He had an idea, ran to the livery, and made a quick arrangement. Then he ran back to the diner's porch to finish his coffee. As the men came out, they loaded their supplies in the several saddlebags. They then walked their horses to the livery. Willy came out on his porch and waved with a big proud smile.

Wayne waited till they came out of the livery, and were out of town before he headed to the livery. "Well sir, how much do I owe you for this service, and can I see the detail of the marked shoe you just installed?" After being shown the masterpiece defect, he paid the extra $4 and settled his livery bill. "In fifteen minutes, your horses, guns and panniers will be ready." "I'll be back in one hour with fresh meat and supplies. Thanks." "Good luck and get the bastards."

Because he didn't want to be spotted, he waited an hour before getting on the trail. He easily followed the marked horseshoe and trailed the gang members for hours before he smelled camp fire smoke. He tethered his horses to tree branches and took his shotgun, Win. 76 and his new telescope. He walked for about a half mile before he spotted their camp. This was a permanent isolated camp with several tents, a corral and lines for laundry. It was next to a stream and a nice grassy area, where the horses were cropping grass, fifty yards away.

Wayne decided to sneak up closer to see individuals and to hear what they were saying. He got to within 150 yards when he put his rifle down, looked with the telescope and listened.

"Are you sure you weren't followed?" "Yes, we kept watching our back trail and never even saw a dust cloud." "Ok, so we'll stay in camp tonight but tomorrow we're going to Cheyenne for a week. That will flummox anyone on our trail."

Hearing their plans, Wayne knew he had to act today. He knew his Win. 76 would be deadly at 150 yards, whereas their 1873 would be highly inaccurate beyond 100 yards. After carefully spying on the camp layout, setting his ladder sight to 150 yards, resting it against a tree, he aimed at someone standing by the fire. With total determination he fired. That outlaw was hit in the upper chest and was literally lifted off his feet and blown backwards. The camp exploded with hustling about, with men trying to find cover and their rifles. They started shooting ineffectively at

Wayne's smoke cloud. Wayne used his telescope and was able to find the location of each outlaw trying to hide behind some tree or tent. Wayne decided that he had to again impress them, that it was time to give it up. He spotted one outlaw sneaking around the back of his tent. Wayne took aim and fired. The tent collapsed, wrapped itself around the outlaw, and the entire mass went rolling backwards.

Wayne reloaded and yelled, "Give it up or I continue shooting till you are all down. You have three choices: you can all be dead men today, or hang within a week. There's a third choice, you can chance overpowering me during our day's ride to Virginia Dale. This is a potential win-lose situation. I'll give you a minute to think about it, then I'll make up your mind once I start shooting again."

Floyd was trying to buy time to figure how to get to their horses, some fifty yards in the tall grass. He asked, "how did you know to find our camp?" "Your buddy with the black mustache had to have his horse get a replacement shoe while in Virginia Dale. I had arranged for the livery man to use a marked shoe." Wayne heard, "you idiot!" He then decided to help them make up their minds. He saw an oats bucket near the ground hitched grazing horses. He fired at the bucket, it went skyward and then rolled about. The four horses ignored their ground hitches and scattered in every direction. Wayne was almost laughing at the results of hitting that bucket. With the horses gone, option three was their only choice.

"Ok, we give up as they dropped their rifles, pistols and put their hands up." Wayne starts walking up to them. When he was within five feet and holding his shotgun, he says, "turn around and put your hands behind your back. They complied and Wayne steps up. With an uncocked shotgun, he pops both of them in the back of the head with the shotgun's butt.

Wayne then follows his routine. He drags both of them to the fire, places a neck collar and locks the chain to a tree. He then locks their wrists behind their backs with handcuffs and ties their feet together with another set of special ankle cuffs.

Wayne went to gather all the horses. It took a half hour to get his two tethered horses, but the outlaw's horses had returned to camp by themselves. He unsaddled the horses, watered them and returned them to their ground hitches for grazing. Brownie and Blackie were left to graze freely since they would not leave camp.

With coffee in hand, he set up a pot of canned stewed beef, fresh potatoes, and onions to cook, Wayne waited for the two scoundrels to wake up. By the time the stew was ready, the outlaws were still out. Wayne threw some cold stream water in their faces and the result was instantaneous. Floyd and his mustached buddy were stunned to find themselves hog tied and secured to a tree like an animal.

Wayne spoke, "You boys better lick the water off your lips since that's the last water you'll get till you're in jail. Guess that neck collar dampens your potential escape plans, and makes you wish you had shot it out against me? Now you're going to hang. So, I'm going to have my dinner and sleep the night without interruption from you two animals, or else suffer the consequences. Isn't justice great, heh?"

Wayne was enjoying his beef stew when he heard the prisoners whispering to each other. "Charlie, tell him we have to go to the bushes, so we can head butt him and kick him in the head till he's unconscious." "Ok, hey Mr. I need to go to the bushes. Wayne gets up, puts his stew down, and steps over to Mr. Mustache. He draws his pistol and plants the hogleg directly on his front teeth. He started to spit out blood and all his front teeth. Wayne asks Floyd, "do you want some of the same?" Floyd shakes his head in the negative. "Now, shut up or the next treatment will be much worse."

The next morning, Wayne was up at dawn. He had bacon and eggs cooking along with coffee. After his breakfast and cleaning up, he had a talk with his prisoners. "Now this is how the day will go. I will release your ankle cuffs, help you to step up on your horse, secure your right ankle to the stirrup by an ankle cuff, secure the chain to the left stirrup by a lock and keep your handcuffs on behind your back. If you fall off your horse, you are going to have some serious hurting because I'm not stopping to pick you monsters up. You'll be on your horse till we get to jail. I don't care about your comfort or your needs. Your life is scheduled to end soon, and I'm going to make it happen."

The last thing Wayne did was scavenge all four outlaws. He found all $2000 plus the loose bills that amounted to $159 and he pocketed that money. The saddle bags revealed the usual

44-40 ammo. Then he started burning the tents, clothing and other belongings that were trash. He cleaned the cooking utensils and left them for other travelers.

Camp was closed and the site left clean for others to use. The horses were saddled, the two dead outlaws were straddled on their saddles, and secured in place with feet and hands tied to stirrups. Before loading Floyd, he asked that he be allowed to relieve himself.

Wayne just picked up a switch from the ground and smacked him three times on his back. "I told you to shut up."

After they got moving, Blackie decided that following was not the place he was going to stay. He stepped up to be beside Brownie. Wayne got a whiff of the reason, both prisoners had relieved themselves in their britches, and the smell of dead bodies just pushed Blackie to a better smelling spot.

The traveling was kept at a steady pace. They stopped several times to rest the horses, water them and give them some oats. By 4PM they arrived in town. They were followed to the sheriff's office. The sheriff came out to greet Wayne. "Well here are the other members some dead and some alive." The sheriff walked to Floyd and said, "boy you stink. He confirmed that these were all Jackson gang members. He said, "it will take two days to get your reward vouchers. The trial will be held tomorrow and you may be asked to testify." "That's Ok. I will wait since you have a hotel and a nice diner.

The president arrived and was handed the $2000. He said, "the town's people and myself appreciate this gift. Are you sure you want me to give your reward to the victim's families?" "Without a doubt, sir."

Wayne settled his two horses at the livery, sold all four outlaw saddled horses to a happy livery man for $175. He also sold six pistols and six 1873 rifles at the local mercantile for $240. Each pistol was worth $15 and each repeating 1873 was worth $25. Willy still expected to make a decent profit, plus Wayne gave him all the spare ammo.

The next day the trial was held. The bank clerks all identified the prisoners as the thieves. The defense attorney could not budge the clerks. Wayne was asked to testify. He was asked to verify that the $2000 was in the thieves pockets. The defense attorney tried to attack Wayne. "Did you go after these innocent men for their old bounty?"

The prosecutor jumped up and said, "your honor, it's not the court's business why our savior went after these murderers and what he does with the rewards." The Judge answered, "sustained." The jury was out ten minutes, and the two were found guilty of murder and robbery. The judge sentenced both to hang tomorrow morning at 8AM.

The next day, he went to the telegraph office to collect his four vouchers. He walked in the bank, the president came to greet him and welcomed him to his office. "How may I help you Mr. Swanson?" "I have four Western Union vouchers for $7200 and another $400 in cash to add to the deposit. Please explain how a bank transfer works and how you can send money to my account in Silver Circle." "Well it's a somewhat complicated process through the telegraph service. We notify the parent company through secure codes, that we have a secure deposit, and wish to send the funds to another bank with the account number. Through several paper forms, you money will be in your account today within a few hours." "What proof do I have that the money will be sent?" "We give you a bank receipt signed by me and you pay a $10 fee. And by the way, here is your receipt for the $3600 deposited by our sheriff and sent to your account." "Very good, would you send these funds by bank transfer today?" "Certainly, for a $10 fee, heh."

Wayne again stopped at the telegraph office and sent a gram to Mandy saying that he would be home tomorrow night. He then spent the afternoon reading his bounty hunter dime novels, having great food at the diner, and sleeping another night on a real bed. In the morning, after a full breakfast, this first job had come to an end and Wayne was riding back to Fort Collins.

***

CHAPTER 12

The Siege

Wayne rode cross country to Fort Collins and then took the train back to Denver. He arrived a 4PM but Mandy was still in school. In half an hour Brownie and Blackie were unsaddled and eating in their stalls. The pannier supplies were brought in the kitchen, and Wayne waited for the girls. At 5:15 the buggy taxi arrived. Mandy saw smoke from the kitchen stove and knew that Wayne was home. She jumped out of the buggy and flew into the front door. They jumped into each other's arms and passionately kissed. It was an emotional meeting for a separation of only ten days.

After a steak dinner, Mandy discussed how school was going. Mandy said, "this last year will be more important than my last two years. It will make my teaching applicable to Silver Circle living in the mid to late 1880's. The training in geometry is very interesting. It explains how the

RR was laid out and how ranching acreage is surveyed.

"How was your first job?' "I gave $500 to the victim's families and I brought back two alive, four dead. I put $9400 in the benefactor account. Tomorrow, I'll meet with Captain Ennis."

After a night of welcomed newlywed intimacy, Wayne had a full breakfast with the girls, before they left for school. Afterwards, Wayne headed to the marshal's office.

Captain Ennis greeted Wayne and stepped into his office for a private meeting that did not officially take place. "You eradicated an evil group of outlaws. It would be nice if there weren't any replacements to take their place, but that's wishful thinking, heh." "So, do you have another situation that needs my attention?" "Yes, there is a small unnamed town some thirty miles west of Colorado Springs. This is a rich town that caters to two silver mines and many ranchers. A RR spur has been built to handle cattle and silver ore."

"The issue is that this community is under siege. Ten gunslinger bullies have taken over the town. Their leader is a well known killer and trouble maker, Amos Strickland. They are charging for protection, and collect 50% of every businesses' profits–similar to Denver's organized crime today. This has been going on for two months. I sent two deputy marshals by train, but they were met by six of these bullies. They were beaten to within an inch of their lives, and thrown in a boxcar back to Colorado Springs. The 'powers to be' have since declared that the marshal service was not to assist a non organized town that doesn't contribute taxes or have national voting rights.

These bullies have beaten the business owners into submission, have killed two ranchers that resisted them, have chased the judge into exile, and both deputy sheriffs resigned after the sheriff was found hanging in his barn. Of course, his death was ruled a suicide by Strickland."

"Town's people are leaving during the night. The bank president is home, recovering from two broken arms. The telegraph office is only open three hours a day, with a gunslinger in attendance that approves all telegrams–plus he can interpret the telegraph codes. The last depredation is the cancellation of accounts on credit. Ranchers and homesteaders are told to pay up the back account or never return for supplies—it's a cash business or no goods. So it's a mess."

We suspect that each gunslinger has a price on his head, but we only have proof that Strickland has a $1500 reward, dead or alive. The other nine are unknown to us. And last, yesterday, one of those deputies rode the thirty miles to meet with me. They're willing to return to work if the gunslingers are eliminated. They're also willing to assist you if you'll take the lead, because your reputation precedes you. We have their home addresses, so you could look them up and present your plan of attack."

Wayne had questions. "Are these ten men on duty every day?" It appears that eight are. The leader stays in his office, a lawyer's confiscated office and home on Main street. Every day, two men each supervise the mercantile, bank, and hardware store. The two saloons each have one man from morning to 5PM and varying numbers for the evenings." "So in the morning, we'll have one gunslinger who could be anywhere." "Yes, but likely at the stock yard, collecting his money."

"This will be a one day reclamation. The first six in the mercantile, bank and hardware store will be arrested and secured alive. There is no guarantee about the two in the saloons and the one who could be anywhere. The death toll could be high when dealing with gunslingers." "That's acceptable if you prevent collateral damage to innocent bystanders and town's people."

"How do I identify these men? I need a name to apply for a reward." "Choose the right man, and you've been known to slowly bend a few fingers backwards. That always works to get names, and doesn't leave any residual marks."

"Ok, I'll take the job. This behavior of killing, domineering, and abusing innocent people must stop. Terminating this siege will show other outlaws that these animals weren't given any mercy. I'll be on the train Monday, set up my camp out of town, meet in secrecy with the deputies on Tuesday, and plan to reclaim the town on Wednesday morning."

Wayne went back to Spring Street, took care of his horses, packed his panniers, and cleaned his guns. He prepared a pork roast with potatoes and onions, set it to slow cook all afternoon, and planned to relax till the girls got home. He spent the afternoon reading another bounty hunter novel. He had to admit, that he was learning some life saving tips, from an author who probably never sat on a horse or fired a gun.

When the girls arrived, dinner was served by the chef. They enjoyed a pleasant evening and retired early to their private bedroom. In the morning, the girls went to school and Wayne rode his horses to the RR depot. After a short trip to Colorado Springs, he rode to the community under siege, set up camp on the town's outskirts, and spent a quiet evening. In the morning he made a rear entry behind Main Street's buildings, tied his horses at the sheriff's rear hitching rail and walked to the nearest deputy's home.

The other deputy joined them and a planning meeting was held. Wayne explained his detailed ideas and summarized the plans by adding: "arm yourself with a double barrel shotgun loaded with #3 Buckshot, and cover my back. Carry six pairs of handcuffs and six pairs of ankle cuffs. There will be a gunfight, but I want you out of that fight. I can handle four gunslingers by myself. Stand aside and pull your shotgun if I get shot and cannot finish the gunfight. When I enter a business, stay outside and shoot any gunfighter that shows up unexpectedly. If you have to shoot, don't hesitate, or you're dead. Shoot him even before he spots you. Once I need you, I'll come outside to get you."

The next morning, the team was on the boardwalk. One deputy was looking east and the other was looking west. Wayne entered the mercantile with a grocery list in his hands. The gunslinger by the door stopped him and said, "give me your gun till you leave." "I don't give up my gun to anyone." The other gunfighter comes over and asks where he lived. Wayne said, "pistol up your nose street." Both gunfighters went for their guns. Wayne, with incredible speed shoved his Colt at one man's nose and swung the Colt sideways and smashed it onto the other gunfighter's forehead. Both outlaws were out on the floor. The store's owner was smiling and pleasantly surprised. Wayne called in the deputies, applied handcuffs and ankle cuffs, tied a cord and pulled up their feet up to their hands, and stuffed a rag in their mouths to gag them. Wayne then tells the owner, "if they try to scream, hit them in the face with a stick. We'll be back for them."

The team then moved on to the hardware store. The deputies took their positions, and Wayne entered the store with the same grocery list. The gunslinger stopped him and said, "this is a grocery list, you're in the wrong store." Wayne raised his voice and told the outlaw to shut up. That brought the other man up to find out why Wayne was yelling. Shortly afterwards, the deputies were called in to do their job. When both were hogtied, one deputy said, "at least you're consistent, one with a smashed nose and the other with an egg on his forehead." Wayne gave the same instructions to the store owner who nodded in agreement.

The third set up was the bank. Wayne walked in with the same grocery list and some paper currency to display. The outlaw stopped him with his hand on Wayne's arm. Wayne raises his voice and says, "don't touch me, I have a venereal disease." The other man came to investigate and both found themselves on the floor. The deputies came in laughing. They hogtied both of them and left the same directions to a shaking head clerk.

Meanwhile, Strickland is getting nervous. He tells the free gunfighter, sitting in his office, that all three businesses were due their payment this morning, and none of the boys have showed up with the money. "Something is wrong. Pick up the two boys in the saloons and go see what is going on."

Wayne and the deputies waited on the bank porch. As expected, three men were seen coming down Main Street. The deputies went to their designated positions, and Wayne stepped into the middle of the street. At fifteen yards, he stopped the oncoming gunfighters. "Stop there, you are all under arrest for murder, robbery and holding this town in siege." "You must be some idiot, there is one of you and three of us. You might hit one of us, but the other two will mow you down." "Gentlemen, if I see those guns lift out of your holster, you will all die.

You would be wise to take your chances with a trial." The head man just said, "now," Wayne drew and shot all three in the head. Their guns fell back in their holsters as they violently fell backwards. The deputies stepped next to Wayne and said, "how did you shoot all three in the head with one shot?" Wayne opened the revolver's gate and pushed out three spent shells—to the deputies shock.

Wayne said, "it's time for Mr. Strickland. Would you go home and get your dog—the one that almost made me pee my pants yesterday."

The deputy took off at a run, and came back with a 90 pound rottweiler on a leash. Wayne said, "each time I wink at you, can you make him attack and hold his bite." "Heck, he'll hold, shake the spot and growl like a,mad dog–and 'mad dog is his name.'" "God, if that doesn't make him talk, nothing will. Let's go."

Strickland had heard one shot and knew his men had taken care of the problem. When he heard footsteps, he lifted his eyes and spotted Wayne, two deputies and a dog. He said, "get the hell out of my office, as he went for his gun. Wayne heard the attack command and saw mad dog grab Strickland's gun arm with a large mouthful of forearm. Strickland screamed blood gurgling screeches. Wayne said, "what's the combination to open your safe?" "Go to hell!" Wayne winks and the deputy says, "attack again." Mad dog lets go the arm and muckles onto the screamer's right nipple. The screaming steps up a pitch but he still refuses to give the combination. Wayne says, "well this should work," as he pulls Strickland's britches down to his knees and winks at the deputy, who points his finger at the exposed genital. He never got to give the next command, as Strickland yelled out 69-14-39, and pleads, "get this 'cur' to let go my chest, and get him away from me."

Wayne unlocked the safe and took out bundles of paper currency. They counted the cash and came up to $39,000. Strickland was handcuffed and walked to the jail. Once in the cell, he demanded to see a doctor. Wayne said, "that's a waste of time since you will hang by tomorrow."

To clean up the mess, the mortician was called to pick up the dead bodies. The six hog tied outlaws were thrown in the cells. One individual was separated. The prosecutor offered him a deal if he named all the other outlaws–twenty years or hanging. He took the deal, as the deputies' wrote down the names.

The ten horses were put up for sale at the livery, and the guns were all packed and shipped by train to Harrigan's gun shop in Silver Circle. The ten pistols and ten rifles were worth wholesale $15 per pistol and $25 per rifle. The $400 was a bit low, but the amount was agreed upon before Wayne left town. Omer Harrigan was reliable and would add the funds to his benefactor account. Wayne sent two telegrams. One to Captain Ennis to determine if these scoundrels had a bounty. Another to Mandy, telling her that the reclamation was completed and would be home in four days. A deputy was sent to bring the Judge back to town for a trial tomorrow.

For the rest of the day, Wayne sent the other deputy to visit all the businesses in town that had paid protection. They were to prepare a listing of each payment and an estimate of the siege's negative effect on their business. For the evening, Wayne closed his camp, moved the horses to the livery, and took a room in the small hotel, with a hot bath added to his pleasure.

The next morning, Wayne and the deputies went around town distributing the cash refunds. They hit every business and when done, they still had $6000 left over. Wayne said, "give $2000 to the two ranchers' widows and $2000 to the sheriff's widow.

Judge Weaver arrived in the morning and scheduled the trial for the afternoon. The witnesses included all the business owners who had been charged the protection money. They identified all the seven living outlaws. The defense attorney asked Wayne if he had rounded his clients for the reward money. Wayne said, "I still don't know if they had bounties on their heads. I went after the money to return it to their rightful owners–the victims.

The closing arguments were short. The prosecutor reminded the jurors that this was their chance to provide justice. The defense attorney mentioned that, Mr. Strickland and his men, always had the intention of returning the money to the business men they collected from. They would only charge an administrative fee.

Everyone in the room started laughing. The sheriff's wife got up and said, "what about the two ranchers and my husband who were killed by these monsters? I presume that was acceptable collateral damage, heh!" The jury was out ten minutes and found the seven guilty of murder and extortion. Judge Weaver sentenced all seven to hang at 1PM today.

After the sentences were carried out, Wayne got a telegram from the marshal's office. All ten men had a bounty, and vouchers would arrive at the telegraph office by tomorrow noon.

That evening, Wayne was planning on a nice meal at the diner, but he was escorted from his hotel room to the local town hall. Banners were displayed, and Wayne walked into a surprise gathering of people clapping and whistling. He walked a gauntlet of town's people pumping his shoulders, slapping his back, and shaking his hand. A local band was playing and people were dancing. A large buffet was set up. Beef was the main entree, to include steak, roasts and stews. During the meal, workers were walking about, accumulating suggestions for a town name. After dinner, the bank president made a speech, appreciating Wayne's work. He then announced that a town name had been chosen, Swanson Hollow. The applause was deafening. He also announced that the sheriff's son, a sheriff in the next county, had agreed to accept the sheriff's position. He would be moving to town, with his family, in the next two weeks. The applause was again loud and clearly supportive.

Eventually, Wayne was pushed into saying a few words. Wayne got up and said, "thank you for the reception and a great meal. Before dinner, I was asked how to prevent a siege from happening again? I recommend that you set up a volunteer citizens watch committee to work with your sheriff's department. Be at the train depot every day when the train arrives. Pick out well armed newcomers with their own horses. Visit saloons and look for tough men that are not local residents. Match faces with reward posters. You will be surprised how often you pick out outlaws. Then report to the sheriff's department. They are responsible for further investigations."

After a good night's sleep on a real bed, he bought a full breakfast at the diner. He left a dollar to pay for the 50 cent meal. Arriving at the telegraph office, the telegrapher handed him ten vouchers to cover the rewards. Wayne went to the bank and met with the bank president. They agreed on a fee. A bank transfer would be used to transfer $12,000 to his benefactor account in Silver Circle. Wayne could not believe the large rewards offered. It would be interesting to find out what evil they had been up to prior to their escapade in this town. He knew Captain Ennis would know all the history of their depredations.

Wayne got his two horses, with minimal supplies, and headed for Colorado Springs. This was an easy ride, so he didn't take the train. After one hour on the road, he came onto a large Conestoga wagon with a couple and three kids. They were trailing two horses, and the wagon was full of belongings. Wayne stopped to say hello. "What brings you folks to the open range?" "We bought a quarter section with a house and barn.

We got directions in Colorado Springs, but it appears something is wrong." "Who gave you the directions?" "The clerk in the land office." "Did you pay with cash or a bank draft?" "Cash" "Uh, did you show a wad of extra cash?" "Yes." "Well, it appears you were sent here to be waylaid and likely killed for your money, horses, and belongings. I strongly suggest we move into the trees, set up camp and get ready for visitors. What do you have for guns?" "I have a Colt, a 1873 rifle, and my wife is good with the shotgun."

"Good, lets set up camp on that knoll. So I can scope the area and find the outlaws before they get to camp." The lady asks, "why are you helping complete strangers?" "Because this is your lucky day, and this is what I do, Ma'am." The family quickly dug a fire pit and built a nice fire for cooking.

Meanwhile, Wayne was using his 8X power scope on his Sharps. He scouted the entire area and finally saw a dust cloud from the east. Watching the area he finally spotted four riders who were pushing their horses to a constant canter. Wayne had the kids safely positioned behind a large tree with their shotgun bearing mother. Dad was positioned behind the wagon with his rifle. Wayne stayed standing by the fire.

The four riders stopped some 400 yards from camp, and sat on their horses. Two of them started to ride their horses toward camp.

When they got to fifty yards, one yells, "Hello the camp, may we step down and set?" "Yes, and tie your horses to the wagon wheel." Wayne had his right hand hidden behind his back. After tying their horses, they walked to the fire. Suddenly, they both drew their pistols and said, "this is a hold up. Show us your right hand behind your back." Wayne obliged them and pulled his right hand out, leaving it next to his Colt. "Gentlemen, if you cock those pistols, I will kill you." "I doubt it, you don't even have your gun out." As they pulled their hammers back, a shot rang out and both outlaws fell to the ground.

Meanwhile, the other two scoundrels looked at each other and said, "how could one shot drop two of them?" "I don't know, what I do know is that the homesteader has a bundle of money that I want. I'm not going against that gun from 400 yards. For all we know, he may have a long range rifle. Let's pull out and we'll be back after they're all asleep."

The homesteader asks, "are you going to shoot the other two?" "No, I'm going to let them make a decision of right or wrong. If they charge, I will pick them off before they get to us. If they come back during the night, they will also meet their maker."

Wayne scavenged the two dead ones. They both had ID's, a receipt from a hardware store for ammo and tack. They had a total of $132 and Wayne gave half to the family. The horses were all stripped of their saddles, and the two outlaw horses were tethered next to a stream for grazing. For dinner, Wayne liquidated his supplies to feed the entire family who were short of supplies and appeared hungry.

After dinner, they set up a perimeter with a cord six inches off the ground. The family was set behind trees for cover. Wayne set up several stuffed bedrolls to look like someone was in the bedrolls. Wayne sat to the side and waited. By the middle of the night, suddenly Wayne saw two men approach the camp fire. As expected, one tripped on the cord and fired his Colt as his knee hit the ground. The other started firing at the bedrolls. Wayne yelled to stop. He gave them the usual double option, continue shooting and they would die, or give up and take your chances with a trial.

Wayne knew they were choosing to fight it out. They knew they would be hanged. So Wayne scooted behind a large tree, the outlaws spotted movement and started shooting at a well protected Wayne. After they slowed down throwing lead, Wayne pointed his shotgun and fired both barrels of #3 buckshot. Both outlaws were torn up with hits over their faces and chests. Wayne stepped up and confirmed that they were both dead. The homesteader came to Wayne and said, "like you told us, they chose to return, heh."

The next morning, Wayne scavenged the new bodies. Found ID's for both as receipts from a hotel. He collected $139 and gave it to the homesteaders. He laid claim to the guns and the horses. They saddled all the horses, straddled all the outlaws on their horses and headed to Colorado Springs.

Arriving at the sheriff's office, the entire event was explained and the sheriff said, "so this is the group that has been waylaying settlers. Now we know that the land office agent was the one sending the settlers in the wrong direction. We have lost two full wagons of innocent people, including kids. Let's go to the land office and arrest that monster."

On arrival, the clerk never suspected a thing till the handcuffs were applied. The sheriff said, "you're going to hang you smart ass!" Wayne looked at the homesteading map and found the homesteader's matching lot number. Wayne said, "you were sent west, and your lot is three miles to the east of town." The sheriff added, "at trial, we'll need you as a witness for the prosecution." "Ok, I'll be here."

The sheriff matched the four outlaws by name and was able to find wanted posters for all four. He went to the telegraph office to notify the organizations who were posting the rewards. Wayne knew he would have to stay overnight. He brought the four horses/saddles to a local livery and sold all four for $360–high values because of city prices. He also sold the 8 guns for $400 at a local gun shop–again high values because of city prices.

That evening, he had a great dinner in the hotel restaurant, had a hot bath and a restful night. In the morning, after breakfast, he visited the sheriff. He was handed four vouchers ranging from $750 to $1500 for murder, kidnaping, robbery and rape. His total was $4500 plus the $760 for the guns and horses. Per his routine, he went to the bank and arranged for a bank transfer to his private account in Silver Circle. These funds were not rewards for an official job—the reason for his private deposit instead of the benefactor fund.

By noon, Wayne and his horses were on the train to Denver. He went back to reading his bounty hunting dime novels. This novel was about train robbers. Wayne wondered how easy it would be for thieves to clean out a full passenger car of well to do travelers. He would have to bring up the subject with Captain Ennis.

***

CHAPTER 13

The Train

Wayne arrived home by 4PM. Took care of his horses by mucking their stalls, adding oats to their feed bags, filling their water troughs, and adding 10 pounds of hay for each horse. He rubbed them down of the trail dust and pollen.

He went in the house to start dinner, but found a meatloaf in the cold room, with assorted vegetables. Instead he put water on the stove for tea and coffee. The girls arrived shortly, and again, Mandy nearly took the screen door off it's hinges, as she ran in the house and jumped in Wayne's arms.

During the evening, Wayne said, "every day spent without you is a permanently lost day. I guarantee you, that come April, we will be together regularly. We may be apart during the day when you're teaching, but we'll be together most evenings." Kissing and fondling started, it was certain that the evening would not be lost.

The next day, after the girls left for school, Wayne headed to the US Marshal's Office. The clerk greeted Wayne, got up from his desk and shook Wayne's hand saying, "we heard the good news by telegram. The Captain is looking forward to seeing you. This way please."

Captain Ennis gave his greeting and immediately went into a tirade. "Remember, 'the power's to be' had denied the Marshall service helping this unincorporated town?" "Yes, that's why you gave me the job." "Well now they have reversed themselves when they heard that you made $12,000. Well, the law is not only about money. My deputy marshals are not gunfighters. In a shootout like you had, they would all have been killed. I refuse to send my men on a suicide mission."

"Now we have another situation. Deadly robberies on passenger trains between Cheyenne and Denver. These trains have many well to do business men, who are not armed, and carry too much cash."

"What's so special about this situation. Just put RR detectives or US Marshals on each passenger car, and the problem will stop." "We've tried, but these killer thieves are dressed like unarmed business men, and even women participate. Once the train is moving, they pull out a hidden gun and shoot anyone wearing a badge. I've lost two good deputies and I'm not bowing to the RR's demands. Resisting travelers have been shot dead. Even the RR detectives refuse to participate. Once the robberies are done, they force the engineer to stop the train at a designated location, and the robbers are picked up by their partners awaiting with horses. In addition, there appears to be two or three teams that alternate from train to train." "What is this you said about women?" "On one robbery, a passenger took the outlaw's gun, and was about to shoot him, when a woman got up and shot the passenger dead.

"Well, I'm willing to help, but I suspect that I would be recognized as a well known bounty hunter by this ring of thieves." "It is true, that if you travel as yourself, a scout on the RR platform would likely pick you up as a suspicious repeating armed traveler, and cancel the robbery. There is a solution and the answer is multiple disguises. There's a company that specializes in making disguises for different occasions. It's used in the theater, holiday events and so on. You need to meet with them and see what they can offer you."

"Ok, if this outfit can convince me that I can be disguised, I'll take the job."

Wayne arrived at Mr. Impersonator and was greeted by a pleasant attendant. When he explained what his needs were, the attendant said, "we can easily disguise you so that your wife wouldn't even recognize you. Let us show you some of our samples." Wayne was escorted to a room full of mannequins dressed and disguised. The attendant said, "now picture these displays with a voice change to match each one." The mannequins had the same face, but the facial alterations gave them a different identity. He saw the different personae: a minister, a Texan musician with a guitar case and a large drooping mustache, a ranch baron with white hair, long sideburns and a high end suit, a city dandy with fashionable attire with a Derby hat, a scruffy looking drunk, and an eastern dressed drummer carrying a large case of his samples.

The attendant added, "we would dress you up, using the more sophisticated disguises, with facial makeup before you leave Denver. The simpler costumes, you would carry in your travel bag, and you would dress yourself on your return trip from Cheyenne. The three would include: once as your normal attire, a minister, and a scruffy looking drunk."

"Great, what is your charge for all five set ups?" "$55 would cover it." Wayne gave him a bank draft and scheduled his first arrangement for 7AM since he was taking the 9AM train, tomorrow. Before leaving, the seamstress took body measurements, in case alterations were necessary. The last instructions came from Wayne, "all my costumes must include a vest, or some type of coat, to hide my shoulder holstered Webley Bulldog."

That evening, Wayne was tutored by Mandy and Kathy. He learned how to: talk with a southern drawl, speak in biblical terms, give orders like a rancher baron, sound pompous like a drummer, and sound drunk.

By 8AM Wayne walked out of Mr. Impersonator looking like a Texan well-to-do rancher. At the RR ticket office, he was speaking loud, and tripping over his tongue with the classic drawl. He was well disguised with a white haired wig, sideburns and facial aging makeup.

The RR company had eagerly provided a single passenger car. Wayne boarded early and took a seat in the front row, but facing backwards.

He figured that the outlaw would come from the rear, since he needed to spy on the passengers. The second man, the cash collector, would likely be sitting anywhere, but near the center aisle.

During the first hour of travel, Wayne worked on identifying the outlaws. A man in a rear seat was way too busy looking at all the passengers. He would remember this man. The second outlaw was the easiest to detect. He was sitting across the aisle and facing backwards. He was reading a dime novel, but not really reading. He would turn pages inconsistently, sometimes too slow, sometimes too fast.

Keeping in mind the possibility of a woman accomplice, Wayne had identified a young woman wearing a riding skirt instead of a dress, like all the other ladies on this train. Feeling sure he had identified the team, he just waited for the robbery to start.

Suddenly, the man in the rear reached in his travel bag and pulled out a Colt. He stood up and yelled, "This is a holdup. If you don't want to die, place your cash in the bag. The second anticipated outlaw drew his gun, and passed his travel bag around. The collector went down his side of the train going rearward. He then turned and came forward. When he got to the woman suspect, she dropped a large bundle and never showed fear like all the other ladies had.

Finally, the collector got to Wayne who said, "no, I won't give you my life's savings." "Then you're going to die." "No, you're going to die." As Wayne heard the hammer's first of three clicks, a gunshot was heard and both outlaws dropped to the floor.

People were stunned, someone said, "there was only one shot, so who shot the man in the rear?" "Another said, "there were two shots from the rancher up front." Wayne then stepped forward and ordered the woman suspect to stand, as she did she pulled a belly gun from her purse and pointed it at the passenger ahead of her. Wayne responded immediately by shooting her in the head—but it was only a superficial graze, enough to knock her out. He then handed a passenger the handcuffs and asked him to restrain her, and apply a bandage to the insignificant head wound.

Wayne and the conductor went forward to speak with the engineer. They were all watching the countryside, looking for a man holding two or three horses. Wayne was holding his sawed off shotgun, which had been hidden in the travel bag.

When spotted, the engineer brought the train to a stop. To the outlaw's surprise, Wayne stepped off the train, pointed his shotgun at a shocked outlaw, and arrested him. He was handcuffed, his horses loaded in the stock car, and the train resumed it's trek to Cheyenne.

Arriving in Cheyenne, the woman kept yelling that she was innocent and wanted a lawyer. The prosecutor met with the horse holding outlaw. He gave him a deal, for giving up the names of the other four outlaws, the leader and his wife—already in custody. The deal was too great to refuse, 20 years in prison and avoid hanging. Wayne took the train back to Denver as himself without a disguise. He also brought the three horses and their guns to be sold in Denver.

Wayne skipped the next day's trip. He figured the outlaws were laying low and trying to figure out what had happened. Wayne was hoping they would not change their mode of operation. Hopefully, they would attribute this last botched job as part of bad luck.

The second day was a holiday and passenger trains weren't running. The third day, Wayne boarded the train as a drummer with a large display case. Nothing happened to Wayne's disappointment.

In Cheyenne, the RR surprised Wayne by adding a second passenger car. Apparently, because of the holiday, there were too many business men that needed to appear in the Denver area. He made a quick costume change to a minister with a full beard, round spectacles, a flat top/low crown hat, and a bible in hand. Of course, the bible was a hollow box carrying his Bulldog.

After the train started moving, Wayne started looking around to identify the two likely suspects. Suddenly, a shot rang out and a deputy sheriff, on holiday, was gunned down. It was clear that the outlaw had made small talk, and had identified a lawman not wearing a badge.

Wayne was sorry for the loss, but he knew he could not have prevented it from happening. The outlaw stood up and made his announcement. The collector was already filling his bag of paper currency. The dead deputy was an unwelcome incentive.

All of a sudden, the collector yelled, drop your wallet or you're dead you old fool. The elderly gentleman was shaking his head no. His wife was pleading with him. The outlaw said, "you're dead," as he pulled the gun's hammer back. Wayne knew he had to act now. He pulled his gun and both outlaws dropped dead. The resisting older man passed out when Wayne's gun was fired.

Wayne asked, "is there a doctor who can attend to the older man. I think he just passed out. I have to go to the other car to see if there is also a robbery in progress." Wayne stepped across the car's linkage and notice two outlaws conducting a gathering. The gunshot had not deterred them, since they assumed it was caused by their partners.

Wayne stepped into the passenger car when both outlaws had their backs to the rear car entrance. Wayne yells out. "Stop, and put your hands up!" The two robbers had no idea who they were dealing with when they turned and saw a minister. The leader cocked his gun but dropped to the floor without firing it. The collector had more sense, and put his hands up, saying, "I give up."

After securing this outlaw, the conductor went with Wayne to see the engineer. Again the train was stopped, and Wayne was the outlaw's unlucky greeter. After again securing the outlaw, Wayne and the conductor got the outlaw's horses loaded into the stock car. Then they went back to see if the unconscious passenger had awakened. As they entered the car, the conductor said to Wayne, "stop, do you know who that man is?" "No, but I would have saved anyone in his predicament." "That is certainly gallant, but that's the president and owner of this railroad. Wait, are you the well known Wayne Swanson under that disguise?" "Yes." "Well. Let me introduce you to our owner."

The elderly gentleman started to say, "I made a mistake by trying to resist. I knew I was going to die because of my stupid decision. Then I heard a gunshot and everything went black. When consciousness came back, I realized that I was alive and that someone had saved me. Who shot that outlaw?" Everyone pointed at the minister.

The conductor introduced Wayne to the RR executive. He graciously thanked him for his quick response and saving his life. The conductor had the dead bodies moved to the back of the passenger cars and covered with a tarp. The two secured outlaws were chained in the caboose to a steel wall anchor. Wayne collected the one rifle and five pistols, but waited to check the dead bodies' pockets till the passengers were disembarked.

The outlaw collector, wanted to make a deal. He told the conductor that for a prison sentence, he would divulge the name of the head organizer above the gang leader. This was a lawyer in Denver and the deal would have to be made with the prosecutor or judge in Denver.

After arriving in Denver, Wayne scavenged the pockets of the live and dead outlaws. He collected $421 which he legally pocketed, with the conductor as witness.

With the job coming to an end, Wayne returned his costumes to Mr. Impersonator, and went home. He waited for Mandy while taking care of his horses. When Mandy arrived, she told Wayne that she had a three day weekend off because of teacher's meetings on Monday. Wayne took the opportunity to suggest that on Saturday, they visit a demo of the gasoline powered automobile. On Sunday they could visit a demo of electricity, lighting, and early electrically powered motors and household small appliances. Mandy added, "that's a fantastic idea. I suspect that our future will include these two technological advances."

The two days of demonstrations were interesting and enlightening. They both realized that in their 20's, they would likely be using these new items, even before their retirement years. On their way home Sunday, Mandy asked what he had planned for Monday. Wayne said, "we have an appointment at an agricultural dealership." "Oh really, and does that have anything to do with the discussion with Uncle George about harvesting hay?" "Yes, Ma'am."

Arriving at Winslow Ag Equipment, Wayne was greeted by the same salesman he had seen in the past. The man introduced himself as Steve. Wayne introduced Mandy and said, "I need more information on the implements I will need, and my wife also needs an introduction to the subject." Mandy says, "I am a combination learner, I learn by functional theory and visual application." "So you need an explanation how each implement works, and you need to see each one working in the field." Mandy says, "Yes, sir." "Well, this is the harvest season, so let's go visit some farms that are working the fields today."

As they arrived at a large hay farm, Steve said, "this farm is in full operation and we have permission to observe and ask questions. You will witness, hay cutting, windrow rake, hay loader, finishing/dumping rake, one horse baler and a storage shed for hay bales.

The first implement was the cutter. A side sickle was made of steel fingers with a cutter blade moving side to side between the fingers. A very efficient, one horse, one man operation. A warning, use petroleum based grease and oil in the grease and oiling holes of all the implements.

The next was the side rake making clean rows of hay ready for loading. "Keep replacing lost teeth, and it will clean quite well. Another one horse, one man operation.

The next was the hay loader. This machine was pulled over the windrows and 90% of the hay was picked up and dumped into the trailing wagon. This was an impressive set up. It required two horses and two men. "One man driving the horses, and one man to stack the hay away from the hay loader. The wagon stacker would also unload the wagon onto the ground next to the baler."

The last field demo was the one horse baler. "This implement has modernized the commercial sale of hay. This is a one horse and six man operation. The power is a horse walking in a circle and turning a cam that transfers power to the main piston. This piston will cut the hay and push the hay through the square tunnel, Two men feed the hopper from the hay mound on the ground, two men add twine or wire to the compacted hay before it exits the square tunnel. One man removes the bales and places it on the wagon. One man stacks the hay and then unloads the hay in the warehouse."

Wayne was seen to be smiling and Mandy said, "what amazing advancements, and you've got us hooked." On their way to the showroom, Steve said, "let's talk about hay. During the war, hay sold for $50 a ton. Today it sells for $30–40 a ton. This baler can bale 1000 pounds an hour. A bale of hay is 1/8 the volume of hay. Each bale weighs the standard 50 pounds. So it takes 40 fifty pound bales to make a ton, or 75 cents a bale. Most fertilized and cultivated hay fields can produce 100 bales per acre. With fertilizer, a second crop is feasible."

Mandy added, "wow, them are interesting facts, now I know why Wayne is interested in growing commercial hay. Out of curiosity, in a day, how much hay does a horse eat anyway?" The answer is 10–20 pounds a day. There are many variables: size of horse, working or stabled, sustenance or supplement, outside temperature, field grazing or not, and I'm sure there are other variables. Can you imagine the hay need of a 1800 pound draft horse pulling a plow all day would be compared to a luxury 1000 pound Morgan stabled all day."

After getting back to the showroom, Steve demonstrated the cultivating equipment. He reviewed the plow, disc harrows, finish harrows, and spring harrows for rocky soil. These usually required one or two large draft horses. The amazing manure spreader required a special explanation. "this new implement has a continuous web that moves the manure backwards to a beater attachment. The entire mechanism is activated by the rear wheels through gears and chains."

Mandy chimed in, "our ranches have our cattle on the range, we don't have cow manure to spread." "I know, but you all have a massive mound of 100 year old composted horse manure. Because grazing lands are deficient of phosphorous, adding half a bag of phosphate on each load of manure will add the supplements to get a good harvest of oats and hay."

"Once the manure is gone, you'll be back for a phosphate spreader to continue fertilizing your hay fields. I expect you will cultivate as many acres you can achieve between spring and early summer. This will be a yearly spring project. Cultivated land produces a profitable yield of hay."

The last items discussed and reviewed were for grain harvesting, especially oats: a reaper and binder, a thresher, and a fanning mill. Steve explained how each worked, and presented his ideas on harvesting oats. "Every year you'll cultivate a piece of land and fertilize it. By July first, you will plant it with oats to get a fall crop. The next spring, after harrowing, you will then plant your hay, of timothy and other local seeds."

"Now oats is the basic grain supplement for horses. There's a profitable market for local bagged oats." "Yes, I agree, but what do you do with the stalks?" "Baled straw. This is another commercial market developed by baling the straw. Straw has several uses:

1. Horse feed. Used to reduce caloric intake, in overweight or horses that need to eat constantly. Used with hay, it makes hay go longer and saves money. Straw sells for less than half the price of hay.
2. Bedding for cows, calves, sheep and goats.
3. Box foundation for laying hens.
4. Mattresses.

5. Can be used when hay runs out during bad winters or droughts.
6. Mulch for flower boxes and gardens."

"I'm certain that there are other uses, and the wholesalers/retailers know all of them. You won't have trouble selling your straw as long as you bale it."

"Great presentation, would you excuse Mandy and I for a few minutes? "Certainly." "Well dear, what do you think?" "I love the implements and love the idea of being a grain/hay farmer. If you want this venture, you have my complete support. I would look forward to working with you during the harvest, when the school is closed. What do you want, my husband?"

"I've been interested in this for a year. I look forward to manage a cattle ranch on the Box B Ranch, and a grain/hay business on the Bar W Ranch. I really feel we need to diversify to survive to the next century. A bad year with ranching would be buffered with a productive year raising grain and hay. I really want this, Mandy." "Great, let's do it!"

"Ok, Steve, we've changed our minds." "Oh, I'm so sorry, I was hoping to work with you on this venture." "No, no, we don't want to order in April. We want to order today. We'll take every implement you demonstrated plus we want four of those hay wagons. I will pay for storage in your warehouse until my implement shed is built. Also, include a freight charge to my ranch, six miles from Silver Circle."

"Wow, this is a very large order and will require a deposit." "Not a problem," as Mandy hands him a bank draft for $3000. "This may cover more than the actual costs." "Keep the balance on my account. We'll need small tools, extra cutting blades, rake hooks, baling twine, hardware to attach implements to horses, and I'm certain many other unplanned accessories."

With the contract finalized, Wayne was given an operator and parts manual for every implement—reading material for weeks to come. Steve's departing words were, "When you start harvesting hay, I will have one of my men spend time at your ranch, to help you get started."

The Swanson's next stop was the telegraph office. Uncle George had sent a telegram to Mandy some time ago, informing them that he had purchased the Box B Ranch at auction for $3500. With the signing of the implement contract, it was time to communicate with Uncle George. The telegram informed him that they had ordered the cultivating and grain/hay harvesting equipment. It requested George to order the construction of a pull through equipment shed with stalls for every implement on the list. It also requested the construction of a storage shed that would hold +-20,000 fifty pound bales, and the expansion of the barn to hold the extra animals. It also asked George to work with Bruce Hawkins to find four teams of draft horses to handle the plow and harrows, and large gelding horses to handle other implements and wagons. The telegram included a Western Union voucher for $3000 to cover these and future expenses.

The next day, the girls went back to school and Wayne planned to see Captain Ennis. While he was in the barn caring for his horses, a telegram arrived from Uncle George. It said, "Great news, all in favor. The construction company has finished my new house/barn and will be done your dad's in a week. Will meet with the design people and will plan construction of the two bunkhouse cook-shack extensions, barn extension, equipment shed, and hay storage shed. Bruce will take care of the horses, and Dan

Evans will build the harnesses once the animals are chosen. This is a great time for Sally and I, as well as your folks. Be safe and tell Mandy that she'll have the Swansons and Wilsons for Christmas guests."

Wayne arrived at the US Marshal Office and was greeted by Captain Ennis. "Welcome, and what a nice job you did on the train robberies. You brought ten criminals to justice, and half of them alive. The most important thing, no innocent passengers were injured or killed. Yesterday I got this extensive telegram from the RR owner. He thanked you for your skill in eradicating these murderers and saving his life. He enclosed nine $1000 vouchers as posted reward by the RR. The surprise lawyer organizer had no reward on his head. He is also adding his personal touch. He has issued you this document. That is a life long RR pass for you, Mandy, and your future children."

"Well thank you. As we are approaching Christmas, do you have a job that could take me to the holidays, when I plan to take a vacation with out families." "Yes, this is a legal job for the marshall service, but I don't have the manpower to spare. So, I would like to make you a temporary deputy on a specific assignment. As a temporary deputy, you will be allowed to collect any posted rewards. Since we don't know who the criminals are, I can't guarantee a financial reward." "That's ok, tell me about this caper."

"We have a new method of rustling cattle. This outfit doesn't steal cattle, they rob the ranchers who just sold some cattle, and have a bundle of cash in their ranches. Since the nearest bank is thirty miles away, it could be weeks for a rancher to spare several of his Cowboys to escort him to the bank. During this interim period, they get robbed, beaten, tortured, and some have been killed when they refuse to give them the money. Since you'll need the ranchers' help to stop this gang, that's why you need to wear the badge."

Wayne was sworn in, and the Captain placed the badge on his vest. As he was leaving, Captain Ennis said, "Stop shaving, you will need a full face beard for your next assignment after Christmas."

***

CHAPTER 14
The Rustling

Not wearing his badge, Wayne took the lifetime free train ride to Colorado Springs. He then changed route to head east on a RR spur to a small railhead for a regional cattle, receiving and transport, to points east. He arrived late and took a room in the local hotel, brought his two horses to the livery for overnight care and feed. Paid the $2 fee and had a great fried chicken dinner and dessert for 50 cents. Left a full dollar to cover the tip and paid the hotel room/bath for another $2.

Following his instincts, he decided to visit both saloons during the evening, again not wearing his badge. He entered the first saloon, Smith's, ordered a beer, and watched the customers. It was clear that these were local business men and ranchers out to play a low key nickle/dime card game and have a few beers. He left after his beer and went to the other saloon., Waterman's. After ordering a beer, he stayed leaning on the end of the bar and watched the patrons. The owner, Horace Waterman, was the bartender and he was watching his working girls. The customers were a hard bunch, well healed, drinking whiskey, and playing a dollar minimum poker game. Wayne made a mental note of a half dozen of these faces. He felt they would meet again.

In the morning, after a nice breakfast, he stopped at the RR depot. Skipping the ticket office, he went to the cattle office. As he entered, he was greeted by a pleasant man in his 50's. "What can I do for you marshal?" After the clerk had seen the badge, Wayne closed his vest to hide it in case someone entered the office. "I am looking for the miscreants who are robbing the ranchers. Do you post the name of the herds you receive and purchase?"

"Yes, let me show you the board of scheduled sales." Wayne turns around and looks at the board. "I see you are expecting 200 head of cattle today, Monday, from the Circle A Ranch and you received 150 cattle last Thursday from the S–S Connected Ranch." "Yes, that is correct and this information is available to the public." "How do you pay for these cattle?" "The funds arrive by train, under armed guards, the day after we take possession of the herd, and we pay in cash." "So today's herd will be paid tomorrow." "Yes, and the owner or his foreman will stay overnight in the hotel till the train arrives tomorrow morning." "You have posted $22 per three year old steer. That means a lot of cash." Yes, but fortunately the owner or foreman are surrounded by several ranch hands, which guarantees the funds will make it to the ranches. The local bank is under construction, and this will change the method of payment from cash to vouchers in the near future."

"So, this information is available to the public. Have you noticed certain individuals who regularly visit this board." "It's impossible for me to say, since every Cowboy hangs around when a herd arrives, trying to land a job with the owner or the foreman." "Well thank you, and where do I get directions to the last two ranches?" "The land office across the street."

After getting directions to both ranches, Wayne headed out some twenty miles to the S–S Connected Ranch. As he arrives, he yells out, "Hello the house," as the wife steps on the porch carrying a shotgun.

"Hello, I'm deputy US Marshall Swanson on assignment regarding the ranch robberies. May I speak to you and your husband?" "Yes, come in and I'll get my husband." Wayne steps up to the house and as he enters the living room, he sees a battered man. He had multiple facial bruises, a splinted left forearm and using a cane to walk.

Wayne says, "what happened sir?" "My foreman arrived Saturday evening with $3000. The nearest bank is 30 miles from here and it doesn't open till Monday. On Sunday morning, all my hands were in the pastures taking care of my herd. We were overcome by five armed men who wanted our money, They beat me up and when I lost consciousness, my wife gave up and gave them our money. Today, my foreman and the hands are trying to track them. I doubt they will be successful since previous robberies always lead back to town."

"Have you contacted the sheriff?" "No, there is no point since the ranchers suspect he is paid off to ignore the situation. We were the fifth of such robberies, and we were lucky to not get killed like one of my friends was two weeks ago. "Well, sir, I'll get your money back, and I'll bring these murderers to justice. I'll be back within a week."

Wayne headed to the Circle A Ranch some five miles away. Upon arriving, he was greeted by the owner, William Hutchins. Introductions were made and Wayne informed him of the anticipated robbery. "Your foreman is delivering 200 head of your cattle to the .RR tomorrow. That means, your men will arrive by Tuesday noon with $4000 in cash." "Yes, and my five men will leave Wednesday morning to travel thirty five miles to the nearest bank before closing." "Where will your men be Tuesday afternoon?" "They'll be working the herd all day since they'll be leaving in the morning." "So that will leave you and your wife to guard your money." "Yes, but only till dark, as the men will be back by then,"

"Do you have a heavy safe?" "Yes." "Let make you an offer. Place your money in your safe and go visit one of your neighbors for the afternoon. I will stay in your house and will be here to greet the thieves. It is clear to me that they already figured out, that the only time to rob you will be Tuesday afternoon when the men are in the pastures."

"Are you sure you want to face those five gunfighters? I'm willing to leave the foreman, who is good with a gun, to help you." "No sir,

I can handle five outlaws. There is no reason to risk the foreman's life." "Wait, did you say you were deputy Swanson, as he picks up the Denver Gazette. The badge threw me off course, is your first name Wayne?" "Yes." "Now I understand. My wife and I will be out of here as soon as my money arrives." "Great, and I'll be here by 10AM tomorrow in case the thieves are watching your men." "No need, deputy, stay the night, there's no need to do all that traveling." "Well thank you, I will set myself up in your barn." "Ok, but come in the kitchen for dinner and your meals tomorrow."

The next day, the foreman and cowhands arrived by noon with the money. Mr. Hutchins explained to the foreman what the deputy's plans were. The Hutchins left after securing the money in the safe. Wayne made himself a cold roast beef sandwich and coffee. He then went to the barn to water and feed his horses, during which time he saw a bear trap hanging on the wall. He came back to the house, and set up the bear trap next to the kitchen door's threshold. He camouflaged it with a thin rug. He sat on the porch with his shotgun and Colt loaded with six rounds, and waited.

An hour later, he spotted a dust cloud some three miles away. He spotted the area with his variable telescope and identified five riders at a fast canter. They stopped, apparently to make plans, and when they resumed riding one rider veered away. Wayne assumed that the separated rider was sent to enter from the rear kitchen—with the surprise bear trap.

Wayne moved to the living room and waited. The four riders quietly walked their horses to the hitching rail, and then rushed the front door with their drawn pistols. Wayne was ready, as soon as the fourth man was in the doorway, Wayne let off two separated shotgun blasts, and one outlaw was blown off the porch while another was thrown through the open window.

The double blast inside the house was devastating. The other two outlaws cringed to the floor, which gave Wayne the time to draw his pistol. As the caustic smoke cleared, Wayne heard the kitchen screen door creak open followed by a loud snap. What followed the snap was a scream from hell. One of the rustlers lost control and wet himself. Wayne then said, "drop your guns or you're dead. The one with wet pants dropped his gun and put his hands in the air.

"What's your name son?" "Randy Ferguson, sir." "If you give me the name of the other four scoundrels, I will speak to the judge in your favor, for being an informant." "I'll do that and this man is the boss."

Looking at the other outlaw with the gun still in his hand, Wayne says, "what's it going to be Mr. Boss-man? Are you going to take a bullet now, or try your luck with a trick lawyer and avoid the noose?" Wayne could read his mind, he knew Mr. Boss-man was going to shoot it out. Wayne did the only think he could do. He shot the outlaw's gun out of his hand, with a perfectly placed shot to the gun's frame. Mr. Boss-man screamed out in pain. Randy then assisted Wayne by handcuffing Mr. Boss-man with his hands behind his back.

Meanwhile, the murderer in the bear trap was still howling, ranting and pleading for help. Wayne noted that the top of the boot had been completely cut off. The trap's teeth were deep in the calf muscles, and the bone was likely fractured. After freeing this piece of crap, he was handcuffed and dragged to the living room.

The next thing on the agenda was finding out where the money from these five robberies was located. Randy volunteered that Mr. Boss-man always brought the cash to an organizer in charge. Wayne looked at Mr. Boss-man and said, "you're going to tell me who you bring the money to. We can do this easy, or we can do it the hard way. What's it going to be?" "Go to hell, deputy!"

Wayne nonchalantly walks over and slams the butt of his shotgun into a knee cap. Mr. Boss-man howls out, Wayne says, "what did you say?" "Go to hell. "Wayne then grabs his pistol hand and slowly forces his index finger backwards, followed by a delayed scream. "Anything to add?" "I'm going to kill you." As the middle finger gets slowly forced backwards and held erect along with the index finger.

"Nothing to add yet?" "No," as he spits in Wayne's face. Wayne regains his composure and says, "I am prepared to cause you pain for the entire day until you give up the name. I guess I'm going to have to become more innovative with my persuasion techniques." Wayne walks to the kitchen and comes back with pliers and a carpenter's awl.

Wayne pushes Mr. Boss-man to the floor on his back, and sits on his chest. He pries his mouth open and applies the pliers to a front tooth and slowly pulls and twists it. Mr. Boss-man is groaning and squealing as his head gyrates and follows the pliers. Wayne pulls out a front tooth and then grabs the other front tooth and pulls it out also. "What do you say now?" "You'll get nothing from me."

Wayne is beginning to think that he will need to get much more aggressive and start cutting off body parts or breaking limbs. He decides to try one more forgotten source of unbearable pain. He opens his mouth again, looks around and spots a rather rotten molar with a black center. He nonchalantly pokes the awl's pointed tip directly in the black center, and Mr. Boss-man's world went into the dark side. His eyes popped out and rotated into his head. The noise coming from his mouth made Randy shake uncontrollably. Wayne kept moving the awl back and forth until Mr. Boss-man sounds mimicked a dying elephant. Wayne pulled the awl out and said, "what did you say?" "No more, no more, his name is Horace Waterman, of Waterman's Saloon."

Wayne looked at his victim and said, "torturing is not my forte, but it is sometimes necessary. However, I learned something today, as he straightens Mr. Boss-man's two extended fingers, with another associated scream. In the future, I will skip torturing and go straight to the awl, boy that really worked, heh."

Wayne proceeded to get things ready for riding back to town. The first thing he did was to scavenge each man's pockets and found $279 which he pocketed. The five pistols and five rifles were place in the pack horse's panniers. Mr. Boss-man had a neck collar applied and the chain locked to a stirrup, with his wrists handcuffed in his back. Randy helped straddle the two dead bodies to their horse's saddle. The bear trap man was also handcuffed and loaded onto his saddle, still moaning and crying. Randy was handcuffed in the front.

As the caravan was ready to depart, the foreman came in from the pasture. "We are done here, I have the five responsible outlaws. Would you send one of your men to get the Hutchins back, and send him out to the other five ranchers who were robbed. They will need to come to town tomorrow to get their money back." "Yes sir, be happy to."

The trip was uneventful except for Mr. Boss-man spitting blood and the bear trap man groaning throughout every bump and stirring on the trail. They arrive at the sheriff's office by late afternoon. A young deputy was sitting on the porch and greeted Wayne. The deputy took control of the prisoners and Wayne stepped into the office. The sheriff was sleeping at his desk with his boots on the desktop. Wayne slapped the boots off the desk, and the overweight sheriff almost smacked his mouth on the desk. He yells with a gruff voice, "what do you want and who do you think you are, you young squirt?"

"I'm deputy US Marshall Swanson. I have in custody the five rustlers and murderers, to place in your jail. I also want a report from you of your investigation. There have been five robberies, men and women beaten and one rancher killed. What have you found?"

"I'm the town sheriff, I don't get involved with outside crimes." "You're wrong, these are your people. You have failed your responsibilities as a lawman and I am charging you with malfeasance. I am relieving you of duty, and give me your badge." The sheriff hesitates to react or to respond. Wayne yanks the badge off his vest and says, "you're fired."

As Randy is escorted to his cell, he says, "Marshal, the sheriff is paid to stay out of the matter and not investigate. He's a friend of Mr. Boss-man." Wayne reacts by grabbing the sheriff by his shirttail, relieves him of his pistol, and unceremoniously throws him in a cell. He then hands the sheriff's badge to the deputy and says, "until your town council acts, you are the temporary sheriff." He then instructs him so send for the doc, since one man has a broken leg and needs stitches.

Wayne then explains to the deputy about the organizer of this robbery escapade. He brings the deputy with him to the Waterman's Saloon. As he walks in, he points his shotgun at Horace and says, "you are under arrest for robbery and murder in regards to the rustling caper." The deputy handcuffs him and they step into the private office. Wayne says, "open the safe, we know you are holding the stolen money." "I'm innocent, you have no proof of my involvement." "Wrong, you have been implicated by your gang leader. Now open the safe, or things are going to get very bad for you."

Waterman answered, "go to hell." Wayne says, "there you go again with that line." As he pushes Waterman onto his back on the desk, sits on his chest, forces his mouth open, spots a bad cavity and shoves the awl deep in it's center. Waterman went into a shaking convulsion, lost control of his bowels, and screamed some gargoyle muttering followed by a scream that chased several patrons out of the saloon. Wayne pulls the awl out, looks at it and says, "most impressive tool, I'll always keep it with me." As Waterman was recovering, he kept looking at Wayne as if he was the devil himself. Wayne said, "want some more of this wonderful tool," as he mimics reinserting the pointed tool. Waterman violently shakes his head in the negative, and says, 69–13–48. The deputy opens the safe, counts the bills and comes up with $43,000. Waterman yells out, "hey, some of that money is part of the saloon." "Where you're going, you won't need any of it, now shut up."

After Waterman was thrown in jail, Wayne and the deputy sat down, with fresh coffee, and made plans for managing this mess. The deputy started, "these prisoners need to be transferred to Colorado Springs since we don't have a residing or visiting judge." "Ok, I'll send a telegram to Captain Ennis and ask for a transfer."

Next, the deputy added, "there are five families that are witnesses to the robberies, they'll have to testify at the trial in Colorado Springs, and will have to come to town for their money." "I've already sent a messenger to the five ranches and they'll be here tomorrow for their money."

"Now that Randy has given me the names of the other four outlaws, I'll send a telegram to Captain Ennis requesting a check to see if any of them have an old bounty on their heads" "You know that the Cattlemen's Association has posted a $1000 on each head, so that will at least give you $6000. I'll send a telegram confirming that all six are in custody or dead, and the Association will send you a Western Union voucher."

With the telegrams all sent out, Wayne told the deputy that he would stay in the jail all night until the money was distributed tomorrow.

The deputy agreed to take the next night and they would alternate till the train transfer was achieved. Wayne brought his horses and the five outlaw horses to the livery. He was surprised to see the livery was out of horses for sale. The livery man paid Wayne $350, as a wholesale price for the five horses and their saddles. Wayne then went to the diner for a nice steak and baked potato dinner. He then returned to the office with his bedroll, his 1873 rifle and shotgun.

The next day, the five ranchers arrived. The first was the S–S Connected. They had lost $3000. Wayne gave them $4000 for their injuries. The next three ranchers had lost anywhere from $4000 to $6000 and the ones that were injured received the extra $1000. The last of the five ranchers was the widow of the killed rancher. Wayne expressed his sympathy and was pleased to hear that the widow had three married sons to run the ranch. Her actual loss was $5000, but as a compensation, he handed her the balance of Waterman's stash, $15000.

The next day telegrams were arriving repeatedly. The first telegram from Captain Ennis, was to inform them that a deputy marshal would arrive on the morning train to transfer the prisoners to Colorado Springs. Wayne would return with the marshal on the noon train. The second telegram was from the Cattlemen's Association. Thanks to the deputy, the $6000 vouchers were transferred to Wayne's benefactor fund in Silver Circle. The third telegram was from Capt. Ennis who informed Wayne that the rustling thieves did have old bounties. The five outlaws had a total of $4500 in reward money, wanted for bank robbery and murder. Captain

Ennis had already sent the funds as a bank transfer to Wayne's account in Silver Circle. The Captain's last words were, "come home, enjoy the holidays and some well deserved time off."

En route, the four outlaws had neck collars with the chain padlocked to the seat. Each one was handcuffed to their backs. The passengers were all local people, and so they all knew that the miscreants were the rustlers/robbers.

The train trip was uneventful and Wayne found himself wool gathering. The holidays would be a special time. School was out for two weeks, the Swansons and Wilsons would be at the house for Christmas, and this was the time that they had planned to finally consummate their marriage. Suddenly his day dreaming was interrupted by a jerking of the train, as the power was transferred to reverse the locomotive wheels. The prisoners were transferred to a jail wagon headed for the state penitentiary. Wayne left his Denver address in case his testimony was needed at trial. He then changed trains, and headed to Denver.

Wayne arrived before the girls came home. He was caring for his horses when the school buggy arrived. Mandy saw Wayne in the barn and ran into his arms. They kissed passionately, and Mandy said, "welcome home and it's finally Christmas. I need you to make special love to me and make me a child."

That evening, Wayne found out that Kathy had been seeing a male senior student regularly. Tonight they had a dinner date and she would not be back till late. As soon as they were introduced to Roy Simms, and the couple soon departed, Mandy and Wayne skipped dinner and went straight to their bedroom.

Their passion was out of control. They badly wanted this moment. Wayne could not hold back and took Mandy in an ultimate climax. Mandy uncontrollably screamed out–out of relief. After recovering from total exhaustion, they repeated pleasuring themselves. This time much more slowly, yet the peak pleasure was even more intense.

Mandy eventually said, "If the intensity increases, I'm going to pass out. I can't believe what we've missed." "The past is over, forget it, we are now truly married lovers, and the future will be the same, till death do us part!"

When Kathy returned from her date, she admitted that she was in love. Wayne and

Mandy were sitting at the kitchen table having a late replenishing dinner, when Mandy got up and hugged Kathy. "Is there a wedding in the works?" "Yes there is, I said yes." "Great and I'm so happy for you. Now what are your plans after graduation?" "We are applying for teaching jobs in the Denver school system." Wayne finally spoke, "wonderful, wonderful. That means you'll need lodging. I'll make you an offer you won't be able to refuse! Let me talk to Mandy about that and I'll get back to you, heh"

After Kathy went to bed, Mandy and Wayne decided to make a list of what they needed to do before Christmas.

1. Decorate the house both inside and outside.
2. Buy a Christmas tree and decorate it.
3. Grocery shopping for Christmas dinner: a turkey for eight with the fixings—squash, cranberries, mashed potatoes, carrots, sourdough rolls and custard pie.
4. Shopping for Christmas presents. Mandy points out that this will be the most difficult task. Wayne adds his six ideas, and Mandy smiles and approves whole heartedly. They would need Christmas wrapping paper.

5. Planned entertainment for guests. Mandy would bring everyone to her school's open house. Wayne would guide a tour of the Winslow implements he had purchased. And if they needed a third event, they would bring them shopping in the downtown district, and include a tour of the city using the horse drawn rail streetcars.

It was a hustle and bustle for several days but Wayne and Mandy were finally ready for the guests. The Swansons and Wilsons arrived two days before Christmas and were greeted by Wayne and Mandy at the RR depot. They spent the arrival day visiting and catching up on events in everyone's lives. The Swansons and Wilsons spent a long time describing their new homes. They both had a two bedroom home with a separate small office. The kitchen and bathroom had running hot and cold water. They also had a water closet. The main room had all new furniture with a huge fireplace. There were coal heating stoves in the bedrooms and main room, and the kitchen had a wood burning cooking stove. They had water piped in the barn for the horses. They had two riding horses and a large gelding to power the buggy. For people in their early 60's, it was a great down-sized retirement home. George added, that they had added hot and cold water, and a water closet in the main house, for Mandy of course!

The construction company had just finished the two cook shack extensions and were planning on starting on the farm buildings right after Christmas. George went over his copy of the designs. Wayne like the expansion of the horse barn from 8 to 24 horses with a large tack room/work bench, hay storage area on the ground floor, and a room for the carriage, buggy and utility wagons. No more loft for storing bales. It also included piped water from the house to water the horses.

The plans for the hay storage was massive post and beam structure. It was constructed for an easy addition if it was not big enough. The designer guaranteed it would hold 20,000 bales. He especially liked the finished walls on the north and western sides—where wind and rain generally hit. It also included a wooden floor to keep the bales off the ground.

The designer was especially proud of his implement shed. He apparently checked with

Steve Winslow and was able to get approximate sizes for each implement. The pull through stalls were sized to fit each implement, and room for the horses to enter and exit without backing up. Wayne was more than pleased, and wished he could be present to see the construction. Yet, with his dad and George to supervise, he had nothing to worry about. They agreed that once the implement shed was done, that they would notify Steve Winslow, and start shipping the implements as soon as possible. Wayne wanted them in the shed when he arrived in early April.

The last items included a guarantee form Bruce Hawkins and Dan Evans that the large work horses, mules, and draft horses would be in the barn and fully harnessed.

Christmas day arrived. At 9AM, everyone was in church for Christmas mass. The festivities started after church. Every one was served a freshly squeezed orange juice with an alcoholic topping. Everyone seemed to like the taste and Mandy had to reveal the ingredients. "My dad liked the taste of corn liquor, or moonshine as it's commonly called. This is the last of his stash. Drink slowly, ladies, or you may find yourself asleep through most of Christmas."

There was a very festive atmosphere, and the ladies were laughing while preparing dinner. At 3PM, dinner was served. The turkey was very much appreciated as an alternative to pork or beef. By the time dessert was served with coffee or tea, and the dishes done, it was 6PM. Mandy then announced that it was time to open the tree gifts. She acted as director and started.

"To Cora and Sally from Wayne." The ladies opened a large box and were both flummoxed until they realized that they were looking at a Singer sewing machine. The oohs and aahs were uttered by surprised recipients. Wayne adds, "the salesman said that this was the current model with many bells and whistles. Most important, the new manual explains all the parts and how to operate it." "Thank you, Wayne, that is very generous."

"To Cora and Sally from me." The box contained bolts of fabric for all occasions, including men. More thank yous.

"To Cora and Sally from Roy and Kathy." A box of patterns for dresses, riding skirts, pants and blouses. It also included a kit of sewing machine grade needles and threads. More thank yous.

"To Sam and George from Wayne." Each man opened their gift and found a brand new Winchester 1876 in the new caliber 45-70. Wayne adds, "This is the new high power center fire cartridge that would likely be the one that would become a standard for years to come. The 8X telescope is for your aging eyes. More thank yous.

"To George and, Sam from Roy and Kathy." A new scabbard made to fit the new rifles. More thank yous.

"To George and Sam from me." A metal ammo box with ten boxes of 20 round ammo in 45-70. "Well George, that range of your's is going to get some use, heh." More thank yous.

"To Roy and Kathy from Mandy. A card is handed to Kathy. Inside was a note:

"Wayne and I have been fortunate and we would like to share our good fortune with the best friend I ever had." Enclosed is the deed to the Spring Street house, barn and land."

Kathy starts crying and says, "We cannot accept this, it is too much money. Give us a price and we will pay it, because we really want this home." "Too late, accept it because it was given with love." "No, this is not right!"

Wayne sees their point, "Ok, I'll make a deal with you, make payments when you can to my benefactor fund to help local people in need. The property is valued by the city at $7000. I will accept payments, up to $2500 as payment in full, over the next ten years. And this deal is not negotiable." Roy adds, "At a beginning teacher's salaries in the Denver area, we can easily make $20 monthly payments, or 125 payments over the next ten years to pay the loan." Kathy adds, "that is very generous and we thank you so much. One day we hope to return the generosity."

"To Wayne from Roy and Kathy" A state agricultural manual on growing hay and grains in Colorado. Also a accounting ledger for expenses and income to help balancing his books. "Thank you and I assure you we'll read this manual from cover to cover."

"To me from Roy and Kathy." A daily ledger for planning school teaching schedules and programs. Also a book on pregnancy and childbirth. "Thank you, one that is useful, and one that is hopeful."

"To Wayne and Mandy from mom and dad." Wayne opens up an envelope to find a bank draft of $9000. "What is this for dad?" "We sold the ranch, land and buildings for $5000 and one thousand cattle for $22000. This is your one-third share of the ranch. We want to help you with your crop harvesting venture." "Wow, I never planned on this but it certainly will be put to good use. Thank you."

To Wayne and Mandy from Uncle George and Aunt Sally." An envelope with a deed to the old Box B and Bar W ranches as well as a new brand that reads W–M Connected Ranch–also included on the new deed. The card reads:

"Wayne you already paid for the Box B with your first voucher. We are giving you and Mandy our ranch now, while we are still alive, and able to enjoy it with you."

Wayne and Mandy knew this was coming. All they could do was to hug them and say thank you. More words were not necessary.

The day after Christmas was play day for the ladies, all learning how to run a sewing machine. Kathy and Roy were out making arrangements for a wedding. Sam and George were enjoying smoking their pipes while rocking on the porch. Wayne came to join them and asked them a personal question. "Now that you are both retiring, I am willing to help support you. So fess up your finances and your needs. Sam answered, "both George and I were successful ranchers and we were both able to put money aside for this day. Now that the ranches are sold and or given as inheritance, we are financially secure."

George got more specific. "We both have brand new homes with all modern conveniences. A barn with three horses, one buggy, a chicken coop, and an enclosed garden. We also have $50000 invested at a special interest rate of 3%, which gives us $1500 per year. More than enough to live comfortably. Plus, we both intend to work part time for you in this harvesting venture."

"Not to worry son, we both have what we want, to keep busy and spend quality time with you and Mandy, and maybe grandchildren, heh."

Wayne closed by saying, "Great, and if in need, we all have each other."

After Christmas, the guests spent three days visiting. The first tour was Mandy's school. This was an open house and each area of the school had a tour guide. This was a perfect way for the in-laws to get exposed to a modern school. It was a two year program at a cost of $70 a month to include room, board, books and tuition. Wayne admitted that he had taken the ultimate degree for granted till he saw Mandy studying, and now seeing the school in real life.

The second trip was the tour of the city on the horse drawn rail cars. They had lunch at the same piano bar, followed by shopping at the large department stores. The ladies went overboard in the kitchen department. They bought small new kitchen utensils that they didn't know existed. In addition, they bought new thicker metal pots and pans, and some porcelain eating plates. Of course, they landed in the fabric and dress department, and loaded up on more of those items. It was a good thing that the men didn't need anything, since it took all arms to carry the ladies purchases. Upon getting back on the rail car, Sam said to George, "it's a good thing that we'll be living in Silver Circle." George answered, "I suspect that Sally will find a way to come shopping in Denver again, now that she's seen the department stores."

The last day was the tour at Winslow Agricultural. The family was greeted by Steve himself. Being the holidays when the store was quiet, Steve volunteered to give the tour. Everyone was escorted to the warehouse to view the implements that Wayne had ordered. Steve went from one implement to another explaining what each tool did and how it worked. The men were smiles from ear to ear. The ladies were surprisingly interested in the agricultural advances, and asked Steve more questions than the men did.

Before leaving, Wayne asked Steve if he knew where he could get a temporary job to do yearly maintenance on these implements. "Yes, you are in luck. I have an elderly gentleman who spends January in southern Texas. He returns Feb 1st to do the yearly maintenance on his equipment. It's a one month job and it pays $30 and room and board for the month." "I'll take the job and I'll do it free of charge, as well as living in my home. On second thought, I'll accept lunch as full pay. I want to learn as much as I can about these implements and how to service them."

"You've got the job, be here on Feb. 1st to meet Clyde King."

The next day, the Wilsons and Swansons were thinking of getting their tickets back to Silver Circle when Roy and Kathy arrived with an announcement. "We have Roy's parents, his brother and the six of you, so we would like to invite everyone to our wedding. It will be held in two days at the Episcopalian church, and we are having a reception at Bessie's diner paid by Roy's parents."

To everone's surprise, Roy's parents lived in Pueblo, only 40 miles by train. Mandy said, "looks like we'll see Roy and Kathy again in the future. The next day, everyone got ready for the wedding. They met Roy's parents, and the ladies were able to find something to wear.

The wedding was held without fanfare. The diner had prepared a special table away from the other guests, and at 3PM a meal of roast pork was served. After the meal, one wedding present was presented to the newly weds. A gift card was given which read:

We decided to put our money in the same pot, but could not decide what to get you, so we are giving you the one gift that all newlyweds need, especially when you are still in school, have new household expenses without income. MONEY." Kathy opens the envelope to find a bank draft for $700. "Good luck, from Wayne, Mandy, George, Sally, Sam and Cora. Roy's parents and brother."

The newlyweds went to Pueblo to visit Roy's old friends and other family members. When they returned to Denver, the Swansons and Wilsons had already returned to Silver Circle. They spent one day moving Roy out of the rooming house. They took two rooms upstairs, one was a study and sitting room, and the other was their bedroom.

While the moving in was under way, Wayne and Mandy were enjoying a beautiful day, drinking lemonade and sitting on the porch rockers. Suddenly, they both hear and spot a rider arriving at a rather fast trot. The rider steps down and walks up to the porch and says, "good day Ma'am and deputy Swanson. I'm the new deputy, Ted Kittridge. Captain Ennis has sent me to ask you to immediately come to the office. It's an emergency sir!"

Wayne saddled Brownie and within minutes, was on the road to the office. Upon arrival, Captain Ennis was waiting in the outer office. He greeted Wayne with a hand shake and invited him to his office. Wayne walked in and handed his marshal badge to the captain. "Keep it, you'll need it on this caper." "Just to let you know, this is my last job, since I've made a commitment effective February 1st."

"I reluctantly accept your resignation, but I understand. Now this last assignment will likely require a serious shootout with many gunfighters. I need your skills with a handgun in a gunfight, your precognition skills in warding off an ambush, and your skills in reading people. Most important, I need someone with sand, one who can make something happen no matter what it takes."

"Tell me more, captain, you've got my undivided attention."

***

CHAPTER 15
The Last Job

"We need to get ten of our innocent girls back alive, before they're addicted to opium and put to work in a whore house. Plus one of the ten is one of our own marshals. Fort Collins has a state representative to the legislature that is pushing for property tax reforms, and has the ranchers riled up. He has been receiving death threats."

"The governor has ordered our service to provide a security detail to escort the representative, his wife and daughter. The daughter is college student and is a bit wild. We have assigned the only female marshal in our unit, Martha Lewis, as the daughter's personal armed bodyguard."

"New Years Eve, the daughter and Martha went to a big dance. On a short walk home, they both disappeared. We have spent all of yesterday shaking down every informant that has ever worked for the law. We have found out this information:

1. We have a kidnaping ring operation in Fort Collins.

2. There have been six cases reported to the local sheriff in the past two days. Two more last night makes eight.

3. The word is that they use a carriage when they have ten women. Assuming they secure two more today, they will be traveling in the AM.

4. It is believed that they travel with four armed men, and they use a carriage to transport their package.

5. It is likely that several informants are correct when they all believe they use an old abandoned stagecoach trail east of the RR to get to Cheyenne.

6. Since this is a 50 mile trip, they will have to stop overnight to feed the hostages and change horses.

7. Eventually, these ten ladies will be delivered to a distributor who is probably the gang's leader. He then distributes them to whore houses who pay the collection fee."

"Wow, how do you get this kind of crucial intelligence?" "These kidnappers drink too much.

and they talk too much. When we shake down informants, we take every tid-bit of information, and then put them all together. That's how I prepared the scenario for you."

"Ok, what do you want from me?" "I want you to locate the stagecoach trail, spot the carriage, follow it to their overnight stop and follow them to the delivery location. Then, I want you to rescue the ladies and bring all these monsters to justice, dead or alive. Presumably some of these outlaws have a price on their heads." "Not important, what is crucial is to rescue these innocent gals. I'll take this job, and I'll resolve this mess."

On his way home, he figured how this caper would come about. He had to go home and load his food and supplies on his pack horse. He surmised that he had to get on the trail today. He had to find the old stagecoach trail today, before the carriage appeared tomorrow.

As he was getting ready, he said to Mandy, "this is my last job for the marshal service. I have a job for the remainder of the winter working at servicing implements, and I'll be home every night." "Mandy said, "I'm due for my monthly in three days. If I'm pregnant, you'll find out on your return." "I'll probably be gone for two weeks, and if you're not pregnant, we'll work on it some more, heh." They kissed and Wayne was off, heading for the RR yard.

Wayne used his life long pass and boarded the train, with his two horses in the stock car. It was a short two hour ride to Fort Collins, and Wayne was on his horse and out on the eastern plains by noon.

Wayne was traveling east-northeast at a slow trot. He was looking for an abandoned stagecoach road in the high plains' grasses. It was crucial that he not miss it, because he would end up wandering for days, and miss the hostage carriage. After two hours, Wayne stopped to water the horses at a nearby stream. After he resumed his travels, he suddenly fell into an area void of vegetation and suddenly recognized wheel marks in the middle of nowhere. He had found the carriage route.

Wayne got out of the road and traveled some 30 feet next to the road, always keeping eye on the road. He was looking for a hidden spot where he could watch the road. He finally saw a clump of cottonwood trees which usually means water. He rode to the spot. It was 600 yards from the road, slightly elevated, with a grassy area hidden behind the trees for the horses to graze and drink, out of view.

Wayne set up camp and dug a fire pit. He started a fire to cook a hot meal. This would be the last hot meal until the carriage appeared. He could not risk the smell of a wood fire/smoke to alert the kidnappers of his whereabouts.

Wayne had time to eat a beef stew dinner with crackers, coffee and a side of bacon. After dinner, he boiled several pots of water and made enough coffee to last at least three days. Wayne liked cold coffee and he had a stream to keep his coffee cold during dry cold camps.

The next morning, Wayne had the leftover bacon and beef stew with cold coffee. He then set his telescope next to a large tree, and sat down in front of the tree for camouflage. He had his manual on growing and harvesting hay/oats in Colorado. He started to read and did so all day as no carriage appeared. By dusk, he knew that the carriage would not be traveling in the night without moonlight. This road was so well overgrown that any night time traveling would veer the carriage off the road. He also realized that if the carriage took off at dawn in Fort Collins that it would be no earlier than 10AM before they would arrive at this location. After it got real dark, Wayne made a small fire in the fire pit, just enough to cook a hot meal of beans, home fries, and hot coffee.

The next morning, Wayne had a cold breakfast. He passed the time by writing down some important facts regarding growing crops that he learned in the early chapters.

1. Choose the soil that is best for growing hay and oats. In western Colorado, that is usually 70% loam and 30% sand. Avoid rocky spots that ruins equipment.
2. Bottom land is ideal compared to dry high plains prairies.
3. Build irrigation ditches for watering and flooding large areas during extended heat and or droughts.
4. The grazing lands need mineral and nitrogen supplementation. After a hundred years of grazing, the soil needs phosphate to yield a productive crop in uncultivated prairies.
5. Composted horse manure is a great source of nitrogen in cultivated acres.

Suddenly, Wayne heard hoof beats. Yet he couldn't see the carriage above the tall grasses until he looked through his telescope. He finally had enough visibility. The carriage's front seat had a driver with a second man carrying a shotgun. Behind the carriage were two well armed men on horses. At the slow rate they were traveling, it was clear that they had an overnight waylaying station to provide housing and meals for the four men and ten hostages. It also would provide for a change of four fresh horses for tomorrow's trip to the receiving station.

Wayne closed camp, saddled the horses, loaded his supplies and started trailing the carriage. He planned to trail two miles behind the carriage and stay in the tall grass next to the road. This would avoid a dust cloud. He postulated that the two men in the driver's seat would be looking ahead, and the two men on horseback would be looking east and west of the road. No one would spend the energy to look at their back trail, and if they did they would have trouble to quickly spot a man on a horse in the tall grasses. The visibility at two miles was adequate to keep track of a carriage, but poor to identify a man on horseback.

Wayne followed all day at a slow trot and ate his lunch of beef jerky while on horseback. For Wayne to be at a slow trot, the kidnappers had to push their two teams hard. By the time they would get to their overnight stop, these four horses would be dangerously spent.

By late afternoon, the carriage was seen turning west over an access road to the forest tree line. Wayne cautiously advanced and saw an old log cabin with a barn. This would be the overnight housing with food, water and the use of the overdue privy.

Wayne hoped that the ladies would not be abused during the night. Yet he knew that it was wishful thinking. These heartless men would rape as many as they selected, and there was nothing Wayne could do. He had to remain undetected till this underground destination was found in the Cheyenne area.

Wayne set back to be out of the cabin's view and set a cold camp. As predicted, the carriage appeared on the access road at dawn. Wayne was saddled and ready to ride. By noon, some of Cheyenne's outlying buildings were seen. The carriage turned west and finally stopped at an apparent warehouse type building. The carriage drove directly into the building and the large hinged doors closed.

Wayne knew that the time to hit them was now. The kidnappers would be tired after the long trip. The ladies would be lined up to go to the privy, some men would be meeting with the leader in his office, and some men would be standing watch over the captors.

Wayne quickly rode to within 100 yards of the warehouse. He added his second loaded colt to the left side of his belt. He then snuck up to the warehouse. He looked inside the window and saw, on the left, two men standing guard over the women sitting on the floor. He also saw the office on the right that was full of men talking. Wayne then ran quietly to the rear of the building. He silently approached a guard watching the ladies enter the privy. Wayne smashed the butt of his shotgun in the back of the man's head. He crumbled to the ground, and Wayne knew he was dead.

Wayne quickly returned to the front of the warehouse. The front door was not locked. He stepped inside, looked at the two guards and said, "Hey, you idiots," as one man reeled back a bull whip and the other turned to draw his pistol. Wayne did not hesitate, he pulled both triggers of #3 buckshot, and both men went flying backwards. He immediately turned around and saw men coming out of the office door with their pistols drawn. Wayne knew this would be a shootout till they were all dead or Wayne was dead. Wayne's colt started firing and men were dropping. Wayne had to access his second colt since his first one was out of ammo. By the time the shooting ceased, Wayne was still in a slow motion trance. Suddenly, he felt a soft hand on his shoulder, and said, "Martha Lewis I presume." "Yes, and it's over deputy Swanson."

Wayne stepped over to the ladies, all laying flat on the floor. Several were crying and some had wet themselves. Wayne said, "you are safe now, and I will keep you safe till I get you back home."

"Now this is my plan to get you home. We'll spend the night in this warehouse. The horses will be fed and watered, to prepare them for tomorrow's trip. There is a cook stove, plenty of food and water for everyone. Each of you will have a mattress and blanket to sleep on tonight."

Martha Lewis interjected, "what about taking the train back to Fort Collins?" "No, not wise.

I expect that the receiving leader would have sent an arrival telegram to the Fort Collins leader. Without this telegram, I suspect they are assuming we would be on the train. That would mean the Fort Collins leader would be sending men to reclaim his captives. That would lead to a shootout and the likelihood that some of you would be killed."

"To use the same abandoned stagecoach trail you came up on would also be a bad choice. I'm sure that they would ambush us before we got to Fort Collins. My plan is to leave before dawn, and travel on the main well used road to home. We'll trail the relief two horse pairs, and change teams at the noon break. With stopping every two hours to water and feed the horses, we'll make it home tonight."

Wayne heard a knock at the entrance door. It was the neighbor who came to check why he had heard the gunshots. After an explanation was given, he was asked to get the sheriff and the undertaker. While he was gone, Wayne went to check on the bodies. He was scavenging the bodies' pockets for money to pay the undertaker. Suddenly one presumed dead came alive. Wayne said, "son, you're dying with that chest wound, you should consider doing one last good dead before you meet your maker. Give me the name of your nine partners, yourself and the Fort Collins ring organizer. The man did not hesitate and rattled everyone's name, and included the ring organizer, a Fort Collins lawyer by the name of Craven Samuelson.

After this man died, Wayne collected $189 from the bodies. He then checked the office desk. In a drawer was a metal box that contained $2000 in cash—presumed pay for the outlaws. He wasn't sure what he would do with this money. For now, he put it in his money belt.

The sheriff arrived with three deputies. Wayne introduced himself as Deputy Marshall Wayne Swanson. He then gave the sheriff a detailed history of the kidnaping, the trip, and finally the shootout. The sheriff was shocked beyond belief and said, "you mean to tell me that you put all ten men down by yourself." "Yes sir, I did." Martha adds, "and the ten of us witnessed the shootout, and it's just as Wayne said."

To clean up the mess, the undertaker picked up the bodies and stacked all ten in a large utility wagon. Wayne gave him the $189 to cover the cost of a mass burial. Wayne added $30 of his own money to add a monument stone that would read, "here lie the ten kidnappers of 1882." The undertaker added that the cemetery office would keep the outlaws ten names in perpetuity.

The sheriff was so pleased to see an end to this ring that he offered his three deputies to stand guard tonight, and escort the carriage tomorrow, while trailing on their own horses. The deputies would return the next day by train. The sheriff also said he would send a telegram to the Wyoming and Colorado central bureaus, to see if any of these ten names were associated with a bounty. He would then arrange for vouchers to be transferred to Captain Ennis in Denver. He would also send a telegram to Sheriff Logan informing him that the captives would return to Fort Collins by tomorrow evening.

After dinner, a fire was started in the heating stove to take the chill out of the warehouse. Two of the captives came to talk with Wayne. "Are you Mandy Swanson's husband?" "Yes ma'am." "Well we're both juniors in the same school and we both know Mandy very well. Thank you for your courageous work, we will never forget what you did for us." "You're welcome."

The next morning, after everyone had been to the privy and had breakfast, the carriage was made ready. Martha was sitting next to Wayne with a shotgun loaded with 00 buckshot. Brownie and Blackie were both trailing the carriage, and the three deputies were behind the trailing horses. It had rained a bit during the night, just enough to keep the dust down but not enough to make mud. The hard packed road was perfect for traveling.

The caravan stopped every two hours to water the horses. A full stop and camp was set up at noon. The horses were rope tethered next to a stream and allowed to crop some lush grass for an hour. During that hour, a fire was started and all of Wayne's food was cooked to feed the fourteen adults. The coffee pot was refilled several times and enjoyed by all. After everyone had been to the bushes, the caravan resumed.

The second half of the trip was also uneventful. As the ladies saw the city outskirts, the mood improved considerably. Upon arrival at Sheriff's Logan office, the ladies were met by lovers, friends and families. The tears of joy were plentiful, suddenly, Sheriff Logan yells out, "ladies and gentlemen, this rescue was made possible by one man, Deputy Marshal Wayne Swanson, keep this name, you'll hear it again."

Wayne had to acknowledge the many hand shakes, hugs and thank yous.

At the end of the accolades, Wayne went straight to the RR depot. He used his lifetime pass and paid for his two horses in the stock car. He arrived in Denver two hours later, and headed to a final business meeting with Captain Ennis. The captain started, "Thank you so much for putting an end to this evil ring, and saving all the captives. I've been receiving Western Union vouchers all day. They total an amazing amount of $10,000. I suspect that it will top and close your benefactor account, heh." "Yes, that will make it high enough to distribute the yearly interest to help people back home. Hopefully, the principal amount will stay constant."

The next item was that lawyer, Craven Samuelson, the ring's leader. Captain Ennis said, "we all know this sleaze-ball, we'll pick him up in Fort Collins. The prosecutor will finally have proof to put him away. You and Martha may need to testify, since you both witnessed the dying man implicate and name this man as the ring leader." "Actually, all ten ladies heard the dying man's last words. If you still need me, I'll return for the trial."

"Well Wayne, that's the end of your crusade and your involvement with the marshal service." "It's been a pleasure," as Wayne hands him his badge. "No Wayne, keep it. You are officially on an indefinite leave of absence. Who knows what the future may bring. You may need it again, I hope, heh."

As Wayne stepped up to his horse and started riding for home, he started feeling like the Cowboy who had just hung up his guns and was riding away into the sunset. More realistically, he was now beginning a new life as a husband, rancher, and a commercial hay and grain grower.

***

When Wayne arrived home, everyone was still in school. He went to the barn, unsaddled the horses, brushed them down, mucked their stalls, added hay and oats and watered them. Some of the tack needed repairs, and so he used his work bench and did the repairs.

As he was walking to the house, the buggy arrived with Mandy, Roy and Kathy. Mandy jumped into his arms, passionately kissed, and said, "welcome home, I knew you would make it back to me after your crusade. We are not pregnant but according to my book, I'm fertile this week." "Well, let's see what we can do about that, heh."

Both couples socialized and caught up with news. Eventually, the pork roast was reheated and fresh vegetables were added. Dinner was a great event, especially when one is home and with loved ones. After dinner, Wayne explained in greater details, what he would be doing one week from today.

"In preparation, this week I will be studying the manual on growing hay and oats, as well as studying the operators manuals of some 24 implements I've purchased. Now I haven't been in school for years, but I want this week to be as regimented as possible. I plan to start studying as soon as you leave for school, and study all day till you return. In the evening, I will continue my studies, to accompany you with yours. Our bedroom will guarantee our private time."

That night, Mandy and Wayne were able to release their pent up passions and sexual urges. Once was not enough, but eventually they fell asleep, completely content. Wayne was up before dawn, started the cook stove and prepared a batter for pancakes. Adding a cast iron griddle to the cook stove, Wayne started cooking. He set the table with butter, molasses and raspberry preserves. The coffee and tea was ready. Eventually, the three sleepy heads showed up, with a half hour before their buggy arrived, they all enjoyed Wayne's pancakes.

Wayne started his studies by starting the chapter on cultivation. He reviewed the operator's manual on the plow, disc harrow and finish harrow. Then he read the method of plowing with one team and using another team to do disc and finish harrows. With good strong draft horses, you would get four hours with each team, or two teams to cultivate all day. On a large commercial operation, four teams would be strongly recommended. Along with the cultivation, manure would be spread on the prepared site before the last finishing harrows. The same ratio was followed, if using two teams, use one manure spreader. If using four teams, then two spreaders would be needed to keep up with the cultivation.

Wayne was totally absorbed and reread this chapter twice. He started to make permanent practical work plans. He would explain and discuss these plans with Mandy, just to keep her following Wayne's newly acquired knowledge.

The remainder of the week was a continuation of the first day. The second day covered phosphate supplementation, broadcast and row planting of hay and oats. It also included a monthly time frame for each planting. The third day started the harvesting. It included the hay cutter, teddering, and windrow raking. The equipment included a side sickle cutter, a tedder and a side rake. The chapter concentrated on drying the hay before raking.

The fourth day concentrated on gathering the dry hay. The equipment included the hay loader and the hay wagons. The important thing was the rotation of several wagons and men to keep bringing loaded wagons to the baler. The fifth day was the use of the one horse baler and the several men needed to keep baling without interruptions—to maintain 1000 pounds of baled hay per hour, or 20 fifty pound bales.

The sixth day was the storage of the bales, protected against rain and wind, and ground mildew. This was the basis of a commercial operation. Without bales to store and transfer to customers and wholesalers, the commercial industry would not exist with loose hay.

The seventh and last day involved cutting oats, threshing, fanning and bagging oats for feed. It involved a reaper, a thresher and a fanning mill. It also included baling the stray for retailing and wholesaling.

Wayne used the eighth day to review the past week with Mandy. She was very attentive and absorbed the information. Wayne reviewed the operation of each implement and discussed the theoretical and practical implications of each subject. By the end of the day, and the entire week, Wayne was ready for his hands on exposure. Monday morning, February 1st, Wayne would meet Clyde King at the Winslow store, and start on his much anticipated month's pay-free endeavor.

***

CHAPTER 16

The Harvest

Wayne arrived at Winslow Agricultural on February 1st by 7AM to meet with Clyde King. He was early, but took this opportunity to have coffee and talk with Steve. Steve said, "I have made up a list of parts that you should have as spares for all of your 24 implements. I'm also preparing a list of accessory tools that are necessary to support such a commercial enterprise. I haven't prepared the order yet, I'll wait till you bring me your list of parts and accessories. Clyde will tell you what you need." "Better still, place the order to cover your lists, and I'll give you my list later. I doubt I'll have many items to add."

Shortly thereafter, an elderly gentleman showed up and shook Steve's hand. "So, I'm here to pick up my order of parts and meet this young man who has volunteered to help me perform my yearly implement maintenance." Introductions were made. "Why would you be willing to spend weeks working for lunch and end up one greasy mess going home at night?" "Because Steve tells me that you're a commercial hay and oats grower. That's also what I'm planning. So I need to see what maintenance is customary. The best way is to do it myself. Plus, any experience regarding growing tips would be greatly appreciated. In return, I'll work hard and cut down your work load."

"Wow, something tells me that I'm going to benefit from your help more than you're going to learn from me." Steve adds, "I don't think so."

"Well, if you're ready to work follow me to my farm. It's only three miles from here and I'll start greasing you up, heh." Clyde and Wayne loaded the replacement parts into the small utility wagon, and off they went. Wayne left Brownie to follow, and joined Clyde on the wagon seat.

The first thing Wayne noticed was that all the implements were under cover. Clyde said, "these implements are too expensive to have rust ruin expensive parts prematurely." "Do you bring these implements inside every night?" "No, it's too complicated to park them inside with horses. They stay outside from spring to late fall." "I'm currently building a long shed with 24 stalls. Each stall is a pull through and I'm planning to place all implements under a roof nightly." "Well that's the best way, good for you."

"Ok, lets start with the winnowing or side rake. The three systems to cover is the gear oil, greasing and replacing raking teeth. The large front wheels activate the central gears that rotate the rake. You lift this cover and add 90 wt. oil to the fill line. Then apply grease to the grease holes and push it in with your finger till it oozes out of the grease hole.

The axles need a lot of grease which requires you to remove the wheels. Remember, grease is cheap compared to worn out parts."

"The last job is to change all broken or lost teeth." The rake needed six teeth replaced. "Why do teeth break?" "It usually is cause by wear and metal fatigue. However if the rake is set too low to the ground, there is too much tension and this promotes breakage. The higher the teeth, the less the wear factor, but too high will leave hay on the ground. The only other adjustment is the angle of the teeth. A narrow angle will make a tight row that is well picked up by the loader. If the hay is not quite dry, use a wide angle. The rake will make wider rows and the hay is more fluffed up to promote drying. But the loader will leave more loose hay on the ground." "It appears that this is a reliable tool, and the only spare parts needed are teeth?" "Yes."

Moving on to the mower. "This is the current model, it has a side sickle with a cutter bar made of V-shaped knives that oscillate between fingers. The first thing I do is to oil all the exposed steel gears, check all belts, refill oil and grease holes, and fill oil cups that add oil by gravity. Most of the work on the cutter is the cutting bar. Remove the cutter bar and check all the knives. Tighten the loose ones by hammering the rivets, change any broken knife and then use this special jig to manually operate a grinding stone. The sharper the knives, the better the clean cut. Now the big thing is that you do the same with the other two cutting bars. Also don't forget to check for loose fingers, which will fail to cut the hay or break knives." "So the spare parts are: extra belts, knives, rivets, a jig/grinding wheel, and two extra cutting bars." "Yes, and add this connecting rod, it connects the wheel gears to the actual mower. It's under a lot of tension and tends to break. I had the local smithy make me one and it seems to be stronger and more durable."

"Well. It's lunch time. Let's go see what the Missus has prepared for lunch." "So you are the legendary bounty hunter/deputy marshal?" "Well, that is me, Ma'am, but I'm not legendary." "The Denver gazette doesn't agree with you." "Well dear, I always said that you can't believe everything you read, heh. So what's for lunch?" "Hot ground chuck sandwich with gravy, boiled cabbage and coffee."

During lunch Clyde asked, "Steve tells me you have placed a large order of implements. Can you give me a list, so we can cover all of them in the next weeks." "Certainly, In Steve's warehouse, I have: the double items: two way plow, manure spreader, hay mower, and the three hay wagons. The single items include: disc harrow, finish harrow, broadcast and row seeder, roller, phosphate spreader, side rake, dump rake, hay tedder, hay loader, one horse baler, reaper, thresher, fanning mill, small and large utility wagons."

"Wow, what a nice selection, and a complete one for a commercial grower. How many acres will you have?" "The ranch is eight sections. Five sections are high prairies with limited water but adequate for cattle. I will fence off three sections with two high flow springs and ponds and the lower end of a stream. The three sections(1920 acres) are all bottom land with rich soil. Most of these two thousand acres are flat and have very few boulders. The soil is free of rocks."

"Your choice of double implements is well chosen. Someone is giving you good advice. When it's cultivating time, plowing is slow and manure spreading is even slower because of manually loading the spreader. With two teams, you can probably plow three acres per day since you have a two way plow. With two plows, you need two more double teams. Now you're talking six acres per day. To keep up with manure, you need two teams of two or three men. When it's time to cut the hay, the mowing is productive only with two mowing teams. Also remember, most teams need to be replaced after five hours–depending on the work load on the horses. So you probably need eight teams of draft horses and eight teams of full size gelding horses to handle a commercial operation."

"With 2000 acres of tillable land, you'll probably be plowing and cultivating from April to November for the next five years. That's why you need so many draft and gelding horses. The heavy work goes to the draft horses, and the medium work and loads will go to the geldings. Also, it takes quite a few men since every implement has a seat for a driver to control the work horses. Well, enough talk, let's get back to work."

The first implement was the baler. "First, remove the cowl over the intake teeth. We need to tighten, replace and repair bent teeth. Afterwards, we remove the two apposing cutting knives. We need to sharpen these two knives on the smooth grinding wheel. Along with greasing the holes, we'll be at it all afternoon. The spare parts only include the intake teeth. The accessories include baler twine for 50 lb. bales and baling wire for 75 lb. bales. You'll also need at least ten bale hooks for handling bales. Before I forget, you need a box of caps that cover the oil and grease holes—they frequently get loose and fall out."

The next morning, we serviced the plow, disc and finish harrow. The plow needed some axle greasing and oiling of open gears. The disc harrows needed axle grease to cover each disc. The finish harrow needed tightening of the spikes. The only spare parts for these three implements were the spikes and their anchors.

Our lunch included cold roast pork sandwiches and coffee. During lunch Clyde brought up the subject of fertilization. "As you know, grazed land is deficient of phosphorous. Fortunately, we have today, commercially available phosphate delivered in 50 pound bags. Since you have a phosphate spreader, apply a light coating of phosphate to as many acres you have time and money to cover. You'll find that the phosphate treated pastures will provide twice to three times the hay. Also, save the composted horse manure for cultivated fields and I would even add phosphate to cultivated fields."

"This year, make an arrangement with your neighboring cattle ranchers. They all have old composted horse manure piles that you can get at a very reasonable price, or barter with them for hay. Remember that your manure pile will quickly disappear. A good business man plans ahead. Well, let's get back to work. This afternoon we tackle the hay loader."

"The hay loader is a finicky implement. There are many moving parts and break downs are frequent. We start by tightening every pickup tooth anchor, replace broken or missing teeth, and straighten the ones we can save." Clyde left

Wayne to do this job as he started to grease the many fittings. "Next part is replacing broken wooden sliders and separators. This job is a pain when you're alone, so let's share this job."

After and hour to replace the broken pieces, Clyde handed Wayne a paint brush and they both painted oil over the flat chains and exposed gears. Clyde then showed Wayne how to replace a broken flat chain with a repair link. After four hours of work, Clyde said, "last year, it took me almost two days to service this hay loader. This year, we did it in an afternoon and one tenth of the work." "So the spare parts include pickup teeth and anchors, wooden slides and separators, short chain sections and repair links?" "Yes, and before we forget, It's time to add a dozen two and three tine hay forks and six manure pitch forks." "Well it's 4:30 and time to quit. See you in the morning."

"For the third day we'll tackle the tedder and hay wagons in the morning, and save the manure spreader for the afternoon. Starting with the tedder, lost teeth had to be replaced. This is a fast moving machine that fluffs up the hay to promote drying. Don't set it too low or it will throw dirt at you. If it's set too high, it skims over the hay without picking it up." After an hour of changing pickup teeth, tightening loose bolts, and refilling the grease and oil holes, Wayne said, "the spare parts are the teeth and their anchors plus whatever belts are used."

The hay wagons were simple. The axles needed greasing with axle grease and the retaining walls needed repairs for broken sections. Then lunch arrived. The Missus provided a hot meatloaf with mashed potatoes and coffee. The lunch conversation covered cultivating and planting schedules.

Clyde described his monthly schedule, "I start plowing as soon as I can in the spring. As long as the frost is out of the ground and the ground has dried, I plow. The cultivation with both harrows has to be done by May 15, when I plant the hay seed. The county agricultural agent has checked out my soil, and with other variables, he has recommended a mixture of hay seeds. My mixture is comprised of perennial rye grass, fescue, bromegrass and timothy. Timothy is the major seed. I seed the mixture at 25 pounds per acre. The mixture guarantees a crop, since different grasses don't do well certain years. Use your county agent, he'll guide you in the proper seed mixture."

"Now after the hay is seeded and rolled, I use a finish harrow over last year's oat crop and seed it with hay. After all the hay is seeded, I cultivate till July 1st. I then plant a crop of fall oats. That finishes the seeding season. If I have time before the hay harvest, I will do some cultivating for next years crops."

"How do you know when the hay is ready?" "The prairie lands have hay that is first to harvest. When the hay has produced a good seed, and the hay begins to change to a light color, I start mowing. Generally, I harvest all the prairie acreage, then I start harvesting the cultivated acreage. I am usually done with hay harvesting by the time the oats is ready for harvest."

"I forgot to ask you yesterday, but do you spread some phosphate every year?" "Yes, the money spent on phosphate is tripled in hay production. Plus, every year, the manufacturers are adding new minerals which increases the value of the phosphate. My agricultural agent encourages me to buy composted manure from the neighbors for the cultivated land, and I buy three tons of phosphate each year. I usually spread my phosphate by May 1st.

"What do you do for labor?" "There is two ways to hire help. Some farmers have a year round team, others hire seasonal help. I only hire seasonal help from April to October. I pay $1.25 per day with room and board. I hire a team for cultivation, and another team for harvesting. Some workers overlap and several return from year to year. I have a solid source of applicants since I'm so close to Denver. As a new grower in a ranching community, you may have to go with year round help." "In that case, what do the men do during winter?" "Cultivate, cultivate, cultivate and cultivate. You have 2000 acres that need to be turned over. They can cultivate till snow and frost closes you down. Then you repair buildings, implements and harnesses. Plus you need men to feed hay to your herd. As last resort, haul and spread composted manure till the frost comes. There is always something that needs to be done."

After lunch, the manure spreader was tackled. To my surprise, the manure had been scraped off and all the chains had been oiled to prevent rust. All we did was push grease in the holes and added crude oil to the exposed gears. There was one floor webbing that was broken and was replaced. The spare parts were sections of flat chains and mending links.

"This is the only implement that needs work before the winter. This is one of those winter jobs. After the scraping, I sparingly apply crude oil with a brush to all the chains. This is a two day job per man."

"The last implement today is the oat's reaper. This equipment had many grease holes, but the cutting knives was the most work. The cutter blade was removed, knives were replaced and all the knives were sharpened on a jig with a hand powered rotary grinder, similar to the hay mower. We then will do the same to the other two spare bars." "So the spare parts includes sections of chains, belts, mending links, knives and rivets." "Yes."

The fourth day, was the last day. "Today we service the remainder of the implements. These include the dump rake, roller, seeder, phosphate spreader, thresher, and fanning mill. Most of these need greasing the axles and the grease holes, and refilling the oil cups. With very few repairs, we should be done by lunch time."

Lunch was a beef stew. After lunch, Wayne asked, "what did we not cover while servicing the implements?" "I saved this one for discussion. You may not have seen me, but on every implements, I checked the brake. Sometimes the tension had to be increased to get a good friction fit. This is the universal safety requirement I demand of all my workers–NEVER GET OFF YOUR SEAT WITHOUT APPLYING THE BRAKE. We are dealing with animals that can spook for very minor reasons. If you're working on the equipment and the unit takes off you will be injured or killed. That applied brake will save your life. Applying the brake includes all the hay and utility wagons."

"Well, I guess my services are no longer needed. What are you going to do with all the extra days on your hands?" "It's been a dry spring and I'm going to start cultivating. I have two men waiting to start hauling and spreading manure, and will be able to spread phosphate and get some extra acreage ready for seeding." "Could you use some help, in return for learning the process?" "Are you free and are you sure you want to work for no pay?' "Of course, when do we start?" "Tomorrow morning."

***

"The first thing you need to learn is the horse harnessing and hooking up to any implement. A nice team of golden Belgium draft horses was harnessed and a neck/breast collar attached by the hames to the extra large leather traces. The team was then backed up to the plow. The tongue was attached to the harness. A wiffle tree was attached to the axle and two single tree eveners attached to the chain tracers. Notice the tracers are wide leather straps to reach the rear legs, then the chains are attached to the eveners and the leather trace. The short chain tracers are more durable." "So why do we use both a tongue and tracers?" "The tongue is used to slow or stop a load when the horses stop, the tracers are used to pull the implement or load." "Oh, of course."

Clyde brought the team and plow to the beginning point. He dropped the right "standard" which holds the point and wing of the plow. A clean furrow was turned that was 6–8 inches deep and almost 16 inches wide. At the end of the acre, the "standard" was lifted, the team did a 360 degree turn and the left standard was dropped to add another furrow. The team knew that one horse was walking in the furrow, and the other was walking on unplowed land. The plow was adjusted as such. Upon returning, the horses switched the furrow or unplowed land, and the opposite "standard" was engaged.

After watching Clyde for three furrows, Wayne was handed the reins after Clyde applied the brake. He did alright, and upon returning for the second furrow, Clyde had a smile from ear to ear. The next two furrows saw Clyde laying on a bedroll taking a nap. Eventually, Clyde went to the barn. He showed up an hour later with a utility wagon loaded with a water tank to water the horses.

By lunch time, at least one and a half acres were plowed. With a cold roast beef sandwich and coffee, we headed to the barn. A second team of Percheron draft horses were harnessed and set aside. Then a team of Suffolk drafts were harnessed and hitched to the disc harrows. The other team was hitched to the plow and Clyde then showed Wayne how to engage the angled disks and start harrowing. He explained that the first harrowing was in line with the furrows, and the second would be crosswise. He explained to always stay on cultivated land by turning ahead of the ends, since the harrows didn't do well on unplowed land.

The afternoon was spent disc harrowing and plowing. By the end of the day we had three acres plowed with a double discing.

These two men, six draft horses and two geldings for the second harrowing, continued their daily routine for the next nine days. Clyde was proud to see thirty acres ready for the finish harrows and planting.

Wayne then offered his services for another week. This added another twenty acres and fifty acres provided half of Clyde's oats harvest.

"I will now hire a man and continue plowing. It is my goal to plant 100 acres of oats each year. The oats harvest is a nice cash crop, and there is always a market for oats and baled straw. In addition, it allows you to cultivate land while the hay is growing and maturing. Your goal with 2000 acres should be 200 acres cultivated each year. So that makes is a ten year project. That's a minimum goal, more is even better."

"Before I leave, would you give me some tips about harvesting hay." "Be glad to. Once the hay is mature, you'll do well with two mowers in operation. Water your teams every two hours, and change your teams half way through the day. Every lunch and evening, grease and oil the unit, and change the cutter bar with sharp knives. The second day continue mowing and add a team of gelding horses to the tedder. Start teddering as soon as the dew is burned off and continue till the entire first day cutting is done. Day three is the harvest day, a team of geldings will perform the side raking after the dew is gone, and another team will pull the loader and hay wagon."

"A single gelding can pull the dump rake. The dump rake is important. There are clumps of hay left by the side rake, loader and the wagons. It yields another 10% and this is a nice ladies job. Now every day the entire process continues, cutting, teddering, side raking, loading hay and finish raking with a dump rake. That way there is baling every day. Now do the math. How many men do you need at harvest time?"

"Two on the mowers, one on the tedder, one on the side rake, one on the hay loader and two in the hay wagon. One man transferring hay wagons from the field to the baler, four on the baler and two to stack bales in the storage shed. Wow that's fourteen men. However, I have six year round ranch cowboys that can help during the harvest, and that will save on seasonal workers." "You got it, and that's a great savings."

"Now, use your county agent, and take advantage of the man Steve Winthrop provides to new customers. Keep in touch with Steve, this industry is quickly modernizing. Don't hesitate to trade an implement for a new model. Keep your spare parts inventory updated. Talk to Steve about a very cheap insurance policy–any major implement failure will be replaced by train the same or next day, with a loner till the implement is repaired. You need this since you won't have neighbors in the same business. And last, you're the owner, but when a man is absent you are the automatic replacement. A working owner always helps the worker's morale, and is usually a successful business man. I've seen you work, and you've got a strong work ethic. You'll do well, thank you for your help, and good luck. "

Wayne left and stopped at the Winslow store. He compared his spare parts list with Steve and made an order for the extras. He then gave Steve his list of operational accessories. The list included: grease in five gallon tubs, 5 gallons each of 90 wt. and crude oil, tools to include wrenches, pliers, screw drivers, hack saw, hammers, vice with anvil, large smooth grinding wheel with foot activator, a wiffle tree for each implement, several single tree eveners, breast collars for the tracers, twine and wire for 50 and 75 pound bales, ten bale hooks, assorted bolts, nuts and washers, 10-two or three tine hay forks, six manure pitch forks, a dozen long handle round shovels and flat shovels, four pick axes, twine for the reaper bundler, three heavy duty wheelbarrows, stall mucking tools, and miscellaneous steel pails.

"So Steve, how much am I over the $3000 deposit I gave you?" "I don't know but this order will do it. I'll bill you eventually. Not to worry." So Wayne mentioned the fantastic three week he had while working with Clyde. After some more small talk, Wayne headed home feeling he was ready to delve into this new venture.

***

Wayne spent the next week packing all their belongings into RR crates, Mandy had chosen a few kitchen tools and utensils, had all her toys as a child, years of chosen book manuals, and clothes. It took two crates to pack her stuff. Wayne had his guns, ammo, trail cooking equipment, two panniers, and his clothes. He managed to fill half a crate and he knew that Mandy would find more stuff to fill that third crate.

"Well Mandy, we are approaching the end of our stay in Denver. Your Commencement Day is in a week. Do we invite our parents?" "Yes, and I agree that the Wilsons are like my mom and dad. Having them in the house, along with the Simms, will be a jovial time for all."

Mandy and Kathy spent the week cooking for the guests, and preparing for the graduation. They had practices to attend and Mandy had a speech to give as head of her class.

Mandy had writers cramps. She could not find a subject to present to her class, teachers and guests. Wayne came to her rescue, "tell your story how the school taught a progressive program that prepared you for the next decade into the 1900's. Let them know that you will be teaching in Colorado and will be bringing their progressive philosophy to a small community. You could get controversial and bring up the subject of pregnant students and teachers. As the head of your class, you might get away with it, but I don't know for sure. Your decision!"

The Simms, Swansons, and Wilsons arrived by train a few days before the graduation. One afternoon, the men were talking and rocking on the porch. George asked Wayne, "are you ready for such a big change in your life. To move beyond being a successful paladin to a rancher/commercial grower, requires a serious commitment!"

Wayne answered, I have had several years as a deputy sheriff and now a full year as a paladin bounty hunter. I have done my share of community service. Being a bounty hunter is a dangerous profession. You are going against monstrous outlaws who are wanted dead or alive. These outlaws will fight it out, since being arrested and brought to trial will mean that they will hang. It is only a matter of time, that all bounty hunters will get shot or killed. I cannot offer this life any longer to Mandy, it's time to settle down, change professions, and I'm looking forward to it. I have always given 100% to whatever I've done and I'll give the same dedication to being a husband, rancher and grower. Oh and by the way, I've heard all the jokes about becoming a sodbuster, farmer, and other demeaning names. I remind you that I'm stepping into the modern world of harvesting commercial crops.

Wayne's dad and Uncle George added some interesting news. "We have had a recent meeting of the Cattlemen's Association. The twenty ranchers are all pleased that you are starting to grow hay. They will gladly sell you their composted horse manure pile. Several are planning to expand their herd now that a local source of hay will be available."

Sam added, "George and I have been conducting screening interviews for farm workers. We have chosen 15 men that will be available, upon your arrival, for your individual interviews. We have two families of local homesteaders with cultivating and harvesting experience, but on a small scale. These are young men who are eager to work for gainful employment."

"Your implements have all arrived, and every piece has a fitted wiffle tree attached to the axle. We are now unloading the several crates of accessories you have sent." George added, "my old foreman, Brett Hanson has moved into the old Box B ranch house. He got married to a widow with three kids. He will be in control of all ranching duties, to free us three. We'll be busy getting the new business started."

"With the new cook shacks and cooks, the Box B bunkhouse will house the cow hands, and the Bar W bunkhouse will house the crop workers. And last, the price of hay in Pueblo just hit $40 per ton–that makes a 50 pound bale sell for $1 delivered."

"Well that is all good news. As soon as I arrive, I will be concentrating my efforts in selecting at least a dozen or more workers, fencing off the lower three sections(+-2000 acres) adjacent to the buildings, start plowing and cultivating, hauling manure and spreading phosphate. Once the fencing crew is done, they will start digging irrigation ditches. The three of us will be supervising all these activities at the same time."

***

The commencement exercise was impressive. Fifty seven students marched down the aisle, dressed in purple and gold gowns, with a strange head cap that had a flat top and a dangling gold tassel. The president gave a lengthy speech about changing teaching values. Mandy gave a riveting speech that covered Wayne's ideas. She added about her teaching in Silver Circle, and even broached the subject of pregnancy in school and on the job. This got her a rousing applause. Her last parting shot was how we were fortunate to be living in the changing times of the 1800's and early 1900's.

After the graduation, there was a gathering with a full dinner in the school cafeteria. After dinner, the school board president, mentioned that of the fifty seven graduates, thirty nine were staying in Colorado to teach.

Getting home after the ceremonies, Mandy and Kathy were showered in small gifts. The list included, a school bell, a clicker, an umbrella, a pocket watch with an alarm, a box of 100 #2 pencils, a rotary pencil sharpener, and several unpractical oddities that brought on many guffaws and smiles. It made for a great home reception party.

With all the guests back home, Wayne and Mandy finished packing. They used their life time RR passes and finally set out for Silver Circle. They arrived in Silver Circle and were greeted by Mayor Hawthorne, President Miller, Ed Sorenson, Sheriff Jim and deputies Oscar and Ray, and Bruce Hawkins. With welcoming hugs and hand shakes, Wayne and Mandy finally stepped onto Brownie and Blackie and headed home.

Riding in silence, they suddenly came to a rise in the road, over looking the access road to the original Bar W Ranch. They both sat on their horses in silence until Mandy spoke up, "what are we looking at, this place looks like a small village." Wayne started explaining, "the original ranch house is painted blue/grey and it has a new windmill. The two small homes next to the ranch house are our retired parent's homes. They share a new windmill. The houses are painted a blue/grey and the small barns/chicken coops are painted red. The bunkhouse has a new attached cook shack and is also painted blue/grey."

"All the out buildings are painted red. The original barn has been expanded to hold four times the number of horses. The expansion also includes a new wagon/carriage barn, ground floor hay storage and a general workshop. The long building has twenty five stalls for the new implements. That large warehouse type building is to store bales of hay and straw, as well as bags of oats."

After the visual overload, they rode directly to the main ranch house. The Swansons and

Wilsons rushed outside to greet them. "Wow, what a nice job building this village. We saw the new sign and brand over the access road gate, W–M Connected. As they were standing outside, Wayne said, "what is that sign over that door, Office?"

George said, "the builder had an idea of building a corner where an attendant can receive money from local ranchers who come to pick up hay, oats or straw. They entered the office, saw a sign that read 'ring bell for service,' and a long counter separated the attendant from the customer. The attendant's side could be accessed from the house or from lifting a section of the counter. In short, anyone in the house can service the counter by responding to the bell, without waiting all day for customers." Sam also added, "it will be the location for payday, and will become Wayne's private business office."

A hot lunch was already prepared, and the socialization continued through the meal. Cleaning the dishes revealed hot and cold running water. A coal burning boiler was added to a nearby shed. Mandy also found a water closet next to the master bedroom. After lunch, the RR freighters arrived with the three large crates. Everyone pitched in and the crates were quickly unloaded and packed away. Wayne's gun room was packed with extra pistols, 1873 rifles, and shotguns–enough to arm all the workers if the need ever arose. For those who wanted to experiment with long range shooting, there were several 1876 rifles and a Sharps with a 8X power Malcolm scope.

Finally, after a private dinner, Mandy and Wayne retired to their bedroom. Wayne reminded Manny, that they were alone in the house since they moved to Denver. That night, their love making was not only a release of passion, but a loud response at the peak of mutual release.

After several contacts, Mandy asked, "was I too loud when you know............." "It was not how loud you were, but the pitch of the squealing that probably broke some windows, heh."

The next morning after a replenishing breakfast, Sam had all fifteen applicants eating breakfast in the cook shack. He would then bring a batch to wait on the ranch house porch and Wayne would meet with each man individually, and then they would wait in the bunkhouse. The interviews were done by lunch. The applicants were given a lunch of beef stew, biscuits and coffee.

After lunch, Wayne, his dad and George, came to the bunkhouse for a meeting. "I like all of you and I've decided to hire ten seasonal and five permanent workers. The five year round workers are Charlie, Milt, Curt, Ben and Lyle. Charlie will be the livery man in charge of the horses and barn. The remaining four of you will be in charge of cultivation and seeding, as well as mowing and harvesting the hay and oats."

"The remaining ten will be the seasonal workers. I will guarantee you work till November 1st. What happens after that depends on many variables and we'll see what we need come winter. Now I need four of you to be the manure loaders and spreaders. Any volunteers?" Two men lift up their hands, Henry and Hank. Wayne adds, "every man gets special boots with rubber linings." Two more hands get up, Stan and Murdock. Wayne adds, "I consider this job similar to combat pay, I will give each man a bonus of $5 for each month you stay on the job." Hooray's and thank yous came back.

The six seasonals are Joe, Ray, Larry, Marcel, Pete and Eric. Your job is to fence, off the grazing land, the northern portion of my three sections. Afterwards, you will build the irrigation ditches for my three sections.

"Now let's talk about the rules of employment, benefits and expectations.

1. The day begins with breakfast at 6:30AM. Each morning at 7:30AM, I will hold a half hour meeting in the cook shack, to discuss issues and give daily assignments. I expect everyone heading to work by 8AM. The day finishes at 6PM with dinner.

2. The pay is $1.25 per day. Every man gets a paid day off every ten days. Extra days off are without pay.

3. Room and board is included.

4. Breakfast and dinner meals are at the cook shack. Lunch is in the field. The cook, with a chuck wagon, will bring out a cold lunch, a cold drink, and fresh water to refill your canteens.

5. The cook will prepare the meals, clean up the dishes and do the grocery shopping. He is an older man and has no other duties.

6. Every man is responsible to do his laundry. The only exception are the manure

workers, The livery man has agreed to do their laundry, and will do anyone's at a very reasonable rate. Talk to Charlie.

7. Each man is allotted four boxes of ammo per month–to maintain your shooting skills.

8. There is no alcohol on the job. The evenings are your personal time to do as you wish, including alcohol. If, in evenings, you go into town, you're still expected to be at work on time.

9. If you don't have a rifle, we will give you one. Although you may not use a rifle in the field, we want you all capable of using a rifle in this violent land.

10. Only two men can be off the same day. Schedule your days off with Mr. Wilson.

11. There are no days off during hay and oats harvesting.

12. My dad, Mr. Swanson will handle the payroll every two weeks, on Friday before dinner, and held at the office.

13. My dad, uncle an myself will supervise all jobs."

"Move in today, choose your bunk, and be here for dinner by 6PM if you want to eat. See you tomorrow morning at 7:30AM, and welcome to the W–M Connected Ranch."

The next morning, Wayne and Mandy were having their own breakfast. Mandy said, "Yesterday, when we arrived, Mr. Hawthorne asked me to meet today with Ed and the builder to order the remainder of the equipment, and perform the renovations to the school. Incidently, school begins May 15th." "Ok, I'll be supervising and teaching the two plow operators, see you at lunch then, as they kissed goodbye."

The morning meeting started at 7:30. "Mr. Swanson will be supervising the fencing operation, so meet with him at the barn.

Mr. Wilson will be supervising and assisting Milt to spread phosphate. Henry of the manure team, will be in charge since he has experience with harnessing and spreading manure, but for today they will work the fencing operation. I will supervise the three plow and harrowing men."

For your information, my dad and uncle speak for me. They have experience and are prepped by me for the jobs of the day. Don't be surprised if they jump in to help. I will help also if there is a need. Now let's get this system started.

***

Wayne took the cultivating team of Curt, Ben and Lyle to the barn. He and Charlie showed them how to harness the draft horse. Then they were showed how to hitch the team to the two way plow and explained how to use the safety brake. He showed them how to attach the tongue to the harnesses, and the traces from the breast/neck collars to the plow. The leather traces changed to chains once the rear legs were clear. The chains were attached to the single tree evener for each horse. Once in the field, Wayne lined up the team, dropped the right "standard" and plowed a perfect 6–8 inch deep furrow. At the end of the three acre plot, Wayne made the horse team turn 360 degrees and return to the existing furrow. He then dropped the left "standard" and created the second furrow to match the first. He noted that one horse was walking in the 16 inch furrow and the other was on unplowed land.

All three men were given the opportunity to take over, and try their turn under Wayne's supervision. Wayne then turned the reins to Curt, and took Ben to the barn to get the other plow. After Ben was set up at his own three acre plot, Lyle was brought to get his own team of draft horses and hitched them to the disc harrow.

Wayne told all three workers that they would work these teams till noon, then would exchange them for the other three teams of Belgiums, Percherons, and Suffolks. Every two hours, a wagon with a water tank would arrive to water the horses, and do some extra oiling and greasing. Also, lunch break would occur once the chuck-wagon arrived.

Meanwhile, George took Milt to the barn, showed him the method used to harness a team of gelding horses. He hitched it to the phosphate spreader. He also showed him how to hitch a wagon to a team of geldings and load it with a manageable load of bagged phosphate. They headed to the field, showed Milt how to open the delivery slide and to proceed to drop a light amount of phosphate. Milt could refill his spreader with the bags on site. When the wagon was empty, he would go to the barn to reload it and could water his horses at the same time. By 10 o'clock, Milt was working independently. George then hitched the water wagon and headed to the cultivators to water their horses, and perform whatever oiling and greasing needed.

Meanwhile, Sam took the six seasonal, and the four manure team workers to the barn. They hitched and loaded one wagon with fence posts, and the other with tools, barbed wire and the ten men. Sam knew that he would only have the manure team for one day. So, he explained to the men that the three section(2000 acres) crop area had to be fenced off from the northern five section(3200 acres) grazing area.

Sam took advantage of having the manure team for today. He set them up with the equipment and wire rollers. Their job was to remove the old fence that had separated the Box B Ranch from the Bar W Ranch. The four man team was perfect for the job. One man removed staples, two men rolled up the barbed wire, and one man pulled fence posts and loaded them on the wagon. The reusable fence posts, barbed wire, and staples were brought to the other fencing team to reuse.

The fencing team was broken up in a team of two and a team of four men. The four men were digging holes, with round shovels and post hole diggers, dropping fence posts, pounding them in and burying them. The two man team was laying wire, stapling, and tightening the wires. At 10 o'clock, George arrived to water the horses. By noon, Sam computed the lineal feet fenced in four hours. He figured this team would take at least three weeks to complete this several mile fencing project, before working on irrigation ditches.

By lunch time, Wayne met Mandy at the house. Mandy asked, "how did the day start?" "Quite well, we have three plowed acres, the discing harrow is following the plow, Milt has spread a half ton of phosphate, the manure team has torn down half of the old border fence, and the fencing team is working well. Dad and George will be working all day with a jaw busting smile. George is the water man, and Sam is the fencing supervisor. Tomorrow they will switch jobs. And how was your day?"

"Working with the builder is an easy task. The man wishes to build what I want. I'll be going for a daily visit during the construction, and the builder expects that all renovations will be complete in ten days. Now for the real good news. I went to see Dr. Sutton. I had a light monthly four weeks ago, and now I'm late one week. To my surprise, he told me that I was eight weeks pregnant and my delivery date was mid December." Wayne exploded, "yes, we are going to be parents. Oh, such good news, now does that mean no more relations, no more riding your horse, no more outside ranch/farm work, and what other restriction?" "Wayne, Doc Sutton said I was healthy and there were no restrictions at this point."

"Wow, that's good news. Now why did you choose Doc Sutton and a hospital delivery, instead of the traditional home delivery with a midwife?" "This is the mid 1880's, and young Doc Sutton has been trained in the new methods to minimize infection and bleeding. He is capable of performing a life saving C-Section. Wayne, I not only want to get through childbirth, but I want to live to raise my child, be with you, have more children and maintain a sexual relationship with you."

"That sounds great, so what do doctors do differently today?" "They use uterine massaging techniques to stop bleeding, use proper hand washing and sterilizing to minimize infection, they suture lacerations to maintain normal anatomy, they can use forceps when necessary, and they can provide anesthesia with the new ether for a C-Section, if the need arises." "Well, I'm in complete agreement with you, and the availability of the Sutton Hospital with an experienced older doc and a newly trained one seems to be a win-win situation." "Plus, Doc Sutton wishes to see me once a month to monitor my weight, health and diet. This is a new approach to childbirth, it's called prenatal care."

"Now what do I do for work today?" "You are going to be an apprentice. I want you to ride with George today, so you can take over his job tomorrow. You will be the water, oil and grease lady, you fill the tank at the windmill, but the men will water the horses with buckets, and grease their own implements. You are the driver. You go from the cultivators, fencing group, the manure team, and phosphate spreader. You do it again every two hours starting a 10AM and finishing at 4PM. Since you don't start till 10 o'clock, you can go check the school construction by 8AM."

The remainder of the afternoon continued as a smooth operation. Every one quit at 5:30, giving them time to get to the barn, put up the horses, grease their implements, clean up, and have dinner by 6 o'clock.

The evening was spent different ways, Wayne and Mandy liked to read or visit with the Swansons or Wilsons. The farm hands would bathe, practice shooting, drink whiskey, play cards, care or ride their own horses, or just sit and talk. Most went to their bunks early, since 5AM came early. Very few men went to town during the week unless they needed personal items or had private business to conduct.

The remainder of the week continued without incidents. Every one was reminded to never get off their implement without applying the brake. Wayne saw the manure team use a productive system. All four men would load a wagon, then one man rode the team and spread the load while the other three loaded the second spreader. When the first driver returned with his load spread, another man would take the second load to the cultivation site. So there was always a new traveling man and three loading. Wayne went up to Henry and complemented him on organizing his men. Sam and George alternated between working the morning and afternoon schedule. Their job for now was reloading the phosphate wagon for Milt since Mandy was handling the water wagon.

At the end of the week, Wayne did an analysis of the work's progress. The cultivators were finishing 42 acres a week–ready for planting. The cultivation would continue six weeks, from April 1 to May 15, when the hay would be planted. That means 250 cultivated and planted acres as a start this year. After the hay planting, the cultivators would start work on the next six weeks of cultivating till July 1st. This could yield another 250 acres for planting oats. The oats would be planted before the July 1st start of haying. Also in another week, Milt will have spread 14 tons of phosphate to the prairies and cultivated acres. In two more weeks, the fencing will be done and the cattle will be allowed to graze north of the crop acres. The six seasonal workers would then be released to dig irrigation ditches on and off till early November–with time off to help with crop harvesting. The first ditches would allow irrigation of the cultivated acres–both hay and oats. Irrigation of future cultivated acreage would come later–next year.

Meanwhile, Mandy's pregnancy was going well. She felt best when active on the farm. Her morning sickness was treated with soda crackers and a brisk morning ride to the school under construction. Her visits with Doc Sutton went well, except she was given a salt and bacon restriction to minimize her feet swelling. Otherwise, Mandy was beaming with joy during this time.

***

July 1st arrived and it was time to start harvesting hay. He was speaking to Sam and George. "The prairie hay is maturing, and since we have fifteen hundred acres to harvest, it's time to start. The yield per acre will be much lower than cultivated lands, and even of lesser nutritional value. Yet the phosphate has made this crop possible. Any area not covered by phosphate is not considered worth harvesting. A lesson for future years. We will dedicate the next thirty days to prairie hay harvesting, because I plan to harvest cultivated hay by August 1st and oats by September 1st. We should be finished the harvest by October 15th."

The four man cultivator team took over the mowing, teddering, raking, and hay loading. Sam would drive the hay loader and George would run the dump rake. The two mowers were a life saver. The two mowers could cut twenty prairie acres per day. It was up to Wayne to select the most productive acreage. At twenty acres per day, they would harvest 600 acres in thirty days since the hay was much thinner in the natural prairies compared to the cultivated new hay. After the cultivated hay and oats were harvested, the crews would return to prairie hay until snow. It would be over matured hay but still usable with inactive horses during the winter. It was clear to Wayne that the baler would not be able to handle the volume of cultivated hay generated per hour, so he ordered another baler, and Steve Winslow had it delivered within three days.

The six seasonal workers, and the four manure worker's jobs were well established. Each of the three hay wagons had one man stacking hay and unloading their own wagons, two men would feed the baler, two men would tie baling strings or wires, two men would load transferring wagons to the storage shed, and unload/stack them. One man was in charge of helping to stack the bales. Wayne believed in rotating the men every day, that way they could perform all the jobs.

Mandy's job was to bring water to the horses and men in the fields. In between watering trips, she would share the office with Cora and Sally, as several ranchers were on site to load their wagons.

They were buying bales at a 10% discount since they were doing their own freighting, and saving room in the storage shed.

The harvesting progressed. Wayne was amazed at the ease of baling. After three weeks of harvesting prairie hay, it became clear to Wayne that the storage shed would hold the prairie hay and the straw from the oats harvest. They needed a second storage shed for the cultivation hay. Sam was sent to town to arrange for the immediate building of another storage shed. He arranged for the construction and paid for the building with a bank draft. Eight carpenters and several wagons of lumber arrived the next day. In four days, the shed was built and painted the usual red color. The first day the post and beams were up, the second day the roof went up, the third day they installed the wood floor, and the fourth day the north and west walls were up and painted. The building was ready for the August 1st beginning of the cultivation hay harvest.

Cutting cultivation hay was much slower because the hay was much thicker. Yet they were harvesting eight acres per day and would be finished the 250 acres withing the allotted month. At the end of the month, the newly constructed shed was full of top quality hay. Each acre would produce 90 bales per acre, or 700 bales per day. Each baler could bale 20 bales per hour, so the men had to bale between dawn and into darkness with lamps. Every man had to chip in to handle the field work and the two balers. Even Sally and Cora helped the man feeding the balers with loose hay. Mandy was running the side rake, and the dump rake was abandoned for lack of a rider. Wayne was filling the need, and managed to change jobs every day.

The worker's morale was high, and they were happy to be staying with Wayne's schedule. The harvesting of oats started Sept 1st. The cutting with a reaper was at a rate of ten acres per day but the processing time was slower because of picking up the bundled oats, threshing, fanning, and bagging the oats for feed. In addition, the straw had to be baled and stored. The process took an extra two weeks, but was done by October 15.

Because of an indian summer, the teams were able to harvest ten more days of mature prairie hay. This filled the original storage shed to the maximum. At the end of the season each storage shed held over 20,000 bales, plus the bales sold and picked up by the local ranchers. Wayne set up a price range for the coming sales. This was established by the wholesaler in Pueblo. The prices for 50 pound bales included hauling the hay to the RR box car, some five miles to town. Quality cultivated hay was $1 per bale, prairie hay was 50 cents per bale, and straw was 25 cents per bale. Bagged oats prices varied by the week as a feeding commodity.

By November 1st, haying came to an end. The cultivators went back to work to get ahead of next spring's cultivation. The manure team also could continue their work and fertilize the newly cultivated land. By November 21st, everything came to an abrupt end with a one foot snowfall.

Fortunately, since the wholesaler was pushing hard for a hay delivery, the six seasonal workers started hauling hay to the RR boxcars. When the cultivation and manure spreading came to an end, the seasonal workers were laid off, and the four full time cultivators and manure team took over the hay freighting to the RR boxcars. They used the three hay wagons and the two large utility wagons, to haul hay to the boxcars. On return to the ranch, the two utility wagons were loaded with bagged phosphate, and stored in the barn for next spring. They hauled hay until the roads were no longer passable. Fortunately, that was February 15 because of a late winter.

When winter hit hard, the road was packed by the town roller, to keep ranchers coming to town for business by using a sleigh. The local ranchers had not anticipated their hay needs with their increasing herds. They were running low on hay because of the snow. Wayne worked with Charlie and they designed wooden skis to replace the hay wagons steel wheels. They were then able to make emergency hay deliveries of the prairie hay and straw. The cultivated hay had been all transferred to Pueblo by that time.

By spring time, when grazing could resume, the hay storage shed had just enough hay left over to feed the horses during the summer months. With the fiscal year at an end, Wayne reconciled his books.

His total gross income was 33350. He separated this income into a percentage distribution:

- 5% for equipment depreciation—five year plan.
- 5% for seed money—starting up costs and labor next April.

- 20% for phosphate, seeds and baler twine/wire.
- 30% for labor—to cover 15 men.
- 5% for miscellaneous expenses.
- 5% for new implements.
- 30% for business profit.

Wayne went over the books with Mandy, she was not impressed with bookkeeping, till Wayne said to her, "our share is the last profit category. We made 30% of $3350, or $10000. Out of that amount, I'm paying Sam and George $750 each. This pays them $3 per day for half time employment from April to November, compared to the full employment daily wage of $1.25 for the other workers. So we are left with $8500." Mandy added, "plus my salary and the 100 cattle we are selling at $22 per head." "Yes, but we have plenty of expenses to account for, on that ranch, which I will reconcile after the cattle sale."

"So how often did you activate the filling of the irrigation ditches to flood the growing crops?" "We flooded the cultivated hay acreage three times and the oats acreage twice. The flooding took two days and the two ponds were emptied. The ponds refilled three days later. I'm convinced that the irrigation saved our crops." "I believe it as well. Next year we'll be cultivating another 500 acres between April to November. So will we be building more irrigation ditches. Yes, we have two powerful springs, and we haven't even harnessed the water from the stream. We have plenty of water to salvage crops from the hot dry summers."

Meanwhile, Mandy's pregnancy was well tolerated. Her check ups were perfect. Her weight gain was not excessive and she showed no sign of the dreaded toxemia. She was tolerating the work during the harvest. Mandy became an expert at using the side rake to form windrows. Wayne had shown her how to estimate the hay moisture. If very dry, she produced tight windrows, if it needed more drying she would produce fluffed up windrows. Raking was a smooth ride, and even as her belly grew, she remained comfortable in her springing seat. The only exception was compensating for her ever increasing frequent stops to go pee. She would hide around the horses, since there were no bushes in the fields.

After the harvest, she returned to teaching until she became too uncomfortable. By November 1st she started her maternity leave with eight weeks of pay. The council hired a late graduate from

Mandy's school. Mandy knew her well, and knew the kids would do well with her.

Mandy went in labor two weeks early on December 1st. Mandy and Wayne were having breakfast, when suddenly Mandy made a face. She looked surprised, shocked, but pleased. She experienced her first contraction and Wayne suspected she would have a hard labor by the painful look on her face.

Wayne hitched the buggy, grabbed her travel bag, helped her to climb onto the buggy, picked up Sally and Cora, and took off for Sutton Hospital. Upon arriving at the hospital, Cora and Sally entered the maternity ward with Mandy, and Wayne was left alone in the waiting room—Mandy didn't even kiss her husband since she was in the midst of a hard contraction that nearly doubled her over. Wayne was trying to talk to Mandy as the admitting nurse dragged the three women past the "do not enter doors."

Wayne was pacing the floor for thirty minutes when Doc Sutton came out to talk with Wayne. "Mandy is in early labor, mother and baby are fine, and Mandy is four centimeters dilated. It will be a long day and Mandy has great support with Cora and Sally. We'll keep you posted."

Wayne had read Mandy's book on childbirth, and wondered if this knowledge would be a help or hindrance. He kept thinking of all the complications that lead to maternal mortality, instead of the many positive facts on the natural process of childbirth.

George and Sam arrived in a state of panic. Wayne settled them down by saying Mandy was in early labor. He had to explain that she was only four centimeter dilated, and it will be several hours to delivery.

George said, "this centimeter thing is too much information, I just want to know that the baby is here and both are Ok." Sam was a bit more realistic and said, "we are fortunate to have a modern doctor and hospital to take care of our girl. Now all we need to do is follow the old saying, 'hurry up and wait.'"

George added, "we need some coffee. I'm going to Simms' diner to get some." He came back with three tin cups, a full pot of steaming coffee and a half dozen bear-paw pastries. The real waiting started in earnest.

Sam went to get the second pot of coffee. Upon his return, George felt it would be good to distract Wayne, who was not tolerating waiting for something that he could not help along. Wayne said, "Mandy told me that the future will allow fathers to be with their wives during labor and delivery." George added, "thank goodness that I'm too old to face that day."

George came back, "let's talk about something else to pass the time—crop harvesting. "What changes do you see happening going in season two?" "Well for the past month, I've been working on this. I'm not renewing my contract with the wholesaler. They don't want to invest in my new venture, and eliminating a middle man will increase the value of our crops. I have signed a contract with the RR and two new retailers—Crescent Feed Store and Haynes Feed Store in Pueblo. They both want 20,000 bales and that will account for all the cultivated hay next year. The RR will build a five mile spur to the W–M Connected Ranch. They will pay 50% of the costs, and the two retailers and us will pay the other 50%. The RR gets a turn table to turn a locomotive around for passenger comfort and they get the increase in freight."

Sam keeps the subject going by adding, "we now have 500 cultivated acres and by next fall we'll have another 500 acres. That will mean more hired help and new implements." "Yes, but it will mean more seasonal workers, not full-timers, and I have budgeted 5% of gross income for new implements."

George asked, "what new implements are you planning to add?" "I have ordered a third baler, a third mower, two extra draft horses and work geldings, one more loader, and one extra hay wagon."

Sam looked perplexed, "how is this RR spur going to make a difference, we still have to load the hay in a wagon, and unload it into the boxcar?" "NO." "Steve Winslow has ordered a factory conveyor that his blacksmith will adapt to a cam wheel. A horse will activate the conveyor just like the one horse baler is activated. The conveyor will carry the finished bales from the baler directly to the boxcar, waiting in the yard, to be loaded. This will save several men during the baling season, and make winter RR deliveries easy to accomplish without using the local winter roads."

The men were both astonished and happy with the changes. George added, "don't you think the wholesaler will change his mind when he loses a great hay supplier?" "Yes, but he will have to pay a surcharge, which I will refund to Crescent and Haynes. I will even propose that other feed suppliers, north of Pueblo, may even become our customers."

Sam looked at Wayne and asked, "The business is getting too large for you to be involved with everyday job assignments. You need a farm foreman." "Yes, and I've already found my man. He knows how to organize men productively, and most men enjoy working with him. I hear that some men ask to work with him." Sam and George looked at each other and simultaneously said, "Henry, the manure man." "Yes, that's the man who can lead our men." They both approved Wayne's choice without reservations.

"Have you talked to Henry?" "Yes, I already offered him the job and he happily accepted. All he said was, "thank you and I'm proud to work for this outfit and your behalf." "He starts Jan 1st, and his pay will increase to $100 a month." George adds, "that's a big salary for a foreman, but I've seen him work and he always gives 110%. Plus he'll get 100% from all the workers."

Sam adds, "I think it's time you abandon the morning meetings. Let Henry take over the assignments and announcements. Instead, have a meeting with him everyday at 4PM to discuss the day's activity and planning for tomorrow. Find out what he needs for men, accessories and implements, and make it happen as the owner."

"Yes, I'm ready to be the owner, act as such, and let the foreman take over the daily activities."

Suddenly, Sally came to the waiting room. "Mandy's labor is picking up, she's six centimeters and all is well." George was about to ask something when everyone heard a loud scream from the labor room. All three men turned white and nearly dropped their coffee.

The tension was naturally mounting and the men were getting quieter. An hour later, the doctor came out and said he had broken her water and was expecting a delivery within the hour. As the doctor left, he said, "excuse me, but I have to scrub and sterilize my hands."

George, was getting more nervous. "Why did we need to know he broke her water? And what is this about scrubbing his hands?" "They are new methods of medical care. Careful hand scrubbing with a powerful soap and sterilizing the skin with grain alcohol, apparently decreases the chances for infections." Sam adds, "well I'm beginning to agree with George, this is too much information."

Cora came out and said, "delivery is imminent, all is well, and Mandy is a very strong person. You have a great wife, Wayne." Wayne was very quiet. This was one event that he had no control over. He had to rely on his wife to handle this. He was heard whispering, "oh how I wish I could help her." Sam heard Wayne and said, "now Wayne, in this situation, men are as useful as teats on a bull. So sit back and patiently wait for the news." Wayne and George both broke out in laughter.

The hour passed in total silence, the three men were listening for the sound of a crying baby. Stillness persisted till the doctor busted through the double doors. Sam and George were so startled that they nearly fell off their chairs. The doctor had a big smile on his face and said to Wayne, "your presence is requested in the maternity department, follow me please."

Wayne stepped up and followed the doctor. He was lead through a doorway where he saw Mandy with a smile and holding her baby. She said, "Wayne, come say hello to your healthy son." Wayne stepped forward, touched Mandy's hand, looked at the baby, and started tearing up with joy.

***

Mandy stayed in the hospital three more days. The baby was nursing well, she had normal bleeding, and there were no signs of infection. Wayne went to rent an enclosed carriage to bring his family home.

With Christmas only eighteen days away, Cora and Sally took over the house. They prepared meals, did laundry, and started decorating the house for the holidays. They sent the men to town to buy Christmas presents and turkeys for the Christmas dinners.

Wayne stayed with Mandy and the baby for an entire week. He then stepped out to check on the shipping to the boxcars in town. The last boxcar was filled and shipped three days before Christmas. The men were all getting a paid week's vacation, Henry's first request which Wayne could not deny.

Christmas eve arrived. The Wilsons and senior Swansons went to church, and afterwards had a turkey dinner and gifts at the senior Swanson house. On Christmas day, George and Sally opened their main room and invited the ten year round farm workers and the six full time cattle ranchers, along with the ranch foreman with his wife and children. Dinner was served by the senior Watsons and Wilsons. It was clear that such a get-together promoted the feeling of belonging to a family. After dinner, Wayne made a unscheduled appearance. He came to thank everyone for their help this past year. Things became more jovial when he gave everyone a $20 gold double eagle– to add to their vacation.

***

The winter months provided a private time for mom, dad and the baby. One day, Mandy says, "I know what to name our baby." "Ok, what is it?" "Jimmy, a namesake for Sheriff Jim, the man who affected our lives, and lead us to meet when he sent you to escort prisoners to Pueblo. Talking to you on that train ride to Silver Circle was the first pleasant and enlightening day of my life."

Every month, they saw changes in Jimmy's development. By April 1st, the three month old Jimmy had progressed to the following level"

<u>MOVEMENTS:</u> He could raise his head and chest when laying on his stomach, open and close his hands on objects, push on legs when standing

on the floor, occasionally stand when holding an object, and could take swipes at dangling objects.

<u>VISUAL:</u> He could watch faces, follow moving objects, smile at the sound of the parents voices, and begin to babble and imitate sounds.

<u>SOCIAL:</u> He could smile at will, enjoy playing, imitate facial expressions, and respond to sounds, especially mom and dad's voices.

As April 1st arrived, the farming activities were starting for season two. Mandy went back to school, Cora and Sally were babysitting, and Wayne got use to being the boss, not the day-to-day foreman. Wayne and Mandy had made their future—and life was for the living.

***

EPILOGUE

The next five years brought four more children for Mandy and Wayne. Cora and Sally were in heaven taking care of the kids as Mandy went to school. One would cook, clean and do laundry, while the other handled the children. They would alternate their daily routines. At harvest time, Mandy continued to work the farm.

The farm quickly expanded to 2000 cultivated acres. This produced 75,000 bales per year. 65,000 bales of quality hay, and 10,000 bales of straw, as well as hundreds of bagged oats. They now had one wholesaler, four retailers and twenty local ranchers as hay customers. The conveyor to the boxcars was a life saver, and to keep up with the baling process, they now had four one horse balers set up on a concrete platform, safely away from the storage sheds. It was lit with safe gas lights and baling was done 24 hours a day when the need existed.

The business was profitable from year to year. The poor years were during rainy seasons, and fortunately these were rare in the Colorado plains. Wayne kept busy, meeting with both foreman on a regular basis. He found that this was the best way to keep reins on the enterprise. Despite the long hours spent on business management, he found time for the children every day. Their special time of play was in the evenings after dinner. Wayne would play hard with the kids, and tired them out by bedtime.

One day, Wayne was in town on business, and had lunch with Sheriff Jim. Jim had semi retired and was working the office desk twenty hours a week. Waiting for lunch, Jim asked Wayne, "do you ever miss the life of a paladin bounty hunter?" "No, Jim. I have a stronger need than the lonely life of a bounty hunter. I need to share my life with my best friend, lover, and our children. I also recognize that if our community and friends are threatened, that I will volunteer my services—because once a paladin, always a paladin."

The End

Printed in the United States
By Bookmasters